out of my heart

ALSO BY SHARON M. DRAPER

Blended

Copper Sun

Double Dutch

Out of My Mind

Panic

Romiette & Julio

Stella By Starlight

The Clubhouse Mysteries Series:

The Buried Bones Mystery

Lost in the Tunnel of Time

Shadows of Caesar's Creek

The Space Mission Adventure

The Backyard Animal Show

Stars and Sparks on Stage

The Hazelwood High Trilogy:

Tears of a Tiger

Forged by Fire

Darkness Before Dawn

The Jericho Trilogy:

The Battle of Jericho

November Blues

Just Another Hero

out of my heart

SHARON M. DRAPER

A Caitlyn Dlouhy Book
ATHENEUM BOOKS FOR YOUNG READERS
atheneum New York London Toronto Sydney New Delhi

This book is dedicated with love to
my two daughters,
Wendy and Crystal,
who taught me to appreciate
the power of wheels,
the beauty of dance,
and the giggles of little girls.

out of my heart

CHAPTER 1

The firefly hovered over the back of my hand, then landed—slowly, effortlessly. I could hardly feel its delicate touch. Two wire-thin antennae, flickering, protruded from its tiny round head painted with a small red dot. I tried not to tremble. My hands often move on their own, whether I want them to or not, so I focused intensely, willing myself to remain still.

Its black wings, so shiny, opened and closed like scissors. I barely breathed. Dark lines that looked like they'd been painted on its back with a fine-tipped pen separated the crimson from the ebony.

The firefly seemed to be in no hurry to leave. It looked right at me.

I wondered about the magic of having iridescent floaties attached to my body—what it would feel like to lift into the air and glide on a whisper of wind.

What are you thinking, Mr. Firefly? As if it could hear me, its wings flexed out and in. And then it happened. One tiny bloom of bright yellow-green light gleamed from its body. It spoke to me! I know quite a bit about speaking out loud without saying a word.

As we sat there in the purpling twilight, just me and that lightning bug, I sighed with happiness. I might have breathed out too hard, because at that moment, the tiny insect lifted its wings and took off on an unseen breeze.

CHAPTER 2

"Ooh! Look! There's another one—and another!" my sister shrieked. She raced across the grass of Mrs. V's front yard, a jar clutched in her hands, trying to convince one of the tiny glowing insects to zoom into it. If my firefly had joined that swarm, I'm sure that he and the others had to be laughing at Penny, sky dancing away from her.

"Come help, Mrs. V!" Penny pleaded. "They won't listen to me!" She plunked down on the grass, her face scrunched into a frown.

Mrs. V, who was our next-door neighbor and Mom's best friend, lounged on a padded recliner on her front porch. She winked at me before saying, "Well, maybe they don't want to live in a bottle—maybe they just want to boogie tonight!"

"Just one?" Penny put on her most pitiful face.

"All right," Mrs. V replied. "But we're gonna let it go after we look at it, okay?"

"Fine," Penny grumbled, folding her arms across her chest. "But why?"

"Would *you* like to live in a jug?" Mrs. V asked.

Penny laughed. "I'm too big! But a bug in a jug even *sounds* right!"

"Well," Mrs. V countered, "what if I found a jug big enough for you to fit in? Would you want to live there?"

Penny seemed to think for a moment. Then she said, "I guess not. I'd feel smooshed and stuffy."

"Exactly! So, what do you think we should do?"

Penny rolled into a somersault and popped up with an ease I couldn't help but admire and said, "Okay—we'll catch us some bugs, then we let them fly!"

Mrs. V, whose full name was Violet Valencia, turned to me. "Let me go help her before she scares them all out of town!" she said, double-checking to make sure the locks on the wheels of my wheelchair were secure. The two of them whirled across the lawn, laughing and reaching for the tiny lights. I couldn't join them, but for once I didn't feel left out—a firefly had already found me.

I could see Mom's blue SUV pulling into our driveway next door. Butterscotch, our golden retriever,
raised his head in recognition. Mom works at a local
hospital as a nurse, her days filled with taking care of
people who have diseases or broken bones or heart
attacks. She tells me her job is a challenge, but she loves
it! She often comes home tired, but still has to take care
of me. And, no joke, I'm a handful. An armful! She's
never, ever complained, but sometimes that makes me
feel bad.

During the school year, the belching yellow bus used
to drop me at Mrs. V's house after school. But now that
we're on summer vacation, Penny and I spend most
weekdays with her.

Every morning she has us do stuff like spelling,
math, and language arts, but before I start to feel
all bad like it's summer school or something, Mrs. V
makes it so much fun it hardly seems like schoolwork.
Scrabble equals spelling lessons for me, and easy word
puzzles become vocabulary fun for Penny. I learn
math from a bingo game and clips from old movies
help us learn history. I try to complain, because, duh,
it's summer vacation! But honestly, I really like it—at
least for a couple of hours. Then in the afternoon we
make Popsicles or play games or watch movies. Once a
week we go to the neighborhood library. Penny fiercely

chooses her own picture books—she rarely needs anyone to help her.

I've got this really awesome computer-like device that attaches to my wheelchair. It's called a Medi-Talker, but that sounds way too boring and grown-up, so I named it Elvira. It's how I talk to the rest of the world. By using my thumbs, when they decide to cooperate—which, luckily, is most of the time—I can tap or type just about anything that pops into my head, then push the speak button, and Elvira will say it for me. I can do complicated stuff like a book report or a math project, or I can ask any question that might pop into my head, like *What makes clouds float?* Or *Where do farts come from?* Or *Why do my armpits smell funky?* Instead of answering me, Mrs. V, of course, makes me look up the answer on the internet through Elvira.

At the end of the day, I like to just sit on the porch and chill. But Penny is four and a half and doesn't know the meaning of chill! That girl only knows two speeds—go, or sleep. She's able to run and hop and spin around in a circle until she's dizzy. She did seventeen somersaults in a row earlier today—she made me count.

As for me? Well, even though my brain blazes, the rest of my body works like a piece of taffy that's been left in the sun for too long. No somersaults for me, unless I accidentally fall out of my wheelchair. I can't walk, can't talk, and can't use my hands and fingers like most folks do, but Mrs. V helps me shut down the pity party. She knows my mind is a vault full of words and ideas just bursting to be let out. So between our weekly library visits, Mrs. V encourages me to swim through the deep and gurgly waters of the internet to explore just about any subject that I'm curious about. I've dived into Egyptian history and discovered the female pharaohs, and I've dog-paddled (ha-ha!) through the history of golden retrievers, the mechanics of car engines, and the mysteries of every planet. By the way, I'm pretty sure I'd be able to walk on Mars or Venus, assuming I didn't get fried by poisonous gases.

So Friday is usually library day—my favorite. First thing Friday mornings, Mrs. V loads me and Penny into her car, and we head to our local branch a few blocks away. I even love the smell of the place—it smells like history and mystery and book bindings. It's an old building, so the floors and bookshelves are dark polished wood. Mrs. V told us that she practically lived there when she was a kid. She knew where they kept the audiobooks as well as old photographs and films, and the rare books. I love audiobooks because I can just put on headphones and listen to anything I want. And hardcover books can be attached to my wheelchair tray with an easy clip.

All those books sit all week on the shelves, silent like

me, waiting to speak to me every Friday. Then I grab a new pile of possibilities and place them on my tray. The librarian, Mr. Francisco, always greets me with a smile and asks me questions about the books I read the previous week as he checks them in, then reloads my bag with the new pile.

Last time I went, I was on a mission. Mr. Francisco, aka Best Librarian in the History of the World, had emailed me that the brochures he'd ordered for me were in! I. Was. Psyched! What brochures, you wonder? Well, my parents don't know it yet, but I want to go to summer camp. The last few weeks of school, it seemed like all anyone was talking about was the camps they were going to. Rock-Climbing Camp. Fly-Fishing Camp. Even Mermaid Camp. Yep, it's a real thing. Mermaid Makeovers. Underwater Theater. Dancing with Fins. Girls go there to learn to swim with attached fish flippers. Seriously. Molly and Claire and Rose went on and on and on about it, how their parents are letting them fly— alone—from Ohio to Florida to go to . . . Mermaid Camp!

When I tapped and told that story to Mrs. V, she'd snorted out loud with laughter.

"What's so funny?" I'd asked.

Mrs. V could hardly catch her breath. "When you're wearing those fake mermaid tails, you can only sit on the beach and look cute in a photo!"

"So?" I didn't get it.

"Melody, think about it. A person wearing a fish tail can't walk!! Those kids get rolled around in what the camp calls a royal mermaid chariot. It's a chair with wheels. . . . It's . . . it's . . . a wheelchair!" She exploded with laughter.

I finally got it! See, last year in fifth grade Molly and Claire used to majorly make fun of me because I was in a wheelchair, and now they go and choose to spend their summer pretending to be part fish and not able to walk! *Ha ha ha ha!*

I sure don't want to go anywhere to pretend I'm a mermaid, but it got me thinking. Maybe *I* could go to camp! It sounds really fun and a little scary and totally different. Plus, except for Mrs. V's house, I've never once had a sleepover or been away from my family for even an entire day. I think I want to do something exciting. And unusual. And maybe scary. If those girls can do it, so can I.

But did they even have camps for kids like me? Here's the thing: people tend to stare at me. Nobody asks out loud, but I know they wonder, *What's wrong with that girl? Why can't she talk?* That freaks me out sometimes, because I can't tell them what they're too polite to ask.

I know a little bit about things not said. I'm unable to say actual words like everybody else, and that drives me bananas. I've got like a thousand thoughts and questions zooming around in my head. Like. All. The. Time. But not much opportunity to have a real conversation, or say something quickly, like in an emergency. The result is some serious frustration.

For example, our family went out to a restaurant a few months ago. We don't do that often, because my let's-just-fling-out-any-old-time arms, and my unfailing ability to knock stuff over by accident, are often more than we want to deal with. Soup? Oops, sorry. Penny's orange juice? Dang, my bad. So people stare. Most aren't judging—just curious. A few whisper to each other. They sometimes point at me. I'm used to it and I ignore them.

But on that day we had ordered our food, and all was going well. Even though we forgot my Medi-Talker at home, which almost never happens, Mom read me the menu, and I hummed when she mentioned something I wanted. Mom spooned applesauce into my mouth, and it was delicious—flavored with cinnamon. When the food and drinks came, I didn't spill one single drop.

Weird, though—Penny wasn't eating, and it was chicken nuggets—her favorite. She had been granky all day (that's our word for a grumpy, cranky Penny), but I guess Mom had figured that maybe a special trip out to eat might cheer her up.

Then I noticed Penny's eyes were getting glassy, and sweat had popped up along her hairline. She was going to blow! I automatically looked down for Elvira, and, of course, she wasn't there. So there was no way I could tell my parents that I thought Penny was about to get sick.

And yep, halfway through the meal, Penny scrunched up her face, burst into tears, and threw up all over Mom and most of the food on the table! What a mess!

Dad and Mom apologized to the waitstaff, paid the bill, and left a massive tip. Then we dashed out of there in a hurry. I felt bad that Penny was sick, but secretly I was so glad that for once it wasn't me making a mess. We still laugh about that one. What I wasn't so glad about was that I hadn't been able to warn my parents that Penny was about to erupt. Yep, serious frustration.

Oddly, I still remember that the bill that night came to $47.47. My brain does that—recalls random numbers, maps, facts, and computations. And don't mess with me when it comes to trivia—like the average summertime temperatures in Alaska, or Argentina, or Armenia. Or the secret ingredients in the grease that's used in fast-food places (you don't want to know), or the shortcut to the final level of just about any online video game. Most of this gets crammed into my head, wandering around with nothing to do. I know mountains of stuff, but I'm pretty much stuck in a valley. Why can my brain do all that, but not know how to tell my body to move? Or talk? Or give my folks a heads-up that Penny's gonna throw up?

So I prefer to focus on the things that I can do. Like, I can communicate with folks through Elvira. Mom and Dad just had her upgraded to System 9.9. She's still clunky, but now she's smaller, faster, and even waterproof, like an iPad that took its vitamins. Plus, she snaps to my wheelchair in seconds. She's got apps and a full keyboard, so I can send texts, write out whatever's on my mind, and check online stuff like everybody else. But it's still impossible to type fast enough to bring up everything I wonder about.

She's got a speaking voice called "Trish." It's the closest thing to a real girl's voice that I could find in the choices. I sure wish her speaking system was better-sounding, though. I think they ought to let me create my own voice for her. Maybe I'd pick a cool accent, or something really glamorous, or perhaps low and mysterious.

Which makes me think—who knows what my voice would have been like? I can actually make sounds—something that comes out sounding like *Uhh* to others, my family and my teachers know mean *Yes*. And I hum when I like something—just not real words. Which kinda sucks. Maybe when I go to college, I can major in creating artificial languages. That would be awesome.

Now that I think about it, I've also got a sort of sign language, too. I can't do ASL—that's got way too many complicated hand motions—but me and my family have adapted a version that works. For example, my sign for "Mom" is my thumb on my chin, with my fingers as straight as I can get them. "Dad" is thumb on forehead with fingers up. And my sign for "Penny," even though she's four and a half and sassy, is both arms hugged together like a baby in a cradle. And I can shake my head to say no, just like everybody else does.

So, it's a little awkward, but we manage to communicate—sort of.

But right that second, when I saw Mom getting out of our car, I would have simply liked to have an easy way to blurt out what I was thinking. And what was on my mind right then was that I wanted to go to camp.

When Mom came into Mrs. V's yard, I couldn't just yell out, *Hi Mom!* like Penny did, but I didn't need to spell out anything for my mother—I just hummed, and she knew.

Butterscotch bounded over and yelped with joy as Mom pulled a treat out of the pocket of her scrubs. Penny was right behind the dog, jumping into Mom's arms. "Spin me, Mommy! Spin!"

Mom kissed her chubby cheek and spun her around, Penny's legs pinwheeling out.

"More?" Penny begged when Mom put her back down.

"Penny-girl, Mommy needs a break," she said, laughing. "Can I say hello to Melody now?" She came up onto the porch and leaned over to hug me tight. She smelled so good—a combination of talcum powder, alcohol wipes, and bubble gum. She keeps a big bag of Dubble Bubble in a top cabinet—away from Penny. She says chewing gum helps her relax, so Dad makes sure the bag never goes empty.

Random thought—I'd love to be able to chew bubble gum. The smell makes my nose tickle in a good way. I'd probably pop right with it if I could actually blow a real bubble!

"How's my girl?" Mom asked.

I hugged her back as best as I could and made that hum sound that we both know means *I'm good*.

"Hey there, Violet," Mom said as she poured herself a cup of lemonade. She then collapsed into the other chaise lounge, took a deep sip, and breathed out "Ahhhh."

Mrs. V pointed to the firefly show. "Glad you got home in time for a little nighttime magic."

"Oh, they're out early tonight," Mom said.

"Mommy! Mommy! Look at mine!" Penny shouted,

running across the yard for her jar and back up onto the porch. She plopped the jar of blinking bugs into Mom's lap.

"They're beautiful!" Mom held up the jar. "Even better than the sparkle lights in your bedroom."

"Mrs. V says I can't keep them, but they like me! So, can I? *Pleeeease?*"

"Well," Mom said, "let's think about this. How did you catch them?"

"They just flew into my jar!" Penny told her solemnly. "And Mrs. V helped me."

"Do you think some of those bugs might have moms and dads waiting for them in the bushes?"

"Hmm." Penny pondered this. "Maybe their parents don't know they're out playing in the dark. Maybe they snuck out!"

"Well then, we better set them free so they can get home before they get in trouble, okay?"

"Good idea!" Penny agreed.

As Mom opened the jar, Penny whispered, "Hurry home, little bugs!"

And, with a whoosh of the lid, a dozen tiny little light bulbs lifted into the darkness.

CHAPTER 3

Firefly catching and releasing must be exhausting, because Penny snuggled into Mom's lap and fell asleep long before Mom finished her glass of lemonade. Butterscotch snoozed by my feet. I hyped myself up. *Okay, now is the time to talk about camp.*

"What a perfect evening!" Mom said, twirling one of Penny's curls—her hair is crazy curly like mine. Above the glow of the lightning bugs, the first stars were beginning to speckle the sky. I nodded in agreement.

"Glad school's out?"

I tilted my head just a little. She knew how school was for me.

I like most of my teachers and classes. I love being a part of all that whirling turmoil—most of the time. But even though I have an aide who helps me with things like taking notes and eating lunch, school can be . . . a bit much.

Not many kids pay attention to the girl trying to get through the halls in her electric wheelchair. They rush past me, their backpacks sometimes whomping right into me as they call out to friends, check their phones, and hurry through the crowds. It's almost like they don't even see me. It's strange—so many kids surround me, and yet I'm usually all alone.

That's why I love being at Mrs. V's—she always sees me. But it's also kinda why I want to go to camp. I bet if I went to a camp with kids like me . . . well, I wonder how different *that* would feel!

Every single day since I was born, somebody has fed me and bathed me and read to me and helped me do every single detail of my life. So lately I started wondering— when do I get to do things for myself? Will I ever be a person who runs her own life? I mean, I know I'll always need some kind of help, but when do I get to be *me*?

So that's what I'm thinking . . . that maybe at camp, especially if it's one that specializes in kids like me, I can just be Melody Brooks for a few days. Whoa! That would be amazing!

Plus, if Molly and Claire and Rose can go to camp, then why can't I? I might need extra help, but I sure don't need fins—duh! I was all set to launch my plan.

I'd searched for just the right place for me. I'd spent several afternoons digging through camping websites and reading those brochures Mr. Francisco helped me order.

Trouble was, most of the camps that I thought looked ideal for me and were within driving distance— because, let's be honest, there was no way Mom and Dad would let me get on a plane alone—were no longer accepting applications. Except for this one called Camp Green Glades.

I'd read the brochure and checked the website something like seventy-three times now. Yeah, I'm a stalker! In every picture, the kids—in wheelchairs and on crutches or walkers—are constantly cheesing. Can they all really be that happy? But somehow, I felt good about this camp.

I glanced over at Mom—for sure she wasn't expecting this! I took my time and tapped out, **"I want to go to camp!!!"** I hit the exclamation point several times. I put Elvira's speaker on its loudest level.

"Uh, camp?" she asked, gulping down the rest of her lemonade.

I nodded several times. **"Yes, camp. I found one at the library."**

"You did? Camp?" she asked again, as if I'd asked to go to the moon. "But, honey, it's probably too late to apply now. It's already the middle of June."

"I already checked. They have a few openings."

Mom raised an eyebrow. "Vee, was this your idea?"

Mrs. V shook her head, her own eyebrows raised. "Camp! Well, this is a surprise! And nope, I had no idea she was looking into this."

"So, can I go?" I tapped, wondering if all these raised eyebrows were a good thing or not.

"Uh, show me the website," Mom said, still exchanging glances with Mrs. V. But she wanted to see, which wasn't a "no" yet.

I'd never really done anything all on my own like this. It felt pretty awesome. And I was totally prepared! I had the camp's website link saved, so I just had to click on it. And there was Camp Green Glades, full of smiling-faced kids with a variety of what some people call "special" needs. Mom and Mrs. V pored over the website, crowding so close to me, I was getting hot.

They read every detail, and read them again, in case, I guess, they'd missed anything the first time. The camp was here in Ohio, not too far away, and most importantly, it had only two or three openings left. That meant we better hurry.

They oohed over the pretty sunsets and forest paths

and the sparkling lake. They smiled at the kids in wheelchairs and on walkers sitting around campfires. There were campers on a boat, in a swimming pool, and even on horses!

I looked at the images for like the seventy-fourth time. I still could hardly believe such a place could exist for me. Not one person looked scared or abandoned. But I guess nobody takes pictures of kids falling off a cliff or drowning in a lake and then slaps that on their website.

And hello . . . were my mom and Mrs. V trying to drive me crazy? Because now they were reading it out loud—gah!

"The Green Glades Therapeutic Recreational Camp has been a support for campers with special needs and their families for twenty-five years," Mrs. V read to my mother.

"Twenty-five years," my mother mused.

Special needs, I was thinking. I don't like that term. It sounds so . . . so . . . vague. It's like people without special needs decided that if they made the term vague enough, it wouldn't hurt anybody's feelings. But when you're the person the term is used for, it makes you feel less than yourself. It makes *me* feel less than myself. Yeah, I'm special. And yes, I have needs. But don't make that my label.

I've been seen by zillions of doctors and therapists and specialists—so many I can't even count. My parents do a great job of making sure I get the best medical and therapeutic care possible. But those doctors sometimes mess up too. Like, they'll say I "suffer from" or I'm "afflicted with" cerebral palsy. Spoiler alert: I'm not suffering from anything. And just so you know, CP is not a disease. It is not contagious. Even if I sneeze on you. For real! My body simply doesn't work like most of the people I know, and cerebral palsy is the name that doctors call my condition. It is what it is. And P.S., the mental part of my brain kicks butt.

By the end of sixth grade, we were supposed to know decimals to the hundredths place. But I can do well past the thousandths, although I have no idea why anybody would ever have to know that in real life. I can estimate the cost of our grocery bill, including the tax, before we even get to the cash register. And if I ever get to go to Europe, I can figure out the exchange rate of euros to dollars in my head, as well as share historical details about each city we visit!

Thanks to Mrs. V, I've studied French, and a few words of basic German. I can't pronounce the words, obviously, but I can read them, or identify them when I hear them. If, for example, a couple in the grocery store are speaking French, I can recognize part of their

conversation, or if the movie I'm watching was origi-
nally filmed in German, I can figure out quite a bit,
especially if it has subtitles. I have secret powers! I'm
all set. For now, though, I just wanted to go to Camp
Green Glades.

"So, can I go?" I tapped again.

It took me a minute to do this. Tapping out words
is harder for me than you might think, especially
when I'm excited about something. My right thumb,
which I depend on most of the time, sometimes gets
the wiggles.

Mom told me to hold on—they were still reading. Then she said to Mrs. V, "Well, it's surprisingly
affordable! There are four girls per cabin, each with
their own individual counselor. That seems like a good
idea—safe, you know."

If I could have rolled my eyes right then, I would
have.

Mrs. V nodded emphatically, then added, sounding
all excited, "There's boating, hiking, swimming, and
nightly campfires." She stopped and grinned at me.
"Optional activities seem to include some kind of . . .
what?? Zip-lining?"

Mom looked at me. "They can't be serious! That's
insanely dangerous!"

Dangerous! I have never in my life been given the chance

*to even think about doing something even a little bit danger-
ous! I've got to go to this camp.*

"Oh, I'm sure they have safety protocols that are
NASA-worthy," Mrs. V said calmly. Then she was back
to excited. "And, oh, Melody, get this—horseback riding!"

Um. Do they think I haven't looked at the website
a million times? And okay, truth, the horseback-riding
part has me a little nervous. Like, how's that going to
work? I can't even sit in my chair without straps. But
these folks have been doing this for like twenty-five
years, right? They must have figured it out by now.

So I tapped out again, **"Can I go? Can I go?"** I
looked at Mom and did my best to conjure up the
face Penny used earlier to get Mrs. V in on the firefly
hunt.

Mom continued to ignore me, but I was cool,
because if they were all excited, then chances were . . .

"Oh, and it's only two hours away!" my mother
practically shouted, as if that had been the deal breaker.
Finally she turned to me. "Well, if we can fill out the
application in a hurry, let's at least try."

Okay, I was super pumped. My legs did their
kickety-kick thing, and my arms looked like I was con-
ducting a million-piece orchestra.

While I tried to calm down, Mrs. V tabbed through

the camp website. "I used to do a bit of riding when I was your age," she told me. "Horses are incredibly gentle and understanding—and it says the ones they use at this camp are specifically trained for working with all kinds of kids."

Mom added, "All those cowboy movies you and your dad watch, Melody—the horses always seem to be your favorite part."

I rocked a little in my chair, thinking about me and a horse and a saddle. Yes, I love those cowboy movies. But in none of those movies were there kids like me. I had never even dared to think about me riding a horse. It had never crossed my mind! Until I discovered Camp Green Glades.

"How do I even get on the horse?" I tapped and Elvira asked out loud.

"From what I can tell from these pictures, they've got some sort of a pulley system to get you up on the horse and back down. Plus, you ride with a counselor."

I'm trying to imagine this.

I think I'm feeling sorry for the horse!

CHAPTER 4

Mom downloaded all the paperwork for the camp as soon as Dad put Penny to bed. Which took *for-EVER* because Penny had left her pet stuffed squirrel Doodle in the grass somewhere in Mrs. V's yard, and Dad had to go hunting for it with a flashlight.

Camp Green Glades did not play around. The application was twenty-two pages long. I sat next to Mom while she typed in answers on her computer.

"These folks are covering every single possibility—and a couple of impossibilities!" she told me with an *uh-huh* nod. "I like that. If I'm sending my baby girl to a place she's never been before, I'm glad to know they are very thorough!"

"Like what?" I tapped.

She read the list to me:

—Please give a full description of applicant's
   abilities and disabilities.

—Does the applicant have seizures?

—Describe any allergies or possible reactions.

—Describe reactions to insect bites.

—List all medications the camper takes, the
   quantities, the times medication must be
   given, and any adverse reactions.

—Has the applicant ever had skin rashes,
   breathing problems, low blood pressure,
   high blood pressure, ear infections . . . ?

She paused, scrolling through the impossibly long
set of questions. "Gee, there are twenty-seven more
questions just in this section!"

Most of them did not apply to me, so that made me
feel pretty good. I'm basically healthy. A few weeks ago,
when we went for my regular medical checkup, the

doctor said I was fine and dandy—a "perfect picture of health," he'd said.

Uh . . . yeah . . .

Mom continued reading the checklist:

"'Does the applicant need help with dressing, showering, bathing, tying shoes . . . ?'"

Yep!

"'Does the applicant need supervision in the swimming pool?'"

Yep! For sure!

"Does the applicant have stinky breath and feet that smell like onions?"

I jerked my head around. **"I see you got jokes!"** I told Mom.

"There are zillions of pages of these questions," she told me with a laugh. "I'm sure that one is on the next page!"

She typed and typed, then got to the third page. "Ooh! Now this is better. Listen to these:

"Is the applicant kind and generous and caring? Yes.

"Does the applicant have a family that adores her? Yes.

"Is the applicant smarter and lovelier than any other twelve-year-old in the universe? Absolutely yes."

I reached out for a hug. My mom is the best.

Mom continued to read what was actually on the page.

"'Is the applicant afraid of loud noises, animals, insects, storms, monsters, or the dark?'"

Hmm . . . Godzilla, maybe.

"'Please write a detailed description of the applicant's home life. This includes typical daily family activities, layout of living quarters, and how the applicant fits into the daily routine of your family.'"

Whoa! That's gonna take a while!

I wondered what Mom was saying as she typed in her answer. Nothing around here is what most folks would call "normal." We have a ramp outside our front door instead of steps. Our living-room throw pillows are permanently tossed on the floor in front of the sofa in case my body decides to do a fancy forward somersault. My bed is set up very low to the floor on the possibility that I might roll out.

The bathroom? Yep! Easy shower access and a sprayer that Penny loves. She calls it the "jungle rainmaker." It's fun for her, but Dad set it up because for me, bathing gets complicated.

As I thought about it, I had to admit that taking care of me was a full-time job, a 24/7 responsibility, a task that would never be completed. Jeez.

But Mom was humming away as she typed. That's what she does when she's in a happy place. No frown of annoyance on her face. She glanced over and smiled at me with genuine Mom-love. She didn't even look tired, and Mom always looked tired.

It took forever, but we finally finished the last form.

"You ready?" Mom asked me one final time.

"Yes. Absolutely!" I told her.

"Okay, then. Send it in, kid!" She rolled my chair close to her computer and gave me a high five. It took me only a few seconds to hover my hand over her keyboard. It didn't wobble. I let it drop, and I hit send.

CHAPTER 5

My application to Camp Green Glades went in on Monday. On Tuesday Mom told me they had sent a reply.

Whoa! That was fast! Maybe too fast. There's a lever on my chair that propels me forward. I grabbed it and hurried into Mom's room.

She made a couple of taps on her keyboard, and there it was. She drew in a deep breath. "Uh, well, let me read what they say," she said quietly. "Thank you for your application to Camp Green Glades. We're very sorry, but all available spots for the current summer sessions have been filled at this time. However, your child's name has been placed on our waiting list. If an opening occurs because of a cancellation, you will be notified. We look forward to meeting Melody Brooks in the near future."

I felt like I'd been punched in the gut. It never occurred to me that they would say no. And, and, and the website had said there were openings!

Mom gnawed at her bottom lip, then turned from the computer to give me a long, long hug.

And I couldn't help it, but I have to admit, it felt a little bit like the time I had been left behind in an airport by classmates who I had thought were friends. They had . . . ditched me! Because, well, I guess I was too much trouble. Was I—was I too much for the camp to handle? Were there too many boxes checked off on those first two pages? Maybe they were just being nice by saying the slots were filled!

I pulled roughly away from my mother, rolled back to my room, and grabbed the specially designed remote from its place on the side of my bed. Dad had set it up so it was on a coiled cord that couldn't really fall far from my reach. The buttons were huge. Penny loved it because it was perfect for her chubby fingers. I turned the TV on, clicked on a music channel, and turned it up loud. Mom came in a little later and asked if I was hungry. I turned up the music even louder and she tiptoed out.

At last, the music started changing colors in my head, and I calmed down enough to fall asleep in my chair.

CHAPTER 6

It was only Thursday and it had been raining and gray all day, just like my mood. So Mrs. V decided to switch things up and take us to the library, even though it wasn't even Friday. Well, maybe because I had *begged* her.

"Girl, you want me to go out in all this moisture and mess up my new hairdo?"

That made me laugh. **"It's for Penny,"** I tapped out, giving her what I hoped was a convincing smile.

"I want to get a book about a dragon," Penny told her. "A shiny red dragon!" She placed her small hand on mine.

"Okay, you two," Mrs. V told us, "I can tell when I'm being ganged up on. Okay, okay!"

Because it was a yucky day, it took us a little longer than usual to load and unload—it's complicated trying to keep me and my wheelchair dry—but by the time we got there, the sky had cleared, and the library wasn't crowded at all.

Mr. Francisco greeted us with a wave as I plunked last week's books into the book drop. "Perfect timing, Penny!" he told her cheerfully. "We're about to begin story time!" He hurried her to the picture book section, where I'm sure he'd also help her find books about dragons.

Mrs. V and I wandered around a little; she usually waited to see what I was interested in. Today I didn't even know. Were there books about feeling mad? Was there an I'm Angry section? There should be. Then I got mad that I was mad. Why was I letting this stupid camp make me feel bad? Ooh, I'd really reeeeally reeeeally wanted to go! But if I was too much trouble for them, then it wasn't right for me, right? Well, that's what my brain was telling the rest of me. My leg kicked over a wastebasket. Was that an accident? Maybe.

"You okay, Melody?" Mrs. V asked.

My head nodded yes, but my head wasn't in charge of the rest of me. Nothing new here!

I told Mrs. V that I wanted a fantasy book this time. "Anything in particular?" she asked.

"No," I tapped. **"Just a good book to sink into."**

We found a really old book called *Atta*, by Francis Bellamy. I read the flap and it was about a man who somehow gets shrunk to the size of an insect and becomes best friends with an ant. Freaky weird. But kinda cool. That worked fine for my mood. And Mrs. V seemed to be excited about a collection of poetry by Rita Dove, one of her favorites.

We headed back to the children's section next, just as Mr. Francisco was finishing up story time. Penny had found her dragon book—about a red dragon, even. By the time we got home, Penny was dozing in her car seat, and I was looking forward to reading my book. I tried not to think about camp at all. I was *done* thinking about that camp. Even though stupid thoughts kept badgering me. If I hadn't checked the "needs help swimming," or the "needs help eating" box, would they have accepted me? I told my brain to stop!

But as we were pulling into Mrs. V's driveway, Mom rushed out our door and tapped her fingernails on the window. She must have just gotten home from work—she still had on her scrubs.

"Melody!" Mom practically screeched.

Mrs. V rolled the window down on my side.

Mom grasped my hand. "Guess what? Guess what? The camp had a cancellation and you're in! We have to respond immediately. What do you think?"

Wait. What?

Mom held her phone out and read, "'We have had a last-minute cancellation and your application has been processed. If you are still interested, we are pleased to inform you that Melody Brooks has been accepted to Camp Green Glades in Greengrass, Ohio. The session begins on Sunday. Please contact us immediately if you are able to accept.'"

Uh, *this* Sunday?

She paused. I paused—stunned at the suddenness of it all. So they turned me down, but now they wanted me? I didn't get it. Was I glad? Uh, I thought so. But I'd let myself dig down into the disappointed hole. I needed a minute to come back up.

Penny woke up and decided she really needed to go to the bathroom. Mom whisked her away, while Mrs. V unbuckled me and rolled me to our house, Butterscotch greeting me with yips of welcome. Mrs. V locked my chair and we sat for a moment in silence in the living room. Sunday? As in, like, just over two days?

Penny came racing from the bathroom and shoved her still-wet hands under my nose. "Mom let me wash 'em with her special raspberry soap!" she said triumphantly. She then climbed up on the sofa with Doodle and her new dragon book.

Mrs. V glanced out the front window. "Your dad's home, Melody. And I've got to feed the cat. Let me know what you guys decide!"

Mom thanked her as she left, then collapsed into the softness of our worn green sofa, grinning at me.

"You're in! You're in! You're in!" she kept whispering as if in disbelief.

Dad gave Mom a curious glance as he sauntered through the front door. He kissed her, then picked Penny up and twirled her around—after she made sure he smelled her hands. He saved his best hug for me, whispering, "What's the music of Melody singing today?"

I gave him my tightest hug.

"What's new, my ladies?" he asked.

Wait till he hears THIS news! I thought. My legs started kicking excitedly. Mom jumped up from the couch, sat back down, jumped up, held her head in her hand for a second, then sat back down.

Dad looked a little concerned. "Diane, you okay?" he asked.

Mom jumped up once more. "Nothing is wrong. Everything is right, actually. Melody got accepted into camp! They had a cancellation!"

"Hey, that's great news!" Dad exclaimed, turning to me. "Congratulations, honey," he added, planting a kiss on top of my head. "It'll give you something to look forward to this summer."

"It's for next week, actually," Mom explained. "Like . . . this coming Sunday."

"Wow." Dad exhaled loudly. "That's fast. Okay, okay. Recalibrate. Can we do this in time?"

"Yes, but . . ."

They both looked to me.

The conversation between me and my parents went something like this:

Mom: "What do you think, Melody?"

Me (tapping out my answer): **"I want to go."**

Dad: "I need to call the Better Business Bureau and check on them."

Me: **"I want to go."**

Mom: "There's not much time to shop and pack and—"

Me: **"I want to go."**

Dad: "But you've never been away from home overnight before!"

Me: **"I want to go."**

Mom (already moving into "mom-planning" mode): "I have to write out instructions on how to feed you and—"

Me: **"I want to go."**

Dad: "But it's two hours away, and we won't be able to get to you quickly in case of an emergency, and—"

Me: **"I want to go."**

Mom: "Oh, Melody! Are you sure? We've never been apart from each other for a whole week!"

Me: **"I want to go. Pleeeeeeeeeeease?!"**

We told them yes.

Oh, snap. What have I gotten myself into?

CHAPTER 7

So, our life kicked into crazy whirlwind mode. The folks at our local stores and pharmacies and malls now knew us by name—we've gone twice a day for the past two days. We're pretty recognizable—Mom had added a large woven shopping bag to the back of my chair, since we can't really use a shopping cart. Each time we got to the checkout, it was usually bulging with stuff.

I was seriously wanting to pick out my own clothes—I'm twelve now! I had a very specific list in my mind. So, by my nodding at or pointing to just the right items, we found shorts—one really cute, really short, with a rolled cuff, and another pair with an embroidered flower on one side. And jeans—stretchy and skinny and just the right hue of blue. We found several cute tops—nice to know that part of me was finally filling out a little! Socks and underwear got tossed into the bag, but only after I'd nodded my okay. This stuff is *important*!

And shoes. Yes, I might not be able to walk, but my kicks matter. They have to be white, not pink with little flowers like Penny's, and they gotta be the latest styles. Yes, I do know the brand names, and yes, those are the ones I like! We found a pair of Nikes—cloud white, perfect—even though Mom grumbled about how a pair of sneakers cost more than three baskets full of groceries. I made Elvira screech **"Thank you"** over and over as we navigated through the stores.

On the final trip, I managed to convince her to get me a fresh Nike sweatshirt—black with a white swoosh. So then she went and tossed a second pair of sneakers— pink Adidas—into the woven bag behind my chair. I squealed—loudly. You just can't DO that—mix brands and colors and stuff! And PINK?

Elvira had my back, for sure. I popped up the volume. **"No pink shoes!"** I tapped. **"Black or white only."**

I kicked. I twisted. I did my best to point to the Nike sign.

Mom, totally baffled by my behavior, said, "What? You don't like those? I think they're cute and kinda stylish—plus, they were on sale!" She smiled hard to convince me.

I finally spelled out N-I-K-E on my board and pointed to the sign with the swoosh. She placed the pink shoes back on the rack. *Whew! That was close!* We found a second pair of black Nikes—Air Zooms—on the sale rack, and she placed those into the shopping bag. I reached back and touched my hand to hers.

Thanks, my eyes said. For getting it. And for getting them.

Mom made So. Many. Lists. She used different-colored highlighters to indicate my medications (not as many as I used to take), my food needs (stuff has to be mashed pretty soft), and food I hated (like green peas—but who's gonna serve peas at camp?). She drew an elaborate chart to explain how to use my talking board and how to charge it at night. She also added a note to remind them that it was fairly water-resistant, but it didn't need to fall into that pretty lake on their brochure.

We packed. Then repacked. We sorted and tossed and added.

Jeans. Underwear. Socks. T-shirts. And shorts to match the new T-shirts—green and blue and purple.

Mom likes stuff to match. It makes her crazy if I go to school in a blue shirt and blue jeans, but come home with a purple top and red pants because maybe I had a spill that day. She always feels like she has to change me again. Yeah, issues!

Mom rolled everything into nifty, curled units, each roll containing a T-shirt, matching shorts, underwear, and socks. "This will make it easy for your camp guide," she said. For once I was glad I couldn't talk because when she saw me cracking up, she put her hands on her hips like a challenge. "And what is so funny?"

I can't wait to get to camp and wear a green shirt with purple shorts, is what I didn't tell her! I just kept laughing. She never figured it out.

The last thing she tucked into the duffel was a dress—a red dress.

"I won't need that," I tapped with a roll of my eyes.

"You never know."

"It's camp, Mom, not the prom!"

She ignored me and tucked it in anyway.

Penny flitted around, aware of the excitement, but not really sure what it all meant, except that she always managed to get a new coloring book or markers or clothes for her dolls every time we made a run to the store.

Saturday evening Mom sat down in the rocker by

my bed and just rocked silently. We've had it since before I was born. One of the armrests wobbles a little now, and most of the red roses that Dad had hand-painted on it had worn off, but when I was little, that chair had pretty much saved us both.

I had been a tiny baby—only three and a half pounds at birth. The doctors kept me in a specialized incubator for preemies for a few weeks. At first Mom could only touch me through ports in the Isolette, as it was called. She sat for hours, rubbing my arms and legs and back, whispering words of love and singing to me. At least that's what she told me. I'm pretty smart, but even I can't remember day one and two and three!

Mom was finally allowed to hold me when I was about a month old. Dad told me that she sat there in that hospital room nearly all day long—just rocking her little Melody. So when I got to come home, Dad had welcomed me with that hand-painted rocker. Every single day, either she or Dad would rock me and sing to me. Every day. All day. Maybe that's why I rarely cried. That rocker soothed me—maybe all of us—during those first few months. And it was soothing still, I guess, for my mom, who was *clearly* having all kinds of feelings about me heading off to camp.

Mom sat and rocked, and I was sitting in my chair, watching. Penny was stacking colorful wooden blocks into wobbly towers, which consistently tumbled onto the floor. I couldn't help her, but she didn't mind—she just gathered them around her once more and rebuilt. She hummed as she stacked. Moonlight was streaming through the window of my room.

Squeak. "Are you ready for this—leaving for camp?" Mom asked.

Squeak. I tapped quickly. **"Yes. Yes. Yes."**

Squeak. "Are you worried about being away from home for a whole week?"

Squeak. **"Nope!"**

The squeak stopped as she stood up and clutched her heart.

"Ouch!" she cried with fake despair. "My baby is growing up on me!"

We giggled at that, but she was right. I was.

CHAPTER 8

It took us most of last night to pack our well-used SUV for the trip to Camp Green Glades. All we had to do this sunshine-bright Sunday morning was to add the cooler (snacks and colas and juice boxes already loaded) and my box of medications. Or so I thought.

Penny scurried in and out of the house, wearing the little blue backpack that Mom had given her for the trip. She kept stuffing things in—two Barbie dolls, a coloring book and crayons, her new dragon book, a couple of juice boxes, and of course Doodle.

I sat in my power chair while Dad loaded the manual one into the back of the SUV. He and Mom darted back and forth as well, adding blankets and bags and more bits of my life here. Dad would have packed both chairs and a locomotive if he thought I needed them! But we had all agreed the manual chair probably would be easier to handle on woodsy paths.

At the last minute, Mom went racing back into the house, then running back out, arms full. She tossed in a couple of pillows, some extra clothes, and a small yellow quilt for Penny, a first-aid kit, a case of water, and even candy bars! Normally she'd never let us have those. I think she forgot we were only driving for a couple of hours, not two days.

"We still have room for the washer and the dryer," Dad teased as he helped her shove the case of water into the far back.

She swatted his arm but cracked up as she looked at our supreme overpacking.

"So tell me again why this camp is so far away?" Dad asked as he wedged in a sleeping bag, even though I probably wouldn't need it. "Couldn't you have found anything closer—in case we need to get to her in a hurry?"

"This is the only camp for kids like Melody that is within driving distance and sounds supersafe," she told him in her talking-to-Penny voice. "We talked about this!"

He mumbled something I couldn't hear, but I smirked. Dad was worried, and he didn't know what to do with all the stuff he was feeling!

It was nine a.m. Time. To. Go. Check-in was at noon. We always like to leave early for stuff these days, because of that time I was left behind by that group of kids I thought were my friends. I've been obsessed with being early ever since.

So now I had Elvira shout out the time. **"Hellooo, folks! Nine o'clock! Time to get the Melody show on the road!"**

But Mom wasn't ready. She peppered my dad with a whole slew of questions.

"Did you load her meds?"

"You just did, not two minutes ago," Dad replied patiently.

"Safety straps for her wheelchair?"

"Check."

"Bug spray?"

"Check—two different kinds."

"Her favorite blanket?"

"Check and double check. I think we're good, Diane." He gave her arm a rub. "Our Melody is going to be just fine. Relax a little, okay?"

Mom exhaled in little puffs, then looked up at him with a small smile. "But she's never been away from us for so long. I'm not sure if I can do this! She's my baby girl!"

"Are you worried about her, or about yourself without her?" Dad asked, his voice teasing.

"Probably both!" She sniffled, then sniffled again. "I'm fine," she said after taking a deep breath. "I'm totally fine."

Dad wrapped Mom in a huge bear hug. "And Melody is going to be just great!"

I reached out to my mother. She grabbed my fingers and squeezed. Kids go to camp all the time! We'd be fine.

And, it was time. I didn't want to be the last camper to arrive. So I turned the volume up on Elvira and I tapped out, **"Powerful adventures await! Let's get this show on the road!"**

Mom ran her fingers through my tangle of curls. "Okay, baby girl. We're ready!"

Just as Dad was about to start the engine, Mrs. V bounded out of her house in a neon-pink dress covered with large blue tulips. I've never seen a blue tulip before, but I bet Mrs. V could grow them if she decided to.

She squatted down in front of me and gave me her eagle-eye, no-nonsense stare. "I am so proud of you, Melody! You are brave, you are intelligent, and you are ready for this adventure!"

Then she reached into one of her dress pockets, pulled out a little orange bag, and spilled several circles of braided embroidery out into her hand. I looked at her, a little confused.

"These are friendship bracelets," she explained. "I made them myself."

I still didn't get it.

"I hope you meet lots of new people. And if you want, when camp is over, you can give one of these to a friend or a counselor to remember you by. But know that the best memories will be in your heart."

She leaned in and gave me the biggest hug, engulfing me in that blindingly pink dress. "You got this, kid," she whispered. Then she tucked the packet of bracelets into my backpack.

"Oh, Violet, how very thoughtful of you!" Mom exclaimed. I flung my arms out in agreement.

"Enjoy every second!" Mrs. V rubbed her hands over her face. Was she getting teary?

It was time.

Mom fastened Penny into her car seat, then Dad placed me in the back next to her. Mom double-checked my seat belt, Dad tucked Elvira in the back by my wheelchair, and then I heard him breathe a sigh of relief as he slammed the trunk with a thud. I was amazed it was able to close!

Was this it? Would we actually drive away?

Mrs. V called out, "Don't worry, I've got the power chair, and I'll take good care of Butterscotch!" We all waved. I held my breath. Would Mom run back inside for one last thing?

No. We were off!

CHAPTER 9

Penny's nonstop chatter helped pass the time and kept me from getting nervous. Not that I was nervous or anything . . . well, maybe.

"Why do red cars go faster, Daddy?" she asked as a cherry-colored convertible, roof down, zoomed past us.

"Because that's the rule, Penny," he told her. "Red cars, especially sleek, fast ones, are required to pass all the other cars."

"Why?"

"So they can get there first!"

Penny seemed to think that made sense, because then she asked, "And why are trucks so big?"

"Because they have to carry a lot of stuff!"

"Like what?"

"Well, every single thing you see in a store came from a factory, or a warehouse, or a farm someplace, and all of that has to be delivered by truck!"

"Wow," Penny exclaimed. "I think you need to be a truck driver, Daddy—they've gotta be rich!"

"What? I'm already the richest man in America!" Dad said with a laugh.

"You are?" Penny asked in shock.

"Sure am. I've got you and Mom and Melody."

Good answer, Dad, I thought as Mom touched his arm. Penny started telling Doodle how rich Dad was.

At the same time, hearing him say that gave me an ache. He *wouldn't* have me! For a whole week! And . . . and . . . I wouldn't have him. Or Mom! Or Penny! Or Butterscotch. Or Mrs. V.

All of a sudden all that nervousness that I didn't have even two minutes ago came rushing in. Maybe this camp idea was a mistake. What was I thinking? There was no way I could do this! *What if I get hurt? What if nobody likes me? What if somebody laughs at me? What if they don't understand what I'm trying to say? What if there are bugs in the beds? Ahhhh!* I let myself worry for the next fifty miles.

I did my best to stuff my worries into the back of my

brain as we drove closer and closer to this camp and I noticed fewer buildings and more trees, fewer cars and more green. Fewer people. More silence.

We passed through some small towns, then by a few farmhouses, and lots of fields—thick with stalks, swaying in the breeze. The crops were—uh—I really have no idea. I'm not sure I could tell the difference between barley and wheat. If Mrs. V were here, she'd expect me to know, and also be able to tell her how I could identify each type of plant. Wow, that lady lives in my head.

Dad said, "Hey, girls—most of these fields are soybeans, I think. The taller ones are corn—Ohio's two biggest farm crops."

Somebody paid attention in school. Or maybe Dad was just smart. He always said I get my brains from him, just to tease Mom.

Miles of pine trees, such a deep green they looked like shadows of themselves, darkened the highway. We turned onto a smaller highway; parts of it looked like they had been cut right through an actual forest. The longer we drove, the less there was to see. We were driving through a whole lot of absolutely nothing but forest! And the nervousness started morphing into panic.

I had no business being out here by myself in a

forest! My mind started to create scenes from a disaster movie. There were probably bears or wildcats hiding in the forest waiting to eat me! No, that was ridiculous—like something Penny might say. But it WAS possible that I could get hurt! Or drown. Or roll off a cliff. Or get bitten by a poisonous snake. Maybe I should tell Dad to turn around and go back home! Yep, we need to go back.

I kicked the back of Mom's seat.

"Yes, Melody? Are you okay? You need a bathroom stop? Doesn't look like we'll pass one soon."

I glumly shook my head no. *How am I going to tell them I want to go home?* Elvira was stuck in the far back with my chair.

I was about to be dumped in the boondocks and left to rot. This was not gonna work.

A few buildings came into view.

—A fire station/police station combined: the sign read GREENGRASS FIRE AND POLICE. *Ooh, we're almost there. I think we're almost there!* And I started to feel that flicker of excitement again, like I had the first time I opened the camp's website.

—Two churches: one with a pointed steeple, one with a wine-colored roof.

—A general store. Wow! I thought those only existed in old movies anymore, but the faded blue banner read BUCKETS AND BOLTS GENERAL STORE. Clever.

—A coffee shop. The sign in front said COUSIN JOE'S CUP OF JOE. A lotta cars in that parking lot.

—Ooh! The next store had a giant swirly cone coming out of its roof like an ice-cream chimney. Yum. DANNY'S ICE CREAM—ELEVEN FLAVORS. Whaat? Eleven? I wondered what the flavors were. And why only eleven? Good thing Penny was asleep, or she'd beg for a cone. Maybe Mom and Dad would stop on the way back— but, gee, they'd be stopping without me.

Then it occurred to me that Penny wouldn't be able to say, *Oh look at that—a humongous ice cream on the roof, Dee-Dee!* Because I would be sitting all alone with strangers while she rode back home.

Okay, when we got to this place, I was going to tell my parents that I changed my mind.

Then I saw it—a large red road sign that said CAMP GREEN GLADES—THREE MILES AHEAD! My throat felt like I'd been traveling through a desert, but my palms were wet and sweaty. How does a body even do that? It was like one part of my brain was feeling prickly excited, while the other wanted Dad to make a U-turn in the middle of this road and head the heck back home. Yeah, I was a mess.

CHAPTER 10

We drove down a bumpy road that you'd think would wake Penny, but that kid can sleep through anything. Bumpity, bumpity, until we saw a petite, youngish lady in a baseball cap waving us toward a sign that said STOP HERE FIRST. Dad lowered his window.

"Welcome!" she said, adjusting her baseball cap. "You're early birds, but we're ready for you! My name is Cassie, and I'm your camp director. I'm also the head cook and the song leader and the trash master. I do a little bit of everything." She gave us a quick, broad smile, then got right down to business. "Your camper's name, please?" She glanced at her clipboard.

Mom whispered, "Well, she seems nice!"

But I'm thinking in the back seat, *That lady sounded more like business than fun.* She did not sound like she was glad for me to be here. Fine, maybe I'd just go back home.

Dad smiled at her and said in his jovial, easygoing way, "I'd like you to meet Miss Melody Brooks, a young lady of extraordinary grace and charm and beauty!"

Cassie smiled at me through the back window, checked her clipboard, scribbled a few notes, then said more cheerfully this time, "We're all set! We're eager to get to know Melody. See that orange sign up there? That's where you'll meet your counselor. She'll help you unload, answer all your questions, and get Miss Melody of the extraordinary charm ready for the Glades."

This place sure seemed organized. I might stick around for a little bit, just out of curiosity.

As we drove to the orange sign, I could see large block letters spelling out FIERY FALCONS. What was that all about? Standing by it was someone who looked like she was in college, wearing a shirt that was tangerine bright, a smiling bird printed on the front—a falcon, but it looked a little goofy. The counselor, I guess, had long, rocking braids and wore a metallic-looking hard plastic brace on her left leg.

"She looks a little old to be a camper," Mom mused. "I thought this session was for kids Melody's age—eleven to fourteen."

The orange T-shirt girl beamed as we slowed up and gave her our names. "Greetings, folks! I'm Trinity, and I'll be Melody's camp counselor this week." She waved to me specifically. "Welcome to Green Glades, Melody! I'm so glad you'll be one of our Fiery Falcons."

Dad opened and closed his mouth without saying anything but got himself together quickly. "Uh, glad to meet you, Trinity! Forgive me, but I thought you were a camper."

"Well, I was—when I was a teenager," she said with a laugh. "I came with my little sister—" Now she looked right at me. "She has cerebral palsy too. And I loved it so much, I kept coming back as a volunteer, and I've been a full counselor for four years now. I just arrived this morning as well—we work on rotating weekly shifts, so we always have our best energy for our campers." She pulled over a cart from a cluster of them behind her. "Here, you can unload Melody's stuff onto this, and it will get taken to our cabin."

Mom and Dad were too polite to pry any deeper, but I had about a million questions already. Like can a person swim in a brace like that? And what was her story?

Just as Dad opened the back of the SUV, Penny announced, "I gotta pee!" Trinity pointed to a nearby building, and Mom hustled off with her.

After he unloaded my wheelchair, Dad unbuckled my seat belt and kissed me lightly on the cheek. "I know you're nervous, baby girl," he murmured, "but I've got a good feeling about this." Then he lifted me effortlessly and settled me into the cushioned seat of my chair.

I looked around. It was, well, even greener than I expected, though the online descriptions were color-fully specific. Tall maple trees lined the paths, and I could see a forest of pines just beyond. I counted at least four sturdy-looking wooden cabins ahead of us, and another four across the road. They looked like they'd been made out of Lincoln Logs, a building toy Penny sometimes played with.

A few other early-bird campers—one in a wheelchair like me—and some counselors sat outside a couple of the cabins; they waved when I checked them out.

As I waved back, I wondered about the girl in the wheelchair. Was she worrying about the same stuff I was? Like, what if I got stung by a hornet? What if there was a tornado? What if there were bears? What if I fell down a mountainside? What if this counselor couldn't handle me? What if . . . ?

But as Dad was adjusting my straps and connecting Elvira, Trinity hunkered down beside me. She looked into my rapidly blinking eyes with her dark ones. "I know you're probably feeling a little skittish right now, Melody. You probably want to turn around and go back home. But give it one day, okay? Just one day."

How the heck did she know? Was this how most campers felt on the first day? Was this normal? A little buzz ran through me—was I doing something *normal*? I looked directly back at her and nodded—slowly. Besides, only *part* of me wanted to go back home!

When Mom and Penny came back, Mom proceeded to snap a zillion pictures with her cell phone. Me with Penny. Me with Dad. Me with Penny and Dad. Me with Trinity. Penny with Trinity. *Gahhhhh!*

"We'll be taking a ton of photos for you, Mrs. Brooks," Trinity assured her. "We've hired a photographer! We'll have a packet for you on the last day. I promise."

"Oh, I love knowing that!" my mother said, a little bit of happy finally creeping into her voice.

"Our pleasure! Now let me give you a quick tour."

"You got lions and tigers here?" Penny asked. "You sure got a lot of bushes and trees! This place looks like a real forest! With wolves!"

Trinity didn't laugh at her. Instead she replied

gently, "They all moved away last year—every one! They packed up and moved to California. You sister is safe with me!"

Penny still gave her a side-eye; I had to swallow my chuckle.

Trinity then showed us the cabin I'd be in, which was bigger inside than it looked like it would be. But it looked so . . . empty. But, whoa—bunk beds! I'd never slept in a bunk bed before!

There were two bunks on the left and two on the right. The bottom ones were all floor level. Trinity showed Mom and Dad the rails that would prevent me from falling out of bed. I rolled my eyes in a *I'm not a baby* sort of way. But Mom, of course, gave the rails a hard shake and a huge smile of approval.

Trinity then pulled out drawers and opened closet space we had not noticed. "This is where we hide our stuff!" she explained with a laugh. "You've probably read this on our website, but, to reiterate, we'll have four girls in our cabin, and each camper has her own counselor, who stays in the cabin twenty-four/ seven."

Even though Mom had indeed read that online, it seemed to make her deliriously happy to hear it in person. *I'm* thinking that eight people in one cabin might be kinda crowded.

"Each cabin," Trinity went on to explain, "mostly does things together—we find that campers bond best that way." Mom was still nodding with approval. I was just hoping I'd like these kids! And . . . that they'd like me.

Trinity then showed us the director's office—photos of smiling campers filled the walls top to bottom. When we went back outside, she pointed out with excitement what she called the fire pit, which was not very impressive—just a pile of dirt and charcoal and burnt sticks.

Mom had a million questions, throwing in some she knew I'd want to know about too. Trinity fielded them like a champion.

"Can we see inside the kitchen?" Number one question.

"Absolutely," Trinity agreed. "I just wanted to give you a general overview and layout of our camp area first."

Mom nodded, then added, "I also want to see where she will bathe and eat and do her various activities. This is all very new to us."

"I understand completely," Trinity said, calm as calm could be. She must be used to worried moms! "I'll show you everything—safety protocols, hiking regulations, our kitchen, the bathrooms—all of it."

I could see Mom visibly relax. Maybe then she'd get rid of the gum she'd been chomping on for the past three hours!

The kitchen, well, I don't actually know what I was expecting, but this place looked ready to feed an army. Next was the garden, which grew strawberries and raspberries and tomatoes. The bathrooms, which they called latrines, had safety rails everywhere, and even nonslip security flooring. Mom gave it all a thumbs-up.

As for me, I was starting to feel impressed. There was gonna be so much to see and do here. I *did* wonder if everything—like, what we did all day—was also gonna be totally organized or if we ever got a little freedom. I didn't want to be monitored every single second like I was Penny.

"The stables are just a five-minute walk from here," Trinity told us, pointing vaguely down the road.

"What can you tell me about the horses?" Mom asked.

"Well," Trinity began, "horseback riding is one of our campers' favorite activities! Every horse has been with us for many years, and they've been specially trained to understand our campers. You're gonna love it, Melody!"

I wasn't so sure. A horse weighed like twenty times

more than me! Mom seemed satisfied, however, as she was about to forge ahead with her next question: "And could you tell me—"

That's when Dad, putting Penny on his shoulders, jumped in. "So what kind of cell phone reception do you have here? Your location is rather remote."

Trinity waved her hand in the air, like *no problem*. "No worries there—every parent asks. We've got a privately installed TQ/XP/Ten Thousand phone line— guaranteed to connect to the moon if we need to."

"And counselors always have their phones with them?" Mom asked, her face both a frown and a question.

Trinity nodded with understanding. "We even sleep with them under our pillows. There is no moment we will not have a signal to reach you, or for you to reach us." Then she handed both Mom and Dad a red card full of emergency contact information. Mom peered at it carefully, then tucked it into her purse.

Penny, who had her legs tucked around Dad's neck, hollered out, "So what's wrong with your leg, Trinity?"

Mom gasped. Dad's eyes went wide. I stifled a giggle. I had wanted to ask that same question, but Mom had taught me to be polite. Penny must have slept through her lesson on tact!

But Trinity simply shrugged. "I was in a car accident

several years ago. It doesn't hurt, and it doesn't slow me down. Actually," she continued, winking at Penny, "I think it gives me superpowers!"

Penny's eyes lit up. "Awesome!" she whispered.

As we continued on our tour, I was wondering when Mom would be done with her zillion questions when I got it. She didn't want to leave me. And every question kept that from happening. Aw, Mom. I didn't want her to go either. Or Dad. Or Penny. At the same time, I was itching for them to get out of here. What was that? Yep, I was a *total* mess.

When we circled back to the parking area, Trinity asked, "Are you ready for this adventure, my friend?"

Yeahhh, so far. I was definitely impressed. At the same time, I kept thinking all I had to do was reach over to touch a button on Elvira to tell them I wasn't staying. *I'm out of here! Yep, I've gotta go back home. Now!*

But then, from the silence, a bird, redder than red—a cardinal, I think—landed on a branch right beside me. One solitary bird trilled a solo, so clear, so sure of itself. It seemed to sing just for me—an anthem of welcome? Perhaps a signal I should stay? And now I was wondering what other birds lived around here. We had robins and a few sparrows and crows where we lived. Lots of pigeons. I wouldn't mind seeing other birds.

After signing another stack of paperwork, a final round of hugs from Mom and Dad, a few Mom tears, and—I couldn't believe it—actual Dad sniffles, my parents headed back to the car with Penny. Trinity laid her hand on my shoulder as if in silent support. *Here we go,* I was thinking. *The adventure begins now!*

But as soon as Mom picked Penny up to get her loaded into the car seat, Penny cried out, "Where's Dee-Dee?"

"Dee-Dee's going to stay here for a couple of days, sweetie," I heard Mom tell her.

"All by herself? In the forest?" Penny looked shocked.

"Yes, it's a summer camp for big girls like Melody," Dad told her. "She won't be alone. We talked about this last night, remember?"

"But I didn't know you were gonna *leave* her! There are wolves in the woods! And dragons!" Penny wailed. She wiggled and twisted in Mom's arms, sobbing.

Mom looked at Dad. Dad looked at Mom. I sat there with this woman named Trinity who I did not know, feeling helpless, and guilty for causing Penny to be upset. Penny shimmied down from Mom's arms, still wailing. Mom moved to catch her, but then Trinity asked, "May I?"

Mom's eyes went wide, but she gave Trinity a nod.

Trinity walked over, took Penny's hand, and led her

back to me. And Penny? She sure was giving Trinity the stink eye! Still, she let Trinity place her on my lap. I hugged her as closely as my arms would bend.

Penny grabbed me around my neck. "I don't want you to live in the forest, Dee-Dee."

Okay, being able to talk would be pretty helpful right about now. But I just held her and rubbed her back until she calmed down.

Finally Mom knelt beside us. "Dee-Dee is going to big-girl camp for a couple of days," she said, her voice soothing and soft. "Just seven sleeps. She's gonna be just fine. Hey, we passed an ice cream store on the way here! How about we stop there? Do you want strawberry or chocolate?"

Penny couldn't resist ice cream. "I want 'nilla," she stated, her voice ragged from crying.

"We'll get a vanilla cone, okay?" Mom teased Penny from my arms. "But we better get there quick before they run out!" She passed Penny to Dad. He winked at me before heading to the car.

"I love you, Melody!" Mom whispered. And yep, her eyes were all glisten-y with tears. "Enjoy camp, okay? My almost teenager! I can hardly wait to see all the pictures."

And, in what seemed like a blink, they were gone. I couldn't even yell for them to come back. I felt a swell of panic, but then I looked around at the well-swept paths, the rows of neat wooden cabins, and a pair of blue jays squawking at each other in one of the maples, and told myself, *Okay, Melody Brooks. This is what you asked for. You are ready!*

CHAPTER 11

Trinity twirled my wheelchair around, saying, "You're the first Falcon to check in. How about we get ourselves a little pre-lunch snack, and I'll tell you more about the camp. Sound okay to you?"

At my nod, Trinity rolled my chair to the kitchen, trying to guess my favorite slushy flavor along the way. Nope, not grape—not lime, either! She dug around in a freezer for a minute, then pulled out two. "Cherry or orange?" she asked. I pointed to the cherry one, and she made a silly face. "How did you know that's the one *I* wanted?" That made me laugh.

Trinity draped a towel she pulled out of her

backpack around my neck as we slurped our slushies. Okay, so it was weird having this strange woman spoon cool cherry ice into my mouth. I HATE having to be fed, but gee, that slushy was good.

We ate in a grassy area in front of a row of cabins, tall pines swaying in the distance. Other campers were checking in. Some kids with walkers and fancy motorized wheelchairs. Others on crutches, and some walking with no apparent devices at all. A few cried. Some had carloads of family members hovering near them. Others had only one adult holding a hand or pushing a chair. And nearly everyone looked wide-eyed and wary—I bet I looked exactly the same.

As a passing counselor-looking person stopped by to say, "Hey" to Trinity, I snuck a better look at her. Her hair, dyed a reddish-brown, was styled in intricate box braids, long and flowing. They were twisted to perfection—it must have taken hours. And her perfume was awesome—was that jasmine and hibiscus?

Her makeup—eyes and lashes and lips—looked like it had been professionally done. Who gets fancy makeup done for camp? Hmm. Maybe she could teach me a couple of things. I don't think it's ever occurred to Mom that I might be interested in lipstick or eyeliner, although Penny got a pretend makeup kit for her birthday. Candy-flavored lip gloss and lavender sparkle eye dust. When she'd unwrapped it with an *ooh*, I'd wondered why I'd never been given anything like that. I'd *love* to sprinkle on a little flowery-scented cologne some mornings.

Trinity told her friend she would see her later and turned back to me. "Here's the deal, Melody. I want you to understand that I am *your* counselor. Only you. We have a one-on-one policy here at Camp Green Glades. So I am here for you one hundred percent."

I tried to keep my nose from crinkling. **"Every single second?"** I tapped.

"Absolutely!" she replied. "Our pledge is to keep you safe and secure while you are here."

She probably thought that would make me feel comforted. My mom would be glad to know that, but . . . *every single second*? No free time at all? Yikes.

Trinity continued, "Here's the basic cabin setup. Like I said earlier, there are four girls on our cabin. And four counselors. We, the Fiery Falcons—" She paused. "I know, I know—goofy name. But all the teams have silly names, and T-shirts," she added, "just to make it more fun."

I wasn't really getting how that was fun, but I was paying attention.

"Anyway," she continued, "cabins are grouped into teams. Two cabins of girls, two cabins of boys. Sixteen kids in total, per team, plus the same number of counselors. Our team includes us and the Green Gazelles for the girls, and the Blue Badgers and the Purple Panthers for the guys. But of course we think the Falcons are the finest!"

I managed a small smile.

"The boys' cabins are across the road, and our team shares a number of activities and meals together."

My face must have looked like a question mark, because she quickly added, "Showers and bathroom stuff, are, of course, in two separate buildings."

That's a relief!

"Even though this place is huge, with lots of 'teams' dotted through the campground, we keep each team small—partly for safety, and partly so we can really get to know each other."

I didn't tap anything on my board, just let her talk, taking it all in.

"I promise to take very good care of you. I'll be with you for every game you choose to play, every meal you eat, and every activity you decide to try. And remember, there's not one moment when any of you will be alone."

Not one moment?? That seemed a little intense; even Mom wasn't with me 24/7! I made a face, but I don't think she noticed.

She paused. "And if you decide to do nothing at all,

I'll sit next to you and do that, too!" I looked at her with genuine surprise. Did she really mean that I could sit around doing nothing and get away with it? So I asked her.

She gave me a sideways glance and grinned. "Yep. Nothing is cool. Boring . . . but cool, nevertheless."

I responded with what I hoped looked like a smirk.

"I'll be with you for your swimming lessons. . . ."

And yeah, even though I'd read about it in the brochure, the idea of me swimming was pretty scary.

"I won't leave your side," Trinity continued. "Basically"—and now she laughed—"you can't get rid of me!" She paused and gave me her full attention. Then she said, "So, did I hit all your questions? Did I miss anything?"

I tapped on Elvira. **"What about the horses?"** My hand went extra shaky, so it took a while to tap it out.

"You want the honest truth?" she asked. I braced myself.

But all she said was: "You're gonna love it. The horses are specifically trained, and they are ridiculously gentle. I guarantee this will be your favorite activity."

From my point of view, the words ridiculous and gentle somehow don't go together. But before I could tap anything, she was saying, "And once you feel the magic and power of a horse, you'll never be the same."

Okay, Trinity wasn't half-bad. But she was gonna lose that horse bet, for sure.

She then rattled off info about meals (they were delicious), activities (lots), and safety protocols (double lots), and finally said, "However, missy, now is not the time to do nothing. Let's go get unpacked."

I gave her a nod of agreement.

"This way, Fiery Falcon," she said with a flourish, sending the dozen or so bronze and gold-colored bracelets on her arms clinking like wind chimes. Okay, another plus for Trinity—she knew her bracelets!

CHAPTER 12

Trinity likes earrings, too. As we unpacked my stuff, she carefully unwrapped a small box wrapped in tissue paper. Mom had tucked in three pairs of tiny earrings— teeny butterflies, red rhinestones, and golden dots. After oohing over each, Trinity showed me her own collection—hoops and loops and one set that perfectly matched her bracelets.

"Wanna wear a pair today?" she asked me, holding them out.

"Sure!" I tapped. I chose the butterflies and she popped them in.

We'd barely finished putting my stuff away in an

overhead compartment when the three other girls assigned to our cabin arrived all at once, along with three more counselors.

The first girl, wearing a pair of really cute pink-framed glasses and a T-shirt the color of strawberry ice cream, bounced in, grinning hugely. It was impossible not to smile back.

Next came a girl in a neon-green wheelchair. She had a stony look on her face, and her arms were crossed. I couldn't tell whether she looked scared or angry. She had on unscuffed brand-new shoes.

The third girl walked in on her own power like the first girl had—no wheelchair or walker or obvious special equipment—but she didn't say a word and made no eye contact with anyone, just plopped down in a chair and began picking at her fingernails.

The room was huge, but with two wheelchairs and four stuffed duffel bags, plus the counselors' luggage and four bunk beds, the cabin felt full, crowded—almost like a house with a family.

An iPad, cranked up high, was playing Bob Marley's "One Love."

Trinity greeted everyone with a hello and then declared, "Cabin Chat! Cabin Chat! Let's make a circle, Falcons."

The other girls froze. The music went silent. *What's a cabin chat?*

I rolled myself over to the center of the room, trying not to look too obviously at the two girls who looked as uneasy as I felt, the girl with pink glasses beaming at us all. Okay, it was totally awkward. But I was curious, too.

Trinity flung her arms out wide. "Welcome, Fiery Falcons! I am so excited to be here with you today, our first day at Camp Green Glades!" she exclaimed. "This is going to be home for the next week, and we want you to feel one hundred percent comfortable here. So again, welcome, welcome, welcome, to our four Fiery Falcons!"

The other three counselors, wearing T-shirts identical to Trinity's, made *whoot, whoot, whoot* noises, like we were at a football game or something, then broke into: "Falcons! Falcons!" The other three girls stayed silent. One was peering at me, one had slid down onto the floor and wouldn't look up, and the girl dressed in all pink was bobbing up and down on her toes. Their eyes darted around the room, observing everything. It was clear none of us was sure what we should do yet.

I guess they were like me—a little scared, a little curious, a little *I don't know these people!* At the same time, I knew that these girls, like me, had been to countless doctors' appointments, and specialist consultations, and probably physical therapy and occupational therapy sessions. They were no doubt real familiar

with schools where we either sat in the back of a class
full of kids without disabilities, or in a room designed
for us, with ramps and pull-up bars and security straps
to make sure we didn't fall. Some of us would have to
be fed. Most of us would need a little extra help in the
bathroom.

Yep, even though I didn't know these girls, I kinda
knew them. Which meant they kinda knew me as well.
Huh.

Right on cue, Trinity said, "Time for introductions.
We'll start with the counselors. I'm Trinity. I was born
on the island of Jamaica, and I grew up in a neighborhood in New York called Jamaica. How cool is that?
I'm really glad to be here with you, and I'm here to
help you with anything you need." Then she waved
her arm toward me, bracelets jangling. "And now I'd
like to introduce my camp buddy for the week. Would
you like to say something, Melody?"

What? I thought the counselors were going first! I
hadn't planned on that. Why did I have to go first? I
tried to keep my face from frowning—not sure if it was
working. Then I told myself to get over it.

So I tapped out, **"My name is Melody. This is my
first time at any camp. I'm a little bit scared, and a
big bit excited."** It took a little while to tap all that, but
they were all surprisingly patient. I looked up as Elvira

repeated my words in her mildly mechanical voice.

The girl in the sharp green wheelchair muttered, "I'm a little scared too. I'm not sure I like it here." I glanced over and she gave me a small nod. I smiled back, I hoped encouragingly.

Her counselor squatted beside her. "I completely understand. But let us show you around, try out a few activities, okay?"

The girl's chin trembled, but she didn't say no.

Her counselor introduced herself next. She was short and muscular and had reddish-orange hair and a face full of freckles. "Hey, everybody! I'm Kim, and I'm from Kalamazoo, Michigan. And you guessed it," she said with a laugh, "my favorite letter of the alphabet is *K*! My mom is deaf and my dad is not, so I grew up knowing both spoken as well as sign language. And this lovely lady in the snappy green wheelchair"—she nodded to the girl beside her—"is my camper friend Karyn, spelled with a *K*, of course!"

Karyn, the girl who was ready to get out of here, managed a smile and a wave. Her wheelchair was really cool—the frame sparkled. She didn't look like she had cerebral palsy like me, but it was clear she wasn't gonna walk out of here on her own steam.

"Hi, I'm Karyn with a *K*"—flashing a shy smile at Kim—"and I'm eleven and three quarters. I've never been to camp before." She paused, then said in a rush, "The upstairs part of my body works fine. The down-stairs part—not so much. They call it spina bifida. I call it a pain in the butt. And I really think I want to go home. Can somebody call my mom?"

The other two girls' eyes went wide, but Kim, all calm, simply said, "I totally get it. Let's just wait until later this afternoon to call her, okay? We've got lunch and swimming coming up. How about we call her after that?"

Karyn said okay, but she didn't look happy.

The next counselor quickly jumped in. "Hello, fellow Falcons! My name is Sage. And this is just my second time here at camp. I like to fix computers and play online games when I'm not camping in the fresh air. And I love music!"

That drew some claps. I was thinking, *Oh, good. Some music kids here.*

Sage, who was lanky and totally toned, went on. "I guess my claim to fame is that I once tried out for the Olympics. Swimming; my specialty was breaststroke and back stroke."

"Ooh! Tell us more about that!" Kim said.

"Well, to be honest, I didn't make the team," Sage said with a shrug. "I wasn't fast enough. The girls who made the team were like sharks. I was more like a sea turtle, comparatively." She let out a laugh. "But then I was hired to help them train, and I cheered them on, and when one of the girls from my hometown won a bronze medal, man, was I proud!"

Hmm, I never thought about that—you almost never hear about the folks who *didn't* make the team. Sportscasters aren't ever interviewing *them*. And yet, without someone like Sage, the Olympians might not be able to get where they get. Interesting!

"Introduce me! Introduce me!" the girl wearing the cool pink glasses piped up.

Sage grinned at her. "You betcha! And sitting next to me, with the glossy black hair and infectious smile, is Athena! On the walk over here, she told me she wants to be an artist. She's going to love Messy Paint Day!"

Athena popped up and took several bows. She was seriously into pink, even neon-pink leggings. She had the best grin, and she seemed *ecstatic* to be here.

"I am Athena," she announced, "and I am royalty. I love the color pink. I have probably twenty Barbie princess dolls at home. I don't play with them—I'm too old for that—I collect and display them. They like pink too!"

She bowed again and added a curtsy before sitting down. Then she popped back up again, reached over to her duffel bag, and pulled something from the top.

"I forgot to tell you!" she said, hugging a well-worn

woven pink blanket. "This is Blankie. Blankie sleeps with me and keeps me warm."

She bowed once more and sat down, but then, a second later, was up again. "And oh, I forgot to tell you—I love horses way more than even Barbies."

Then she bowed one last time, sat down, and stayed down. So we clapped at last.

I already liked Athena—I hoped she'd like me. I think Athena might have Down syndrome, but I'm no expert.

"Well, Athena," Sage said. "I'm pretty sure you'll get to ride a horse while we're here!"

Athena hugged herself. "Yay!"

The last counselor wore a backward baseball cap and some sleek purple Doc Martens. She must have been at least six feet tall.

"Hi, I'm Lulu. I was this tall by the time I was in the eighth grade. But my mom taught me to be proud of my height and ignore what other kids might say. So that's what I did. I've got serious basketball skills, and, believe it or not, ballet!"

I imagined her leaping for the basket doing a jeté, and grinned.

Lulu then swung her arm toward the girl sitting cross-legged on the floor.

"This here is my camper buddy, Jocelyn. She just

turned twelve, and she sometimes likes to keep to herself, but hey, that's true for all of us, right?"

Jocelyn seemed much more interested on tracing
the pattern of curves of the wood grain with her finger
than in meeting us.

But just as Lulu finished, Jocelyn tilted her head.
"So we just gonna sit here all day? Let's get this party
started! Started. Started." And she popped up.

All right, then! Everybody laughed.

"We've got twenty minutes till lunch—let's go check
out the lake," Trinity suggested. "It's just sitting there,
waiting to say hello." She grabbed the camera hanging
on a peg by the door and strapped it around her neck,
and we headed out into the sunlight.

CHAPTER 13

So, my cabinmates didn't seem so bad, and the cabin was just like the one on the website, so I was trying to find something awful, something to complain about, but the weather wasn't going to be it either—at least not today. The air was soft, with the breeze barely a breath on my skin. Sunlight trickled through the leaves of the trees overhead, making design shadows on my arms. I had an urge to paint the pattern, it was so pretty. Not that I've ever painted, but I can in my mind. And thinking of that made me realize that I hadn't even *thought* about being nervous since we set out for the lake. I looked back for Karyn, wondering how she was feeling.

The path was dusty and covered over with boards—
to make it easier for wheelchairs, I guess, though mine
was doing plenty of bumping. But the boards kept the
dust out of the chairs' gears. Points for that, Green
Glades. As we rolled along, I didn't think I'd ever seen
so many shades of green. Must be how the camp got its
name. I mean, yeah, we have trees and plants at home,
but this was a whole other level. How many shades of
green were there in the world? I think I was looking
at them all!

As tree limbs swayed, they created their own breeze,
cooling us as we headed down the path, which was taking forev—ooh! Ohhhh! If I could stop short, I would
have stopped short. Because, wow.

"Campers, I have another introduction," Trinity
exclaimed. "Meet Lilliana. Lake Lilliana!" She grinned
like she was introducing her best friend. But I didn't
blame her. The lake was pretty big; I could barely see
to the other side. And it was the most gorgeous shade
of blue. I'd sort of assumed the website had photo-
shopped the color—it seemed impossible. But nope.
It was the exact same, the prettiest blue I'd ever seen.
Actually, it wasn't just one blue; it shifted from teal,
to navy, to turquoise, even to green. The sky above
was another expanse of blue—cornflower broken up
by feathered white clouds. I wished again I could

paint—I'd have a ball with the blues in my palette.

That's when I remembered Trinity's camera! I twisted in my chair to get her attention, then tapped, **"Take a pic!"** Thanks, Mom, for adding camp phrases to Elvira.

"Great idea, Melody!" Trinity said. She lifted her camera, snapped a photo of the lake, then took another one of me, grinning with the lake behind me. Yeah, fine, I was smiling. It had only been a couple of hours, and they already had me with a smile on my face. Then she snapped photos of the four of us, blinking in the sunshine. A white bird suddenly flew past us. Its wingspan was ginormous!

"Wow! A crane!" Lulu cried out as we all looked up. *Wait till I tell Mrs. V about* that*!*

Trinity took a pic of us watching the crane fly off—I hoped it would show up. "You know, we'll have a zillion photos for you by the time you leave," she told us. "We've hired folks to take photos of everybody and every activity while you're all here. You'll get a chunk of a photo album when you go home."

That was cool. Mom and Dad and Mrs. V would love that—so I told Elvira to say thank you. That was one less thing for me to worry about!

I wanted to learn more about the lake, but I was also getting hungry, so I was glad when we turned back toward camp. One of my secret worries when I'm in a new place is always food. Would I be able to eat it? Would they know how to feed me? I'm not fussy, but my mouth needs mushy. I wondered how they planned to do meals—this was gonna be interesting.

CHAPTER 14

Okay, so I got myself all worked up over nothing. The first meal at camp was not the ordeal I expected. Folks here have organization *down*! It turned out that each counselor had a list of all the feeding details for their camper. Trinity already knew I needed my food sorta soft, and that I had to be fed. Truth? I *hate* that. I'm practically a teenager—less than a year away!—and having applesauce and blended hot dogs shoved in my mouth like I'm a baby is just plain embarrassing. Especially in front of a bunch of people I didn't even know!

But as I looked around our table, which was basically just an indoor picnic table, I saw each of my cabinmates had some type of food issue as well. Karyn complained loudly that she was allergic to carrots, so Kim jogged off with her plate.

After she left, Karyn leaned over and whispered, "I'm not allergic—I just hate carrots! It works every time!"

I've got to remember that trick!

Jocelyn, apparently, had a thing about condiments. She smelled her hot dog, then pushed her plate away.

"Mustard feels like sand, sand, sand!" she declared. Lulu didn't comment, but simply fixed another hot dog for her. Jocelyn looked at it, smelled it, asked for ketchup, then ate it with no trouble.

As Trinity spooned blended baked beans, hot dogs (smashed up!), and then applesauce into my mouth, Athena scooted close to me. "Applesauce is magic, you know." She then chomped down on her apple.

I tapped out, **"Explain."**

"You get the best part of the apple, plus cinnamon, and you don't have to deal with the peeling!"

True that. So then I tapped, **"Okay, then, what's so great about squished hot dogs?"**

She tilted her head, thinking, then said slyly, "I can't tell you—it's a government secret!" I laughed out loud, already glad she was in my cabin. As she began trying to pull the stem off her non-magical apple, I looked around at the other groups of kids—some girls, some boys. A few were being fed, just like I was. Others ate without help. Yikes—putting together meals for a bunch of kids with various issues had to take some serious planning.

Just as I was feeling almost stuffed, Cassie, the director, popped her head out of the kitchen. "Anybody want ice cream?" she hollered. "We've got chocolate sundaes!"

Everybody shouted yes! Well, except for me. I'm a strawberry or vanilla girl. Mom keeps telling me she's gonna make me a chocolate lover one of these days—no thanks!

They had sherbets and nondairy ices for the kids who couldn't do milk-based food. So that's what I had instead of the sundae. Okay, more points for Camp Green Glades.

After lunch the counselors took us to the latrine. Get this—we each had our own separate stall! And big! With super-supportive toilet seats. Okay, they've got me admiring the toilets. Sad, I know, but hey, necessities matter.

When we got back to our cabin, Sage told us to get out our swimsuits. "Now remember, while we'd love for you to try all the activities, you're not *required* to, except maybe dinner. I'd hate for you to starve while you're here—it tends to upset parents," she joked. "So swimming will be our first official activity of the week, followed by arts and crafts."

At the mention of parents, Karyn mumbled that she would be leaving for home in a few hours.

But I was thinking, *Hmm. Art projects? That might be fun to try. But swimming? Good luck with that! A whole summer wouldn't be enough to teach me.*

Trinity must have seen the look on my face, because she asked, "You're not a swimmer, Melody?"

I tapped, **"No. I'm a sinker."**

Even Karyn giggled.

Actually, I didn't know what I was. Last year Mom had signed Penny up for swimming lessons, and she took me a couple of times to watch. I liked sitting by the pool, listening to the echoes of the happy yelps and shrieks of the littles. I wondered how the pool people got the water to be so perfectly blue. When I got home, I looked up enough about chlorine to become a chemist.

It was fun watching Penny learn to kick and roll and paddle with her little safety baby floats on her arms and around her waist. But me? Swim? Not gonna happen.

"I tell you what," Trinity said, her voice all honey. "Let's just get your suit on and you can sit by the side—watch the others splash a bit, and maybe just let your feet get wet. Okay?"

I could tell she wasn't going to give up, so I tapped **okay**. But she wasn't gonna win this one.

So I added, **"The lake is dangerous! It could have rip currents! Or a fast-moving tide!"**

"Well, lakes don't have tides, oceans do . . . ," Trinity explained. "But regardless, we're not swimming in the lake. We're swimming in the pool right by it. It's eighty-five degrees, warm and shallow, and about as scary as a bathtub!"

Ooh, a pool, huh? I'd forgotten about the pool! Eighty-five degrees? Okay. Okay, fine. Let's get this over with. We got my suit on quickly—actually, it had never been worn in the water, ha! It was a bright yellow—I probably looked like a stick of butter. Then we headed down to the pool before I had a chance to change my mind.

Along the outside of a long, low building by the pool—another awesome blue—hung a variety of swimming aids and hookups, as well as several different kinds of life vests. All of them were Crayola-bright, as if to say, *Nobody drowns in our pool!* A ramp was perched by the pool edge, apparently to help counselors lower a plastic-wheeled woven water wheelchair into the pool.

And was there music? Yes, soft classical music, the kind Mrs. V likes, was playing from loudspeakers. Classsssssy!

Karyn was clearly a quick changer, 'cause she and Kim had reached the pool first, so they were just going in. I watched, fascinated, as Kim transferred Karyn into that pool wheelchair. It was the same color as those highway cones that Dad always complained about. Karyn was then slowly, slowly rolled backward down the ramp into the water, Kim beside her, close as could be, every centimeter of the way. As the water touched Karyn's tush, I heard her growl, "I told you—I wanna go home!" But Kim gently persisted. A few more inches, a few more feet, and . . . wow, I actually saw Karyn smile!

"It's . . . like a giant bathtub!" she cried out. And when water splashed up onto her face, she only laughed. She let Kim take her out of the chair, and as they bobbed in the water, I could tell she'd at least temporarily forgotten about her plans to pack up and leave.

Trinity, her suit a pattern of dark blue birds, tapped my shoulder. "Looks pretty fun, eh? Wanna try next?"

Nope. I refused to be swayed. I crossed my wrists and stared at her defiantly. No way I was doing this. No way. If someone let go of me for one second, down I'd go. So, no thank you.

Okay, to be fair, when I first saw the lake, I hadn't even noticed the small swimming pool set off to the side. Now that I thought about it, the idea of putting kids at *this* camp into a large, potentially deep lake—full of who knows what kind of fish—would have been a pretty terrible idea. So I gotta admit, these Green Glades folks thought of everything. But I still wasn't going in. Sinker. That's me.

Trinity raised an eyebrow. "Look, girlfriend," she said. "I am the one who will be taking you into the water." I raised a *so what* eyebrow. Well, I think I did.

She paused and seemed to be thinking of what she could say to convince me. "Do you like my hair?" she asked all out of the blue, flipping her long, long braids.

I nodded.

"Do you know how much I paid to get these lovely braids?"

I had no idea—my hair never gets much past my shoulders—but I figured it was probably a lot.

She pursed her lips, then spun around, her braids extending in a glorious circle. "Check this out, Melody my friend!" She gave me a saucy look. "There is NO WAY I'm getting my hair wet today, or *any* day!"

I couldn't help it; I cracked up.

She pulled her braids up into a giant pile on top of her head and secured it with the biggest rubber band I'd ever seen. "So you are plenty safe, okay? If you go down, I go down, and there goes my hair. No way, no how, no, ma'am!"

I honestly could not think of one counterargument. So I started to laugh again. **"YOU WIN,"** I finally tapped out.

But as we approached the edge of the pool, a volcano of *nope, nope, nope* took over. *Not gonna do this. Not gonna happen.*

Trinity must have been used to kids freaking the first time going into a pool, because she added, "I. Will. Not. Let. You. Go." She paused, then repeated it. "Trust me?"

I did. I think. So I nodded yes. Then, I couldn't help myself, but I glanced at the brace on her leg. Did it make a difference in the water? Then I remembered she said she'd been doing this for years, so I guess she had that covered.

She whisked me out of my wheelchair and strapped me into another one of those swim chairs that, now that I saw it up close, looked like it had been constructed out of pool noodles, a cross between a lawn chair and a pool toy. I found myself sitting on the side of the pool like any other swimmer, well, almost. Trinity sat next to me, swinging her feet in the water.

At this point Kim was literally trying to coax Karyn out of the pool. "We do this *every* day," I could hear Kim promising her. An attendant brought over fluffy towels for them as Karyn was wheeled and transferred back to her own chair. As she passed by me, wrapped in the towel, she leaned over to say, "Maybe I'll stay until after swimming tomorrow. But then I'm gone!"

Huh! But before I could respond, Trinity was wheeling me to the ramp. "You ready, kid?" she asked.

I couldn't even give her a grunt of response. Because—*what was going on with me?*—I was too busy wondering if somebody's heart can explode from terror. Even if I could talk, I wouldn't have been able to speak. I felt like one of those characters in a scary movie just before the monster pounces.

Trinity could tell I was not, in fact, ready, because she said, "We're going to roll down the ramp in this fancy water chair, just like Karyn did. And the pool's only a couple of feet deep. You good?"

I heard laughter, splashes, cries of joy, shrieks, giggles of other kids in the pool. Maybe the Gazelles or the Panthers? I really didn't care at this point, because all I knew was that in just a few seconds, death was gonna swoop in and take me. Yep, this was it.

"You good?" she asked again. Wow—she was as persistent as Penny. Penny! How was I going to go home and tell Penny I was too scared to swim? In what was essentially a giant bathtub! I couldn't do that. So, oh so slowly, I nodded my head to tell Trinity to do it. She didn't wait for me to change my mind. "Here we go."

And then we were rolling backward into the water. Backward? *What?* I mean I *saw* Karyn go in this way, but it didn't *register* then! I couldn't even see how deep we were getting! And this ramp? It looked like plastic! Thin plastic! Argh! Yet slowly, smoothly, we kept rolling, despite the fact that this skinny little thing was gonna break into a million pieces, and I would plunge to my death in seconds. I wanted to scream so bad, but I forced myself to hold it in.

And I braced myself for the coldness to seep through my bathing suit. My butt actually hit the water first, and I gasped. But wait—it wasn't cold at all! It was warm—really warm. And even felt soft, like when Mom lets me have a bubble bath.

I was so glad I didn't howl a second ago—that would have been totally embarrassing.

Now the water was at my waist, then mid-chest, and I felt myself relax. Gee, what the heck had I been so worried about? This was easy-peasy.

Well, it was easy until Trinity decided it would somehow be fun to take me out of the swim chair. As soon as she undid the strap, I grabbed the water in a panic, but there was nothing to hold on to. Nothing! My fingers clutched and clawed, at nothingness.

One part of my brain was wondering how water could be something and feel like nothing at the same time. The other part was yelping, *Nope. Nope. Nope. I changed my mind. Forget the embarrassment—I gotta get out of here!* I started to struggle. I arched my back. I had to get out of the water! I let out something that sounded like a cross between a yowl and a yelp. No, this was a jumbo-sized, earth-shattering, gut-exploding HOWL!

I'm sure Martians on the next planet heard me.

Trinity didn't seem even remotely bothered by the fact that I was going to die right that second. She held me tightly and just kept whispering, "I got you, Melody. I got you. Just relax. I promise on my life that I will not let you go. Just breathe. Let it in. Let it out. There you go. Just breathe." She rocked me back and forth, slowly, gently.

"Look at you," she purred. "Just look at you swimming. You're doin' it, girlfriend. You are doing it!"

My arms had stopped flailing, even though I still knew I was gonna die any minute now.

"Feeling better?"

I think I nodded.

"Feel the warm, Melody," Trinity was saying now. "What color is warm? Orange? Turquoise? I'm feeling a little lavender here—how about you?"

That caught my attention—did Trinity feel colors too? And then I was thinking that the thought of the feel of a color made sense. The water felt soft, silky, and

I dunno—it felt pink. Yeah, I know water looks blue in a pool, but this water felt pink, maybe pale rose.

"Looking good, Melody!" I heard Athena call out.

Trinity rocked us to the other end of the pool as Sage and Athena were getting in. As they rolled down the ramp, I wondered why they were using the special loading system like I had. Then I figured it was camp safety rules. Made sense.

Athena was the exact opposite of me when she hit the water. "Whoopie-woo!" she shouted, and immediately wanted to get out of the chair.

"Like *my* suit?" she asked me, waving, splashing water everywhere. But she sounded so happy I didn't even care. I nodded yes. Her suit, of course, was pink. It had cute embroidered starfish all over it—so very Athena.

"I like yours, too," Athena said. "You look like my mom's canary!" I almost choke-laughed at that.

"Okay, girlfriend, let's try bouncing a little," Trinity said to me, getting my focus back on swimming. Or, more accurately, not drowning right that second. She bounced up and down, just once. The water splashed on my shoulders. I only flailed a little bit this time. Hey, not so bad!

"You're doing great, Melody! Let's try a few more bounces, okay?"

I nodded and tensed, but the movement was so slow and gentle, I barely felt it. And I got what she was doing, sneaky Trinity! Getting me deeper into the water. And it wasn't so bad at all. Then she stretched me out on my back and, with her arms tucked safely under mine, began to swirl me back and forth.

My body felt ripply-loose. It was actually sort of amazing. It was like, I was me, but I didn't feel like me. I couldn't believe I'd been so scared. Jeez.

Finally Trinity said, "Let's try some kicks."

Kicks?

"Just let your legs do their usual thing. They move all the time, even when you don't want them to, am I right?"

Yeah, they do sometimes move anytime they want, without any input from me. Seriously. I can be sitting in class, everyone is quiet and concentrating on the lesson, and boom, my legs will simply decide to kick and jam. No music necessary.

So I let my legs do their thing—and they kicked. Ahh—that felt great! I kicked again! The water even splashed a little. Like . . . a swimmer! It sure wasn't going to get me into the Olympics, but I was kicking and moving in a swimming pool. I wished Penny could see me. I felt like I'd just won a gold medal in the advanced freestyle butterfly category—whatever that is.

When Trinity said it was time to get out, I couldn't tell her, but I pretty much wanted to spend the rest of camp right here in the water. Stick some floaties on me, come by and feed me once in a while, and I'd be good.

CHAPTER 15

Once we were all dry—ah—warmed towels—*ooh la la*—and dressed in our shorts and T-shirts, we headed back the way we'd come on the board path. But instead of going back to our cabin, Lulu announced we were taking a detour, which led us back to the mess hall—for pie! We had a choice of key lime pie or apple. Key lime was one of Mrs. V's favorite desserts. As Trinity spooned it in, I closed my eyes so I could *feel* the flavors. *Nope! Not even close to Mrs. V's recipe!* But this was camp—I was just glad it was tasty.

Jocelyn asked for seconds of her apple pie—three times, so I guess that's called thirds! Karyn was cool with the key lime. And Athena seemed to love both, but she *did* ask if we could have strawberry ice cream one day. I had Elvira shout a big "Yeah!" at that.

As we finished, Trinity reminded us that we had art next. Sounded cool. I've always liked to *look* at art. Dad's taken me to the art museum several times—I love it. There are zillions of pictures of pale European ladies, who, frankly, looked to me like they were bored out of their minds. I felt sorry for them—all dressed up in really uncomfortable-looking high-necked dresses, sipping tea or gazing out a window.

What I really like is the modern art wing, where a purple-edged square can be a political statement, or a glop of chartreuse is supposed to represent birds in flight. Dad always makes up crazy stories about the paintings to explain what the painter was thinking of when he or she decided to draw that truck or that bird or that baby.

I thought back to the patterns the trees made, the palette of blue making up the lake. Hey, maybe this was actually a chance to make the paintings I saw in my mind—at least with color! We headed over to what Trinity called the art department, which turned out to be a wide, sunny barn filled with tables that were splashed and speckled with multiple layers of every possible color.

"Sorry, not sorry about the mess," Trinity announced as we looked around. "But great art sometimes emerges from incredible chaos. And you can't mess up here. Whatever you create is yours, and if you create it, it's art!"

Our counselors cut necks and armholes out of the sides and bottoms of massive green garbage bags and slid them over our heads.

So, my fashion statement for the afternoon is a giant green plastic trash bag! Look out, *Seventeen*, I am your next cover model, for sure! Don't know why I even worried about choosing the exact right earrings this morning . . . do butterflies go with garbage bags? NOT!

Karyn wheeled herself back and forth in front of us. She turned, posed; turned, posed. "I'm wearing a one-of-a-kind outfit from a brand-new designer—La Green Glades," she cooed, pretending to pout in front of cameras. "Okay, please, please, no more photographs!"

I typed, **"I'd like to order two, please! But you gotta find some sleeker styles."** Athena, catching on, said, "I want four!" Even Jocelyn chimed in: "Three, three, three for me!" We all cracked up. The counselors just shook their heads, laughing. Kim motioned for us to pull up to a table, then brought over a stack of poster board.

"Okay, campers," she said. "How many of you have

ever made a massive mess at home or school and kinda got in trouble for it?"

Athena waved wildly. "Me! Me! Me! I make a mess ALL the time!"

Jocelyn looked away, but I spied a little smile on her face.

Karyn said, "I never make a mess."

"Yeah, right!" I typed, and we bumped elbows.

"Well," Kim said, "I'm giving you permission to make a mess. Actually, I'm encouraging you to be messy. No, let me be more emphatic—I'm *requiring* you to MAKE A MESS!"

We looked at her like she was crazy. I was sure none of us had ever been told that before. I thought back to all the times I'd spilled my spaghetti or my juice and how Mom would never actually fuss at me, but she'd sigh a little as she cleaned it up. I always felt bad when that happened. Really bad. And now this lady was telling us to do it on purpose? *All right then!*

"Falcons, you have your canvases," she announced. "There are no rules. Do your thing!"

Trinity had set up plastic jars of paint all around the table—cherry red and bluebird blue and the purple of real sweet grapes. Jade green and candy yellow. Sage added bright pink for Athena. And double jars of orange, since that was our color!

"Now go for it," Trinity told us. "There is no way

you can be wrong here. Creation is never neat! Be a messy Matisse! Let the mess begin!!"

We hesitated. Jocelyn lined up all the jars in a perfectly even row, looked at me, shrugged, then dipped one fingertip into the red paint. Karyn reached for the blue, paused, switched to yellow, paused, then, with a teasing smile, grabbed the pink . . . but before Athena could begin to protest, Karyn handed it to her in triumph. Athena laughed and laughed. She dipped her entire hand into the pink, and all the walls of hesitation came crashing down.

Trinity had prepared small paper plates with a big plop of color in each for me. I went for the green first, and I gotta admit—globs of paint felt good! I smooshed my hands into its silkiness. Then I looked at my crocodile-colored fingers, and, because my hands already kinda wobble on their own anyway, I turned to Jocelyn like I was a fierce green dragon. She did the same—one hand red and the other grape-colored—and for the first time since we arrived, she flat-out laughed.

We crammed our poster board with a kaleidoscope of colors. Jocelyn's paper began to fill up with different-sized ovals—each one perfectly symmetrical. Then she filled each one with three more perfectly shaped ovals. And then each of those had three. Whoa.

I almost couldn't paint myself because I wanted to see how many ovals she could cram onto her paper.

As for Athena, she looked like she had bathed in cotton-candy pink paint. There was more paint on her hair than on the paper.

One of my hands dripped with purple and blue; the other with lime green and a bit of random red. I smooshed them around on the paper, but sometimes I missed the paper completely! I'm not sure what I ended up creating, but it didn't matter.

The finished project was a gloppy mess, and so was I, but no one cared, and no one tried to fix or change anything. Splashed in a dozen shades of color, we stopped first at the huge industrial sink in the corner of the room to clean up before leaving. As Trinity ran a wet paper towel over some paint on my forehead, I thought, *One day I hope to be able to do stuff like this by myself.*

Paint from my hands mixed with the paint of the other girls, down the drain. Best mess ever!

CHAPTER 16

I couldn't believe how fast the day went. It was already time for dinner. Trinity explained that we'd eat in shifts every day. So I guess half the camp was there. I counted eight other wheelchairs besides Karyn's and mine. Cool. But the food? This was the most disgusting-looking dinner I'd ever seen! We all stared at our bowls in horror. It was some kind of broccoli mash-up—a deep avocado green—like Penny's Play-Doh after she's mixed all the colors together. One purple T-shirted boy at a table across from us made a loud, deliberate, gagging noise, and we all cracked up.

Athena asked, "Uh, does this come in pink? I think I

might be allergic to whatever this is." That made everybody laugh some more.

It seemed like no one dared take a first bite. But I was really hungry, so I got my brave on and nodded to Trinity. She held a spoonful out to me. I did a quick survey—other kids were about to be fed too. Okay, then. Let's see if this broccoli-hooey stuff was as gross as it looked. I swallowed the first bite, and I immediately thought of Mrs. V, who always told me never to judge things by how they look. I hated to admit it, but this stuff was the bomb!

"What do you think?" Trinity asked.

"Not bad," I tapped. Then I gave her a big green smile. **"You gotta give this recipe to my mom!"** She couldn't spoon it in fast enough. Even Jocelyn ate it without complaints.

By the time we finished, the sky was beginning to darken and an uneasiness came over me. What would it be like to sleep in a strange wooden bed? I've only ever slept in my own bed—maybe Mrs. V's a few times. What if I had a bad dream? Dang! What if I had to go to the bathroom? What if I missed my mom and dad and Penny? I felt tears pricking at my eyes. Good thing Mom wasn't here. She'd whisk me right home!

But before I had the chance to say anything, Trinity

clapped her hands for our attention. "Okay, my Fiery Falcons, are you ready for Fire Time?"

Fire what? Despite our confusion, our counselors shouted, almost in unison, "Yes! Fire Time!"

Karyn looked over at me and shrugged. "Doesn't matter," she whispered. "I'm outta here! They said try one day. I did. Tomorrow, after swimming, I'm gone."

We stopped by our cabin to quickly finish unpacking. Athena had clearly brought the state of Ohio's entire supply of pink clothes. Jocelyn—yay—was a sneakerhead like me.

Trinity informed me she had a very fashionable sweatshirt for me. Well, for all of us. She handed out the brightest orange sweatshirts in the universe. Seriously. But we all looked the same, and it was camp, and we were gonna have fun, right? Right. So I let Trinity tug it over my head, and we rolled and bounced and thumped over to the fire pit. It looked pitiful at first. But ha-ha, so did dinner. The fire area was stacked with logs and branches, and others were also rolling or walking up to . . . whatever this turns out to be!

Pretty soon the other three cabins in our little team—I could tell by their T-shirt or sweatshirt colors— had made their way over, half of them boys. I'd only seen the boys in passing so far or at meals—their cabins were on the other side of the dirt path that I think led to the woods. I was a little surprised at how many kids in total were here—and how many different color T-shirts.

When enough of us had gathered, a counselor I'd seen only once before introduced herself. Instead of a sweatshirt, she wore a long, flowing, multicolored dress. "My name is Kya," she said, her voice both quiet and powerful. "And I was born in Ghana. My name means 'diamond in the sky.' So I offer you welcome to both fire and sky tonight." She bowed her head slightly. "I run the zip line here, so I'll meet most of you over the next few days."

We all looked at each other, not sure what was going to happen next. Kya knelt by the logs with this literally foot-long match and lit the twigs at the bottom. At first I saw only smoke, but then a flicker of orange licked skyward, and *whoosh*! With crackles and pops, suddenly that flicker became a flame, and the flame found fuel in the wood and sticks and charcoal around it. Orange and red and yellow began dancing around each other, changing, merging . . . just becoming.

Becoming . . . pretty. It was a little strange—the evening air was cool, but the flames were hot and bright, decorating the night.

Athena clapped happily. A boy across from us reached out to try and catch a stray spark. As if they were starving, those small flames gobbled those branches and grew and grew. More sparks rose into the sky, and as I looked up to watch them—whoa! I'd never seen so many stars!

At home, if I'm out late at night, I might see a few milky white dots in the sky—maybe the moon if it wasn't hiding behind clouds. But here, each star popped proudly through the inky darkness. There had to be a million of them. If she were here, Mrs. V would have had me learn a million adjectives to describe what I was seeing. Blazing. Dazzling. Glistening. Luminous.

The bonfire. I mean, it's not like I haven't seen pictures of bonfires. But nobody I know even has a real fireplace in their house. Mrs. V has a little square heater that has a fake fire inside made out of lights that flicker and glimmer, and look almost real. She once told me if I closed my eyes and imagined, I would know what a real fire felt like. She was wrong about that one.

The dancing flames gobbled the logs in the pit, turning them red hot, then ashy white. I could have watched it forever.

I glanced around the circle of kids—they, like me, seemed entranced by the fire. It was awesome to see so many confident-looking kids in wheelchairs. Like we were all the insiders instead of the outsiders for a change. One girl had streamers woven through the spokes of her wheels—cool. How had I never thought of that? And one boy rolled back and forth, back and forth, with a fire-engine-red motorized chair—pretty sweet.

But even though everyone was chattering and giggling and pointing at the flames, I also bet that most of them were as unsure as I was about what might happen during our first full night at camp.

Cassie jogged over, baseball hat off. Her hair was short and spiky—the tips dyed blue and orange and green and purple. I guess she was aiming to claim all of us! Mom says I can't do anything to my hair until I'm sixteen. We'll see about *that*!

Small as Cassie was, as she stood in the firelight, she loomed large. "Welcome to Fire Time, campers," she called out. She stopped and smirked. "Well, actually, every night around here is Fire Time—we do like our bonfires—and anything made with chocolate!"

As I sat there in my massive sweatshirt, a shiver ran through me. Not because I was cold, but because this was actually kinda awesome! And also, what *was* it with these folks and chocolate? I chuckled. There *are* other flavors, you know.

"Since we have lit up the night with fire, let's fill up the night with some songs! But I hope a few of you can sing better than me." That broke the ice—we all cracked up. She had set up a cool-looking speaker system. She fiddled with the back of it until something that sounded like *WEE-WOW* erupted from the speaker. That sure woke me up!

Athena shouted, "Volume control!"

"Sorry, people!" Cassie apologized. "I think I have it working now."

When the music started, I recognized the guitar strum, strum, strum of the song. The Black-Eyed Peas started singing, *"I gotta feeling . . ."* I knew that one! And so, apparently, did everyone else. We started chanting, *"Tonight's gonna be a good, good night . . ."* Well, I didn't exactly chant, but hey, I was right there in it, humming along. And when I hum, I can actually stay in tune! And you know what, it really did feel like a good night.

Just as the last notes of that song were ending, Cassie shifted to "Girls Just Want to Have Fun." We sang even louder, really feeling the words, *"Oh girls, they wanna have fu-un/Girls just wanna have fun!"*

By this time Athena had jumped up and started dancing to the music all by herself. Jocelyn rocked in place, singing softly. It turned out that Jocelyn had an amazing voice! She'd hardly spoken ten words all day, but whoa—she could really sing. Even Karyn sang, so maybe she was having fun too?

Then a boy's voice shouted out, "Hey! So do we!" And every time the word *girls* came on, all the guys screamed, *"BOYS!"* And suddenly we were all in a screaming war! If Cassie wanted to fill up the night with sound, we'd sure made *that* happen.

After a few more songs—which nobody seemed to know all the words to, so we just made stuff up, which made us laugh even harder—the fire began to dwindle, and so did I. That's when I saw it—flitting over Jocelyn's head, as if it was attracted to the sound of her voice—a lightning bug. Then another. Then—wow—dozens! Where did they all come from? Had someone sent out an invitation to the Fire Time celebration? Had they traveled here from Mrs. V's?

Then, as if someone had flipped a switch, the whole night sky began to blink. So many fireflies darting and zipping, each one brightening the night for less than a second, until the next flash. Hey, maybe Penny was looking at fireflies right now at home. . . . Wouldn't that be cool?

Suddenly a boy in a slightly dirty purple T-shirt came barreling past us on a walker. He let go of it as he reached out and grabbed into the air. "Got one—got two!" he shouted, nearly tripping over my wheelchair.

"Ooh! Let me see!" Athena begged. The boy pivoted

around, leaned on his walker for support, and partially opened his cupped hands to reveal a pair of fireflies.

I was wondering, *Who is this kid?*

"Ooh, pretty! Pretty. Pretty," Jocelyn said, coming close, peering into the boy's hand.

"Do they bite?" Athena wanted to know, bouncing on her toes. I knew the answer to that! I made a soft grunt so she'd look over, and shook my head no.

"Melody's right!" Trinity agreed. "No. All they want to do is fly around and make the night sky pretty. Oh, and to find other little fireflies to hang out with."

"Why do they glow like that?" Karyn asked, straining to see. The boy bent forward to show her, too.

"To send a message!" I typed out quickly. The boy looked at me for a moment, then nodded his head in agreement. He had thick, tousled curls and almond-shaped eyes that reflected the firelight. He. Was. Cute. And he never really stopped moving—sort of like the lightning bugs in his hands.

"Points for Melody—right again," Trinity agreed. "Their blinking backsides are like a text message to other lightning bugs that says, 'Y'all come on out tonight—we've got a party going on here!'"

The firefly boy gave a laugh, but then said, "We should let them go. Maybe they can find some glow-worms and have a party!" His voice sounded a little hoarse, like he'd been gargling dirt or something.

Karyn looked thoughtful, then said, "I bet they're scared and just want to be home with their moms."

"True, that," the boy said with a nod.

Jocelyn murmured, "Scared. Scared. Scared."

Athena pursed her lips. "Yep!"

"Anything that's got wings ought to be able to zoom where it wants to!" Karyn added fiercely.

And I tapped, **"Yes, yes, yes."**

A bunch of other kids had gathered to see the fireflics too, and now we circled around the boy as he spread his hands open like wings themselves. For several long seconds, nothing happened. Then the fireflies blinked their black and golden bodies and lifted themselves into the darkness.

Free.

CHAPTER 17

By the time Trinity got my face washed and teeth brushed, and we'd gone back to our cabin, where I changed into my pajamas and was tucked into my bunk, I was wiped out. The bed—actually just a mattress on a rectangular wooden box—wasn't soft like at home, but it wasn't lumpy, either. And Mom had packed my favorite blanket—the turquoise cotton one that lived at the bottom of my bed. When Trinity snugged it around me, I could smell Dad's bean soup and Mom's scented candles; Penny's raggedy old Doodle, which actually smelled pretty funky; and the hot doggy breath of Butterscotch. Interesting, I thought, to be not at home

and still smell home at the same time. This place, I guess, smelled kinda brown—not ugly, mud-colored brown, but the brown of tree bark and paths made of earth. Not so bad.

It was dim in the cabin, but not really dark. I guess they didn't want anybody to get scared and freak out. The windows had shutters that filtered the moonlight from outside, but not so much that we couldn't see what was going on. Once we campers settled in, our counselors climbed into the beds above us, those bunks hardly even shaking. I guess Mom would approve, but boy, they weren't kidding when they told us the counselors never left our sides!

I was thinking that it was probably fun to be on top, to hang over and talk to the person below you, when Athena, in the bed across from me, whispered, "G'night, everybody!"

Karyn mumbled something I couldn't make out—I bet she was just about out. Jocelyn, however, who sounded wide awake, called out, "Nighty, nighty, nighty!" I took a deep breath and forced out, "Nuh!" I wish I could have said more. But I'm pretty sure they knew that.

Flickering camp lanterns dangled from each counselor's bed. Not oil—that would be way too dangerous—just a battery-powered flame, like a mini bonfire. It actually made the cabin seem sort of pretty.

I lay there for a long time. Sleep seemed to be having a hard time finding me. The cabin was quiet now but nowhere close to silent. Athena snored! Karyn coughed every so often. Jocelyn mumbled in her sleep. I heard her say, "Go, go, go," and then something that sounded like "Mushy, mushy, mushy"—I wasn't sure. Even in her sleep she spoke in threes!

I wondered what I did in my sleep. I hoped it was nothing embarrassing like farting or anything.

I could hear tree frogs outside—at least that was what I thought was making that chirpy sound. I remembered that from studying for Whiz Kids in fifth grade—Mrs. V would be so proud. Besides, birds wouldn't be up this late, would they? I guessed they were probably asleep. But then I started to wonder, How do birds sleep, anyway? Do they just close their eyes while sitting on a branch? Why don't they fall off?

I never did figure it out.

CHAPTER 18

I woke up with a gasp. Where was I?

Camp. That's right. Camp. So it was Monday. And I was still here. I looked across to the next bed. And, ha-ha, so was Karyn! She didn't even mention going home last night!

Birds were chirping so loudly outside I couldn't believe they hadn't woken everybody up. I guess for them, living here must be like hanging out in paradise all the time—zillions of trees and bugs and worms, and limitless sky.

Trinity came over and squatted by my bed. "Good morning, early bird," she whispered, smoothing my blanket, like Mom does. *Hey, how'd she climb down from her bunk without me hearing?*

I smiled, just to let her know I was awake.

"You ready for day two?" She was clearly one of those people who woke up looking like they had professionals to do their face while they slept: her makeup was perfect. And her braids were tight—not one bit of frizz. She probably beat the birds getting up!

I knew from experience that my hair was a tangled mess. My face felt sticky. Hopefully, I had no dried drool on my chin—yeah, I'm a drooler when I sleep. Maybe that meant I didn't fart? That would be a good trade-off.

So I nodded hard, genuinely eager to hear what was up for today.

"Let's see what we've got planned. . . ." She glanced down at her tablet and kept her voice low. "Ah, the first is a surprise, but you'll love it! Then probably another swim—gotta get you from tadpole to guppy—and maybe we'll be able to squeeze in a boat ride. And, of course, Fire Time tonight."

Gotta admit, I was relieved that she didn't say horseback. *Mom* was the one who'd been excited about the horses. Me? Not sure yet. I was gonna take the wait-and-see approach. Because, duh, my balance was like zip! How was I supposed to stay on top of a thousand-pound animal? But I *was* curious. At the same time, riding a horse had never been on my just-gotta-do-it wish list. Horses were big. And fast. And I was not. So there was that. But then, I didn't have fins, and yesterday I swam! Man, I was getting good at arguing with myself!

"Okay, girlfriend," Trinity said, patting my arm, "we've got lots to do today, like taking a shower!"

So we got up and headed to the showers, which were across the yard and beyond the latrine, passing a few other early birds on the way. A pair of chipmunks chased each other, right in front of my chair!

When we rolled in, wow—what a surprise! The room, instead of being morning-chilly, was warm and cozy. They had special shower chairs just for kids like me. It still felt weird having a total stranger see me naked, but I just shrugged it off. It is what it is, Dad always says. Trinity rolled me in, set my shower gel and sponge in the basket attached to this shower chair, and let me wash up without her. I really appreciated that—I'm way too old to have anybody washing me! Mom had packed pink peppermint shower gel, and the whole washroom area smelled like melted candy by the time I was finished.

Back at the cabin, everyone else was just waking up. Like me, Jocelyn had serious bed head going on, but

she just yanked her hair into a ponytail and she was
done.

"We've got a ginormous box of Fiery Falcons shirts,"
Trinity told me as we were getting dressed. "Want
one?" She held up a Falcons shirt in one hand and the
lime-green one that Mom had packed in the other. I
really liked the green shirt—Mom and I had found it at
Target at the last minute. But I pointed to the orange
one. No one's gonna say I'm not a team player. Unlike
other people—but I pushed that thought away. The
Whiz Kids stuff was more than a year ago. I needed to
be over it!

As we headed out to breakfast, Karyn, also in a
Falcons T-shirt, rolled up next to me. "Hope they have
pancakes," she said. I answered with a head jerk and a
flinging of my hand. "What's your fave—blueberry or
chocolate chip or caramel?" she asked.

"Chocolate chip!" Athena called out. She also wore
her camp shirt, but she had a bright pink tank top
underneath it. That girl was gonna get her pink on, no
matter what.

"Caramel for me, please!" I tapped.

Karyn rolled on ahead, I guess to check out the
menu.

No pancakes today, but even better—cheesy eggs,
one of my favorites, and oatmeal, as well as plenty

of bacon. Can't eat bacon, too chewy, but Karyn and Athena gobbled a stack of it, keeping count to see who ate the most slices. Jocelyn, who today insisted she didn't eat meat, even though I watched her eat hot dogs yesterday, downed three sausages. Exactly three. Trinity and I took our time as we made our way through that pile of eggs and caramel-drenched oatmeal.

Just as I ate my last bite, Elvira beeped. It was Mom. She sent a text message with a half dozen smiley faces and thumbs-ups, saying how she hoped I was having fun. I was able to quickly answer by tapping on phrases and sentences already saved into my machine; Mom and Mrs. V took lots of time typing in "camp conversations" before I left. Clearly they were more bugged out than I was about me going away! Trinity helped me find some phrases to send to Mom so she didn't worry.

Hi Mom. I am fine. I went swimming and did not drown. Ha-ha! Camp is okay. Bye!

Before the first full day of camp, there was apparently a general all-camp meeting right there in the dining hall. It's not really a hall—it's just a big inside area that can hold a bunch of kids and picnic tables. Cassie stood up in front of us once we'd all crammed in. I did some quick math: four kids per cabin, times sixteen cabins—whoa, that's sixty-four of us.

That's an awful lot of kids who fit the qualifications to be eligible for a camp like Green Glades. But it sure felt good to hang with kids who were just like me.

Cassie was trying her best to get everyone's attention. She reminded me of a drill sergeant as she held up a clipboard and read from it. "Welcome to your first full day at Camp Green Glades, and I hope the tree frogs didn't keep you awake! We have an exciting schedule of activities planned for today."

I was right—they were tree frogs!

"Some of you will start your day on a luxurious lake cruise. Some will create masterpieces or symphonies. Others will work off their breakfast with a swim. The rest will learn to . . . *fly!!*" At that, she wagged an eyebrow mysteriously.

Fly? Literally every single kid glanced at every other kid. Murmurs filled the air.

"Settle down. Settle down. We'll be on a rotating schedule. But don't worry, everyone will have a chance to do *everything*—including flying!" she assured us. "And of course we'll end the day with a bonfire."

Oh, I was psyched for another bonfire. But I was mostly wondering what the heck she meant by flying.

CHAPTER 19

After the group meeting, we stopped to quickly brush our teeth and make a bathroom stop. Then we dropped back by our cabin to grab some waters and juice boxes.

"Well," Trinity asked us as she stuck the boxes in her backpack, "are you ready for this morning's big adventure? Because today we're going zip-lining!"

My cabinmates looked up in surprise. So that was what Cassie had hinted at! I thought back to that photo of somebody else flying through the air, held by just a strap and a cord . . . and it seemed sooooooo cool. Even a little dangerous. Me, doing a little dangerous?

Soooo, huh . . . yep. This might be a little over the top.
But what was wrong with that? I thought about Mom—
she'd have heart failure! And that made me want to do
it even more. And yet . . . it was so high. . . .

"You will LOVE it!" Trinity told us.

"This will be the part of camp you'll remember the
most!" Lulu chimed in.

Jocelyn had started walking in circles, then paused
by the window. "Flying? Flying? Flying?" she kept
repeating, worry in her voice. The morning sky was
the bluest of blues. She stared out the window for a
long, long time. Finally she said, "Okay! Okay! Okay!"

I couldn't tell what changed her mind. But it got
me thinking. These folks have done this with probably
dozens of groups of camp kids. For sure they've figured out how to avoid sending a camper to Mars on a
zip line!

I looked over at Karyn—we were the ones with the
wheels here, after all. She must have been thinking the
same thing because she turned to me, too. We silently
exchanged a look that said, *If you go, I'll go.* After a
moment, Karyn shrugged. So I nodded.

"Ah, I see smiles!" Trinity said victoriously.

I touched **okay**, and before any of us could change
our minds, the counselors practically sprinted us down
the trail to the zip-line loading station.

And yikes! Trinity and I got there first, which meant *I* was gonna be the cabin guinea pig!

Kya waved as we arrived. Most of the counselors here wore blue jeans or shorts and camp T-shirts, but instead of jeans, Kya wore her camp shirt with bright yellow silky-looking slacks that rippled as she walked.

"Greetings, Falcons! It's great to see you again. You're gonna love this. I'm an expert on zip-lining—I've been zipping and helping campers slide and glide for a decade now," she told us. "I was honored to be asked to run the zip-line program here at Green Glades. Most important thing to know? No one has *ever* fallen on my watch. Actually, I've never seen *anyone* fall, ever!"

I managed to nod, in spite of the fact that I was worrying about dying for the second time in as many days. 'Cause today might be the day Kya's luck ran out. That would be just *my* luck!

Kya took her time explaining how it was all going to work. "First," she said, "you and Trinity will ride our little elevator to that platform you see above you."

I peered up. That platform sure was high in the sky. I mean, I practically had to squint to see it.

"You'll be fastened into a harness and the bucket, and then Trinity and I will double-check the safety straps."

I was gonna be harnessed into a bucket? Dad says I

have an overactive imagination, but I never imagined I'd hear those words. Me. In a bucket. Those photographer people better get a shot of this!

"So, any questions? Are you ready?"

I wasn't, but I nodded . . . or maybe I trembled. I'm honestly not sure.

Trinity rolled me onto a platform, pushed a lever, and oh my! I gasped. I'm not trying to sound like Jocelyn, but we were heading up, up, up! In less than a minute, we rolled off onto another platform, but whoa! It was like a million feet in the air! Well, maybe a hundred. In front of us I saw a bright red cushioned chair attached to cables that were attached to . . . I have no idea! It was almost too much to think about in one swallow.

"Okay, girlfriend, here we go!" Trinity said as she lifted me into the bucket-seat thingy. It was curved to the size of my butt, and it was even padded. Kya clicked the seat belt around me. Next came the harness, and holy moly, there were like ninety-nine buckles on that thing, which was attached to the seat with another ninety-nine clasps, and they all needed to be hooked together.

"These hooks are called carabiners, just like the folks who climb Mount Everest use," Kya explained. "And yeah, we check the safety straps. And check again.

Then once more." She gave me a wink. "Like I said, no one falls on my watch!"

Trinity gave each clasp a second tug. And, as promised, Kya checked once more. Then she plunked a helmet on my head. Chin strap? Check! Check the check? Check, check! *But wait, if I'm not going to fall, why would I need a helmet?*

"You're all set, Melody," Kya said at last. Then Trinity got in behind me, and she got helmeted and harnessed in as well. She circled her arms around me, the ninety-nine buckles, and let's be honest here, my trembling heart.

"Okay, it's fly time, fly girl!" Trinity said, all psyched. "And don't close your eyes. You're gonna want to see this. It'll be over in like twenty seconds, and you don't want to miss even one."

So I gave my helmeted head a tiny nod, and Trinity yelled out, "Go!"

And then, just like that, before I even had time to freak, because for sure I was gonna die in like thirty seconds, I was flying! Trees hurtled past, their leaves a blur. I swear the very air whooshed right through me. I was an eagle, a hummingbird, a creature of feathers and air. I got it now—why birds soar and swoop and float on the air. This was pure joy! I had never moved so fast.

My disobedient legs swung loose in the air, finally taking advantage of all that uncontrollable movement. They got the chance to kick and kick without it mattering at all. And it felt so good!

But in a snap, it was over. A gentle slowdown, and we were done. No trees hit. And no more soaring. Like a flash of lightning that slices the sky, it brightened my world, and then was gone. I wondered if they'd let me do it again.

"Thumbs-up?" Trinity asked after all those buckles and clasps were unclasped and I was back in my chair.

I focused super hard and held both thumbs up.

"Wanna do it again?"

"Yes! Yes! Yes!" I whacked Elvira.

Athena went next. She was begging "AGAIN!" even before they'd unhooked her.

Jocelyn asked to go three times, but Lulu reminded her she had to give everybody at least one turn before anyone got a second. Karyn was at first hesitant, but the look on her face when she landed on the platform on the other side was stunned happiness.

"I . . . I was like . . . the wind!" she whispered to me as soon as she was down.

After everyone got a slew of chances to zip down that incredible contraption again, we headed back to camp. Rolling in my chair seemed soooooooooo boring.

Karyn caught up with me, and, looking slightly embarrassed, said that she probably wasn't gonna go home today after all.

And I totally got why.

Because today we learned we could fly!

CHAPTER 20

Swimming was next up on the schedule. This time, with Trinity supporting both my head and my stomach, I lay flat on the water—facedown—almost like the swimmers I've seen on TV. But not really—I made *real sure* that not one drop of water touched my nose. I was able to use my arms to move me a little, and it felt SO good! I felt closer to being a guppy, for sure. Trinity's hair stayed dry; mine was a soppy mess. She wasn't kidding about saving those braids!

When we got out, we headed back to the cabin, made a quick change into dry clothes, and gobbled down our mac-and-cheese lunch. More cheese, less mac, would be my review if anyone asked. And for dessert we had something called snickerdoodles, which sounds like a type of dog but turns out are freshly baked cinnamon cookies—really awesome. Trinity soaked mine in milk so I could eat them easier. How come I'd never thought of that?

Then Trinity announced we were doing more water! These folks were seriously into wet activities.

"So, are you ready for our deluxe ocean-liner cruise?" she asked.

Not sure what she meant by ocean liner, we all waited.

"I got jokes—sorry. We're going on a boat ride! It's not a cruise ship—sorry—we'll be on a little flat-bottomed boat on Lake Lilliana."

She watched for our reaction. Since I'd never been on a boat, I only had ocean-liner movie scenes in my head. Hmm—now was probably not the time to be thinking about *Titanic*, one of my favorite movies of all time. So I had *lots* of questions, starting with how would they manage to get all of *us* on a boat?

Karyn had questions too and didn't need time to type them out, so I was glad she began to pepper Trinity and Kim with them.

"So what kind of boat do you have? There's too many of us for a rowboat."

"It's called a pontoon," Trinity started to reply, but Athena interrupted with "What's a pontoon? That's a silly word!"

My thoughts exactly!

"A pontoon," Sage explained, "is basically a giant metal floatie." We must have looked skeptical, because she added, "Let's see. . . . Look at it this way: a pontoon boat is like a floating living room with a sunroof!"

"What's great about a pontoon is that it's 99.5 percent impossible to sink—honestly. I don't even know how one could even be sunk!" Sage added.

"Is that all?" Karyn said with a frown.

"I've got you, Karyn," Kim told her. "One hundred *zillion* percent!" She gave Karyn's arm a quick rub. Karyn, I noticed, did not pull back. But she still looked worried. Kim explained further, "The boat makes runs with campers every day. Trust me, they're experts." Karen still gave her the side-eye.

As for me, riding an ocean liner or a pontoon or tugboat made very little difference—I was about to go on a b.o.a.t.! My legs started crazy kicking.

Sage opened a closet and pulled out a stack of life jackets.

Athena reached for one. "So, you think we're gonna have a flood in here?"

Karyn giggled.

Sage shook her head. "We just keep these here in the cabin to save time. Plus, the ones down by the pool are usually wet."

"They sure are orange, orange, orange," Jocelyn commented.

Karyn gave Jocelyn's arm a gentle poke. "Safety, safety, safety," she murmured. Jocelyn glanced away, but with a sly grin.

Athena insisted on putting hers on by herself, and after a struggle, turned around triumphantly. We had to hold in giggles—she had it on backward! Not that I had any right to comment—I can't even get one arm in by myself.

Trinity, however, had the foam-filled jacket around me and clipped in about ten seconds. "All set, kid!"

Hmm—I sure hoped I didn't need to use this. Then I got to thinking about logistics—got *that* from Mom. I tapped, **"Wheelchairs on boats?"**

Trinity then opened a closet I hadn't even noticed before. It was full of . . . neatly folded wheelchairs! Okay, these people probably had backup plans for their backup plans!

"No worries," she told me. "Special treat—we're all riding in chariots today. It's a camp requirement for boat safety. The pontoon is specially designed with fasteners to hold our chairs in place."

And what if those secure fasteners come loose? I chose *not* to ask. But I thought it, oh yes I did.

"And you'll love the way the boat rocks on the waves."

Karyn sat ramrod straight. "Did she say WAVES?"

"*Small* waves," Kim assured her.

Trinity was dashing around the cabin, cramming suntan lotion and a first-aid kit into her backpack. First-aid kit? What was she expecting? Then she added sweatshirts for both of us, and a couple of pudding cups for me.

Karyn was back to worrying about sinking. "Uh, what if the boat flips? Or crashes into a rock? Or hits another boat? Or it sinks? I just gotta ask, you know."

Kim was so patient. "Okay, fair enough," she said. "Let me answer you this way. How many of you had a rubber duckie or a toy like that when you were little?"

I sure did. Most of us smiled as we thought about baby toys.

"Well, this boat is like a giant, unsinkable toy. It's been made supersafe, and it's designed for fun. So let's go have some!"

I looked over at Karyn. She still looked doubtful, but she let herself be strapped into her life jacket without further questions.

What if . . . I heard the snap-thud sound of the unlocking of my brakes. We were out of here. Other counselors and their campers were already heading down to the dock. All the campers were sitting in wheelchairs too. I guessed that was a good idea.

Athena plunked right into the wheelchair Sage held out, then waved at me cheerily as she and Sage rolled out the cabin door. "This is gonna be so awesome!" she singsonged, then asked Sage to please push faster.

Jocelyn sat super straight in her chair, wobbling with every bounce but never leaning back.

At the dock, we paused as Kim told us about the lake. "So Lake Lilliana's just a large bucket of water surrounded by all the land you see. It's pretty deep but not very large, not like, say, Lake Erie, which is HUMONGOUS. We're super careful to keep it clean and healthy—no trash, no diesel-powered boats. We even have a lake ranger who patrols it, on the lookout for folks who break the rules. That's how much we love this lake. And you're gonna love it too."

I'd never actually thought about the idea of a healthy lake, but hey, lakes need love too. I liked that idea—folks here looking out for its health, sort of like how Mom makes sure that me and Penny take our vitamins and wash our hands and get our yearly doctor checkups.

A ramp led from the dock, where at least I felt like I

could manage a little, to the boat, which was like a foreign country with a different language. I didn't speak boat very well. I didn't speak boat at all!

"Ah, I see we've got the large pontoon today," Trinity said happily, looking down at the chunky, rectangular-shaped vessel.

"Look," said Athena, "it *does* have floaties! It'll never sink!"

Karyn scoffed, "I've watched that movie about the *Titanic* like ninety-nine times. Trust me, 'unsinkable' boats can go down."

Another *Titanic* fan, and yeah, she wasn't wrong.

Sage adjusted her baseball cap, her ponytail dangling out the back. "Well," she replied, "I've seen that movie a million times as well. But since we have no ocean storms or icebergs in the forecast, just calm, placid lake water, I think we're safe for this trip."

The boat rose up and down with the motion of the water, but it was secured to the dock by really, really thick ropes. I'd actually never seen a rope that huge and so tightly woven. I doubted my dad could even wrap his hands around it.

And those things called pontoons? They really *were* like giant metal floaties attached to the bottom and sides of the boat. And I gotta admit, it did look pretty much unsinkable, but what did I know?

Athena begged to go on first and called out, "Ahoy!" as she and Sage rolled down the wooden ramp and onto the shifting boat.

I flapped my hand at Trinity—I wanted to go next! As we wheeled down the ramp backward, Karyn waved from the dock. I didn't have time to wave back, because a second later I was on a boat! Me!

I couldn't help looking in every direction at once while Trinity positioned my wheelchair and began snapping and hooking and connecting it to several tie-downs on the floor. She triple-checked each fastener, giving each a big tug, then declared me "hooked solid." I guess I'd graduated from guppy to trout.

Karyn and Jocelyn came down next, and our counselors set our chairs so that we could see each other as well as the lake—yay. Another group of girls was already safely secured on the deck—the Green Gazelles. Cool.

I thought now we'd launch off or take off or go full steam ahead—however you say *get going* in boat-talk—but then we heard loud, deep laughter coming from one of the paths. Karyn and I looked at each other in surprise as a group of boys in blue and purple shirts, wearing life jackets, burst out of the bushes with shouts of, "Hey, wait up! Don't leave us!"

Kim rolled her eyes, but in a joking way. "Those are

guys on our team—the Purple Panthers and the Blue Badgers. Last year," she explained, "they managed to miss the boat—literally!"

Trinity added, "My bad! I actually forgot they might be joining us! I'm glad they made it 'just in time' this year!"

I opened my mouth and closed it again as the guys were being boarded, one at a time. They were also secured in chairs, just like we were.

Lulu explained how each wheelchair was hooked to a specific spot, and that spot revolved.

I looked down at the circle around the bottom of my chair, which had to be what swiveled us around. "You can do a complete three-sixty and see everything!" Lulu exclaimed.

As I was getting over both surprises, I looked from the boys to the lake behind them. I still couldn't get over the colors. Azure, indigo, sapphire. I ran out of blue words in my head! I mean, I knew lakes were blue, or maybe green, but not all the ding-dang blues with glints of white at the ripples. I couldn't stop staring. And it wasn't at all like a swimming pool.

Swimming pools are tame, docile, chlorinated, and medicated. Okay, I read that in a book someplace, but it fit. And no joke, this lake never stopped moving. It was like blue power! And here I was, Melody

Scared-of-the-Water Brooks, floating on it—well, part of it. I could hardly believe it.

When everyone else was declared "hooked solid," Lulu signaled a man who just had to be the captain—he was wearing one of the little navy-blue hats with a brim, right out of a movie.

He walked over. "Ahoy, mates! Welcome aboard, my friends!" he said. His voice was deep and sandpaper rough. "I'm Captain Frederick Carter. We're mighty glad to have Camp Green Glades with us again this year. This boat here—her name's *Silver Sarah*—is safe and powerful and knows what she's doing."

"Why Silver Sarah, Sarah, Sarah?" Jocelyn asked, eyes cast sideways.

"Great question!" The captain adjusted the brim of his hat. "Well, most boats are named after females—good luck and all that. So I named this little dream of a ship after my wife—because she bought it! Talk about good luck!" He cackle-laughed, slapping his leg, and we all laughed as well.

"Now first, a little vocabulary lesson. This part you're sitting on is called the stern, or the aft." He pointed to the front of the vessel. "And up there is the bow. So if I say I look toward the stern, you'll know to look at the back of the boat and won't miss a rare sea monster sighting!" He went on, clearly enjoying explaining how boats float and propel themselves and stop. The part about stopping, it seemed to me, was pretty important!

I wish I could have told this guy how much I appreciated that he took the time to talk to us—we certainly weren't his normal set of passengers, but he acted as if we were like any other group that would board his ship.

Athena raised her hand.

"Yes, ma'am," the captain said.

"He called me ma'am!" she mouthed to Jocelyn. Then she asked, eyeing the water suspiciously, "You ever seen any sharks?"

"No, ma'am," he said seriously. "No sharks. They live in the ocean, and this is a lake. The only thing you might see in this water are small fish—blue gills, sunfish, and maybe some bass. That's it."

A girl from the Gazelles blurted out, "What about mermaids?"

Captain Carter responded to her just as seriously as he had to Athena. "I've yet to have the pleasure of seeing a mermaid out here," he said, "but that doesn't mean there aren't any hiding at the bottom of the lake. I certainly hope so."

"Me too," the girl agreed.

Then one of the boys I'd seen at the campfire last night, who had really cool, totally white hair, asked,

"So, how many of these boats can fit on a cruise ship? Like, uh, the *Titanic*?"

Lotta Titanic fans at this camp, I thought.

"Dozens, I imagine," Captain Carter replied with a shrug. "Believe it or not, I've never had the chance to go out on the ocean on a big ship. My little watery kingdom here on the lake is plenty 'nough for me!"

There was something I was curious about as well. I tapped out, **"What's the best part about being a boat captain?"**

Captain Carter's smile went huge, his teeth so white against his ruddy face. He didn't seem to be the least bit fazed to be asked a question by a machine.

"I'm so glad you asked! The best part of my job is that I answer only to the wind and the waves. I get to suck up the sun in the morning and spit out the moon at night. For me, that's a mighty fine life."

Just then a horn blared and I totally jumped in my seat. Good thing I was strapped in!

"Well, me ladies and gents," the captain said, lowering his brim an inch. "I'll simply say, 'Thar she blows and off we go!'" He paused, his eyes crinkling as he grinned. "Nobody really talks like that, except in the movies," he confided. "But it *is* time for me to get to my wheel. Enjoy the ride!" He gave a little salute, and off he went. Then off we went!

CHAPTER 21

As the motor rumbled to life, I could hear splashing as the propellers, way out of our view, began to spin. Thanks, Mrs. V, for showing me YouTube videos of boats and ships and planes as part of our lessons on transportation. And suddenly we were moving, motoring, boating on the deep blue sea! Okay, so maybe just a small blue lake, but still, we were moving! At sea. Oh, did you even say "at sea" when you were on a lake? I didn't have a clue. Something else to check out later.

The vessel backed away from the dock and turned to the left. Was that north? South? I had no idea. All I knew was that trees that had looked so large just moments ago began to look smaller and smaller. The land, the shore, drifted away from us. But they didn't—it was us, floating on liquid blue.

As we picked up speed, the air pressed against us like we were pushing through a windstorm. Whoa, this boat was really going fast! What was the speed limit on the water anyway? Was that even a thing? Trinity's braids flew out behind her as we sped past thick stands of trees. I could feel my cheeks flattening in the wind—it almost felt like a wind massage, *ahhhhh*. So *that's* why Butterscotch hangs his head out of our car window.

And the sound of the boat cutting through the water—a sort of sloshing, sizzling sound—was so soothing. I wanted this on my sound machine back home to help me sleep!

Trinity pulled her braids together with a scrunchie. "Hey, look behind us!" She swiveled my chair around. Streaming from the back of our boat was a huge trail, not blue, but almost silver, glistening and frothing. It foamed and churned, but at its center was a pathway, maybe to that underwater palace where mermaids were hiding? Why not?

Oh, and I saw two motors. Well, that was good. If one conked out, we wouldn't be stranded. And in the distance, our dock, our path, our trees—so far away. And so many trees. I mean, I knew there were a lot—the camp *is* in a forest—but when you're in it, the trees seem huge in size, but not in number. But out here, whoa—it's the opposite. They look like leaf-topped toothpicks, but like a billion of them. Okay, a million. Thousands? A whole lot. And a lot to think about!

I tore my eyes from the scenery to see if the other campers were as jazzed as I was, and with my chair turned around, I noticed for the first time a kid to my right—not an arm's length away. He was being turned around in my direction. When he saw me, he waved.

I blinked. He was the firefly kid from last night. I gave a sort of wave back.

The boat chugged along as we began to pass other boat ramps, and soon, other boats. I caught the boy's eye and pointed to a pair of fishermen in a canoe.

"If they catch a big enough bass, it would pull that canoe right over!" he said.

I was just thinking the same thing!

Then we both noticed a shiny black speedboat that left a massive white spume behind it as it roared past us at double our speed, so fast its front—its bow— was in the air! It seemed to disappear from view in seconds. I gaped after it. *It must be* awesome *to have such power!*

The boy was shaking his head almost dreamily. "Speed beats slow any day!"

I laughed, agreeing with him, and he smiled back, his almond eyes arching into moons—supercute.

We then passed a kind of ferryboat carrying a load of—I couldn't tell, maybe housing shingles or building supplies? A water delivery truck—oh, I needed to remember to tell Penny about this one!

A family group passed us next, fishing from the side of their comfortable-looking cabin cruiser. Not something Dad and Mom would do—they pretty much stay on solid ground. The family waved as we went by. Me and the kid waved back, like we were part of some kind of secret club: the Folks Who Boat on Blue Water!

And now I felt a rush of determination. I had to get Mom and Dad and Penny on a boat, even though Penny would drive us bonkers with thousands of questions about the water, the waves, and the wind; about fish and sea serpents and dragons living under the water.

As the pontoon made its way through the wet and the blue, the foam and the froth, the boy pointed up. Birds, their wings spread wide, glided on invisible currents, too high up to identify—maybe hawks or falcons. Not that I would have been able to tell the difference anyway, even if one landed on my hand. I read somewhere that birds sing while they're perched in a tree, but they call out when they're flying. I wondered what the ones overhead were calling out right now. *Enjoying the view?* I sure was.

The lake ahead of us shimmered in the sun. The lake behind us frothed white from the propellers. The wind in my face held the power of the boat and the lake and the sky, and I inhaled it all—all that energy.

If only I could transfer this intensity into my body! *Ahhhhhh!*

Just then I heard the cookie-crumbly voice of the firefly boy. "I think I'd like to live on a boat," he said.

I had to nod my head in agreement.

The boat suddenly slowed down, the motor fading to a hum. No more froth. No more wind. Even the birds, whatever they were, had ceased their cawing. All that power dimmed. I thought about that. It faded—we couldn't see it, but wasn't it still there, just waiting to be used? A flick of the switch, or however the heck you rev up a boat engine—and the power, the energy, would come flooding back. It was all stuck inside, waiting.

And all of a sudden I felt like crying. Because . . . well, that was me—so much on the inside that still could not get to the outside. Energy trapped. Not all of it—I'm glad I have my board to let burps of it out. But, yeah, I'm tangled inside myself. And there's no magical key to unravel the coils. What the heck? I get on a boat, and boom, I got feelings!

Of course I didn't cry—not with this boy sitting so close. I wondered, though, if he also felt that way. I bet he's lived through some stuff too.

But then I began to understand something else. Just because it was sometimes trapped, I still had power—it was *there*, waiting. I had power. Like that engine, the wind, the waves. Yeah, power.

I had a sudden sense that the boy was watching me. I turned my head and blinked. He was! He grinned. I managed to smile back.

"What's your name?" he asked.

You know, I'd thought about leaving Elvira in the cabin for the boat ride. I am *so* glad I didn't! I touched one tab. **"My name is Melody."**

He tilted his head. "Hey, Melody. That's a really pretty name. I'm Noah."

I'm sure I looked ridiculous—cheesing like Penny did that birthday when she woke up to balloons in her bedroom. Still, I made myself tap out a question. **"I'm a first-timer here—how about you?"**

"This is my second go-round. I had a blast last year, so I asked my folks if I could come back." Then he glanced at me shyly and added, "Do you like it so far?"

"It's much better than I thought it'd be!"

"I'm glad," he replied. And it was only then that I realized that the reason we'd slowed down was because one of the counselors had been telling us about the area we were in—I hadn't even noticed. Noah mustn't have either, because he said, "Hope there's no quiz at the end of the ride!"

Then the thrum of the engine shook my chair as we started moving a little faster again. The boat turned in a wide arc—we were heading back to our starting point, I guess.

As we cut through the blue of the water and the white of the foam, I dared another glance at Noah. Yeah, if there was a quiz, I'd bomb it. I laughed out loud.

Noah laughed too. "See you at Fire Time," he said.

I wobble-nodded *okay*. He was wobble-nodding back when a tall, bearded guy walked over, squatted in front of Noah, and pointed out something in the distance. I couldn't tell over the motor's roar.

Trinity in turn crouched in front of me, an eyebrow arched. "Well, Sailor Girl, what did you think of our boat ride?" she asked as distant trees came back into focus.

I touched my board. **"Not bad."**

She found that incredibly funny. I decided to ignore her completely.

Branches, which a few minutes ago had been just a dark blur as we sped by, stood out now like specific personalities, with dangling leaves and rough bark.

We backed into the dock, bumped gently against the wooden pier, and eased into what I guessed was a boat parking space. Captain Carter swiftly tied the boat to the pier with huge ropes. The counselors unhooked our chairs, and moments later we were on solid ground. We waved goodbye to the captain—Athena like she was Miss America, Karyn all smiles. Even Jocelyn gave a rare thumbs-up. My arms didn't want to wave right then, but my legs wanted to kick, so you know what? I did. And that was good enough.

And as the Purple Panthers rolled off, I watched Noah until he was up the ramp and out of sight.

CHAPTER 22

Was it the sunshine? The buffeting breeze? The rocking of the boat? Whatever it was, once we got back to the cabin, we all crashed. Even the counselors, and Karyn, who claimed she never slept during the day, were snoring away.

Good thing Jocelyn smelled pizza in her sleep and woke up to announce that she was hungry, or we would have totally missed dinner. We changed into fresh orange T-shirts, then literally ran to the dining hall—Jocelyn won! They still had plenty of food for us, and Jocelyn was right—it was pizza night. I ate mine without the crust—yummy sauce and cheese with bits

of olives and sauteed pepperoni. Athena named it a
bowl of pizza and asked for one too.

We were so late getting dinner that I didn't realize
it was almost campfire time. Most of the kids from the
other cabins were already there, and the fire crackled
red and gold as we approached. When we got to the
edge of the fire circle, I looked around and saw the
guys from the boat ride not far from where we were.
And yeah, I'm a dork, but I actually gulped.

Trinity grabbed hold of the awkwardness and called
out, "Hey, Jeremiah! How'd your crew like the pon-
tooning?"

"Awesome!" the tall, bearded guy I'd seen talking to
Noah on the boat answered. "Perfect weather today!
Captain Carter really knows how to get that boat mov-
ing! How about your girls?"

Trinity made a sheepish face. "Ha! When we got
back, we totally crashed. The pontoon ride will do it
every time. We almost missed dinner!" Then I swear
she looked from me to Noah before adding, "You know
what? We haven't introduced our cabins to each other.
Who are your mighty Panthers?"

"Well, I've got a rocking crew here." Jeremiah
pointed proudly to his four campers and the other
counselors, and then directly at the boy in front of
him. "This young man is Devin. He's got two pit bulls

at home named Noodles and Doodles."

Must be hard to be fierce with names like that!

"And this big red-bearded guy," Jeremiah went on, "is Devin's counselor, Charles."

Charles, who also sported a thick reddish Afro, stroked his beard and gave us a nod. "Hey, y'all," he said, Southern in his voice. "Glad to be part of the Green Glades crew. And glad to have this dude Devin to hang out with this week." He placed a hand on the back of Devin's chair.

Devin gave a chin nod and a "Hey." His wheelchair was incredible—he pushed a button, and it lifted him to an almost standing position! I'm a wheelchair expert, and I'd *never* seen one like that before! His head wobbled a little and his arms seemed to be connected by invisible puppet strings—kinda like my legs—but his smile was gorgeous.

"Awesome wheels," Athena breathed.

Totally!

The next guy Jeremiah introduced sat in a manual chair like mine, but now I was feeling like I needed to start checking out new chair styles, because this one was the coolest wheelchair I'd ever seen. Painted bright neon orange, it was built sort of like a motor scooter, but that's where the similarity stopped. This was the bomb chair-bike! It had two wheels in the back, and one thick wheel in the front. The spokes, painted a metallic gold, glimmered in the firelight. It even had a rearview mirror and a horn!

When the kid in it spoke, I looked up in real surprise—he had a talking machine like Elvira!

His Medi-Talker spoke loudly for him, in a voice I recognized as "Douglas" from the Medi-Talker system library. I couldn't really see it from where I sat, but I couldn't wait to check out the techs of his system up close. **"Howdy, everyone. I am Santiago Delgado,"** his machine said. **"And I just turned twelve. I sure hope we get to make s'mores one of these nights!"**

Jocelyn whispered, "He's kinda cute, cute, cute!"

True that, I thought. *And he taps lightning-fast,* was my next thought.

A counselor in cutoffs and Timberlands standing next to Santiago gave him a playful nudge. "So you gonna introduce me, dude?"

Santiago laughed. **"Naw. No need for all that."**

After another nudge, Santiago looked back at the guy and laughed. **"Okay, okay!"** he said. **"This is my counselor, Harley. And you know what? He actually *owns* a Harley motorcycle! At least that's what he told me!"**

Harley smiled wide. "Hey, everybody. Glad to meet you all. And yeah, I've got a bike in my garage at home.

Unless my wife has taken it out for a spin while I'm here at camp!"

Cool, a motorcycle! I wonder if that felt anything like zip-lining? Actually, Santiago's chair almost *could* pass for a motorcycle.

"And this is Malik, and his counselor Brock," Jeremiah said, placing a hand on a sunburned counselor's broad shoulder. Malik, the kid with the awesome white hair and the pale eyes, put his hand to his forehead and gave a small salute.

"Malik is my personal hero," Brock told us with a grin. "He showed up to camp with a suitcase full of gummies and Skittles and my favorite—mini Butterfingers! So now we call him the Candy Man."

Malik sat in . . . I'm not kidding . . . a gold-colored wheelchair—manual, but GOLD! Where do these guys find such cool chairs? The ones I've had over the years were useful and clunky and, well, not really cute. I couldn't tell if Malik's had come like that or been painted at a later time, but yeah, I was having major wheelchair envy.

But when Jeremiah introduced the last Panther, my focus quickly shifted. It was Noah, leaning on a neon-blue walker, his right hand clutching a bag of Takis. He waved at us with orange-stained fingertips, his left hand balancing on the walker.

"Hey, all," he began, his head bobbing a little. "I'm psyched to be here! I thought camp would suck, but it doesn't. That's why I'm here for another round!"

Karyn sat up at *that*, I noticed.

When it was my turn to introduce myself, last this time, Elvira's mechanical-almost-close-to-human-sounding voice said for me, **"Hey there. My name is Melody. This is my first time at camp, and I'm having more fun than I thought I would."**

Mom had loaded that message too, trying to anticipate anything I might need to say. She'd put in a phrase for just about everything. Thanks, Mom!

"Now that we all know each other," Jeremiah said with a glint in his eye, "let's *really* fire things up!" Before anyone could ask what he meant, he and Charles dashed off into the trees and came back with an armful each of pine cones. "Who wants to see nature's fireworks?" Jeremiah asked.

At the chorus of "We do!" he tossed a handful of the pine cones into the fire.

Whoosh! Crackle! Wow! The fire flared. Who knew pine cones did that? I guess I did now. Then he and Charles handed each camper a couple of pine cones.

"On the count of three, toss them in!" he challenged. Then he skipped one and two and just shouted, "THREE!"

Everybody threw a cone in the direction of the fire. A few, like mine, fell way short, but many landed in the middle of the flames. *Whoosh!*

That was freakin' awesome! The cones sparked with an intensity even brighter than the logs. Blue-green flames rose into the night sky. I loved how we were all seeing the same thing at the same time, all huddled together around the fire circle. For a few minutes, nobody even spoke. It was just us and the darkness of the night and the brightness of the fire.

Athena—a silhouette against the glow—lifted her fingers toward the pine-cone sparks. Her dark hair looked glossy in the firelight, and she seemed to be entranced. She looked beautiful.

Trinity nudged me with her elbow. "You want to get closer to the fire?"

I tapped **"Yes."**

"Closer to our guests?"

I hesitated, then touched **"Yes"** again.

"You got it!"

She maneuvered me to the perfect spot where I could feel the warmth of the fire mixed with the chill of the night.

Then Cassie broke the silence—and the mood—with a crazy song.

"Schoooool's out for summer!" she hollered out.

And, almost immediately, we all yelled back, *"School's out forever!!"*

I say *we* because in my mind, I was singing too!

I banged on my tray—just making noise. *Woo-hoo!* I was right there with them!

Next, Cassie started singing about hot fun in the summertime. And I realized that was exactly what we were doing!

I think we sang that one like ninety-two times.

Then Jeremiah walked over and handed Trinity a guitar. Who knew? She was actually pretty good! She led off with "The Banana Boat Song." When she sang the refrain, *"Daylight come and me wanna go home . . . ,"* I realized I was loving this, and I was *not* ready to go home! I glanced at Karyn. Her face was glowing, and she was wheelchair-swaying to the rhythm. (And yeah, that's a thing!)

When Trinity was done, Cassie started up "A Million Dreams"—one of my favorites! It came from that movie about how the circus got started.

Oh, yeah. That's me. The kid with the dreams inside. But here, somehow, when I looked up at the night sky, I could see my dreams up there, too.

Next, one of the guys in blue—the Badgers—told some second-grade knock-knock jokes that were so extremely corny they were actually hysterically funny.

We were laughing our heads off. You know what's cool about laughter? Funny is funny whether you can talk or not.

As the campfire glowed, cracked, and sparked, I watched the faces of the other campers. Jocelyn hummed a little song to herself. Karyn must have sensed me looking, because she caught my eye and poked me with her elbow. I was so glad she decided to stay. And I guess I had a new friend! I used to wonder how to make friends. Maybe all you need is moonlight and starlight, a bonfire, and . . . pine cones!

Gradually, the laughter and the giggles quieted. I looked up at the inky sky. Starlight now dotted it like crystals. Last night—fireflies. Tonight—diamond stars.

And more. One incredible thing more. When I looked back at the campfire, I noticed that kid Noah looking right at me. And smiling. Right at me.

How was this even possible?

CHAPTER 23

It was late. Everyone in our cabin was asleep. Karyn sometimes mumbled when she turned over. I smirked because Athena's snores had actually become oddly comforting. I could hear crickets, and a new noise— sounded kinda *hooty-hoot*—maybe an owl? I was sleepy, but all the stuff stuck inside my mind twirled and twisted and kept me restless. The little lanterns dangling from each top bunk cast a soft glow, and I wondered how dark the cabin would be without them.

And this got me thinking about the time when I was around four or five—before Penny was born. A really bad storm swept through our neighborhood. Lightning crackled, and suddenly we heard a transformer blow. All the lights in the house blinked off. The current simply flatlined. Even the streetlights went dark.

No matter how many times Dad clicked the light switches, nothing happened. So we sat there in the dark, huddled together, waiting for the lights to come back on. There was nothing we could do. Of course, Dad found flashlights and candles in a kitchen drawer, but those were just tiny beams in all that darkness. The main power source had been cut off.

We waited a really long time. I remember being scared.

Eventually, the workers from the power company climbed up on poles and fixed the transformer, and the lights came back on—most of them. But some of the wires had gotten fried and they simply could not be fixed. There's a light fixture on our back porch that Mom says has not worked since that storm. Electricians have come by to try, but it simply Does. Not. Work. anymore. The fixture still has a beautiful crystal globe. I love the way it looks because I can see inside its intricate parts. But it has no power.

For me, the inside wires that connect to my physical body are sort of like the ones inside that fixture. They're pretty much fried. But the wires to my brain— ah! Absolutely, exceptionally excellent!

And that made me think about how here at camp, no one was doing what so many people I've met seem to do. Lots of folks still have a tendency to just look at me from the outside. They notice the wheelchair and the head wobbling and the fact that my hands just can't hold still. I drool sometimes—which, yes, is totally embarrassing. Folks don't often look deep enough to see the kid who knows the names of every single bone in the human body. I'm almost twelve, but I read on a twelfth-grade level. Lots of that is thanks to Mrs. V, who never saw me as unplugged, but only saw my power.

But of all the conversations we've had, and all she's taught me, she and I never talked about what to do about someone who made my heartbeat race and my fingers tingle.

CHAPTER 24

On Tuesday morning I woke up to see that our paintings from Sunday were now on our cabin wall. They were gloppy and crazy-looking, but I felt kinda proud anyway. Athena was quick to point out her pink contributions, and the one dot of yellow. Jocelyn, however, reached up and rubbed her hands all over her painting, like she was feeling the colors and the bumpiness of the clumped paint.

Once in my chair, I rolled over to the wall feeling the need to touch mine too—I'm not sure why. The green felt different from the red, and the blue had a different texture from the yellow. It was like each color had a personality. Trinity snapped picture after picture of us . . . it was like we were at a gallery show.

Then, tucking her camera away, she announced, "Today we're gonna do some stomping in the woods. We're going to get up close and personal with some nature—maybe even hug a tree."

Just as she ended with a laugh, Karyn let out a scream. Actually, it was more a bloodcurdling shriek that pierces the silence during one of those Halloween movies, when the bad guy is about to slice and dice somebody with a buzz saw. Then Karyn screamed again and pointed, her arms as trembly as mine usually are.

All four counselors raced to her side. "What's wrong?" Kim asked, grabbing for Karyn's hands. "Are you okay? Did you hurt yourself?"

Karyn frantically wheeled her chair backward, her eyes wide with fear. Kim checked her chair, her arms, her legs, her hair, and still Karyn screamed.

Athena and Jocelyn and I backed away as well. I didn't even know what I was afraid of, but it had to be terrible to make Karyn react like that.

"Tell me what's wrong, Karyn," Kim pleaded.

I looked around. Nothing seemed out of order. None of us could figure out what was upsetting her.

Finally Karyn's scream turned into one single word. "SNAKE!"

A snake? Where? I wasn't afraid of snakes, but I didn't want one to be my best friend. They were apparently Karyn's worst nightmare, however.

"I don't want to be here! Call my mother! I'm going home NOW!"

Trinity, clearly the queen of calm, merely asked, "Where? Where did you see it?"

Karyn pointed to a corner. We all warily looked in that direction.

"There are no dangerous snakes in this area," Lulu quickly assured us. "I bet it was scared of you, too!" she said, trying to joke a little. Nobody laughed.

"What did it look like?" Kim asked.

Why would she ask that? Was she going to invite the snake over for dinner?

Karyn was still clutching her wheelchair rims, breathing hard, but she managed to say, "It was horrible!" She paused. "But it was a pretty color. . . ." She took a deep breath, I guess trying to get her brave on. "It was, maybe, orange and brown and yellow."

"Will it bite us?" Athena asked, creeping close to Sage. "It won't eat us, will it?"

"No! Snakes don't eat people," Kim told us emphatically. "Besides, the group of us would give him really bad indigestion, don't you think?" Another joke bomb.

Jocelyn wanted to know why a snake would even want to come in here.

Lulu answered this one. "Probably because our cabin's warm. It was a little chilly last night."

Jocelyn nodded as if this was perfectly reasonable.

"Listen up, my brave campers," Lulu continued. "First of all, the snake that Karyn saw was probably a corn snake. It's harmless, and like Karyn said, actually quite pretty. It's orange and gold and brown, mostly minds its own business, and eats small mice. It does not bite."

"I don't believe you!" Karyn argued.

"I understand," Lulu told her. "But trust me—it's not poisonous, and it was probably more scared of you than you were of it. Corn snakes are very shy."

"If that's true, why would it come in here with all of us, even if it *was* cold?" Karyn wiped her forehead. "I don't like snakes."

"Why?" Kim asked.

"They're nasty and slinky and evil."

Jocelyn shook her head. Three times.

"Snakes have a pretty bad reputation, I admit," Lulu said calmly. "But think about it—it's hard to be a snake! They don't have arms or legs, which means they have to slide on their stomachs everywhere they want to go. Plus, they're cold-blooded, which means they have to find sunshine to get warm, and they have to eat bugs and mice for dinner! No s'mores for snakes!"

Okay, so that was a little funny. Poor snake!

Then Karyn screamed once more. "There it is! I see it!" She backed up so fast she bumped into the wall behind her.

There, in the corner closest to the door, was our visitor. It seemed to me that it had emerged on purpose. It curled into a small shaft of morning sunlight.

Did that snake just blink? Nah—I was pretty sure snakes couldn't blink.

Then, as breezily as if she were picking up a dropped headband, Jocelyn shocked us all by scooping that snake right up! Karyn gasped. I did too! Athena pressed against Sage.

Even Lulu looked a little alarmed. "Jocelyn, uh, maybe you should give me . . ." But Jocelyn shook her head and began whispering to the snake as it wound itself around her forearm.

I couldn't believe she was letting the snake do that. What if it *did* bite her? I was barely breathing.

Jocelyn whispered, "Hey, there, Miss Snake. Are you lost, lost, lost?"

The snake didn't answer. Ha-ha!

Lulu glanced from Jocelyn to the other counselors. Trinity shrugged. Lulu asked, "So, you like snakes, Jocelyn?"

Jocelyn nodded. "My brother," she said in a soft, small voice. "He has a few like this. It *is* a corn snake. They're not scary, scary, scary at all."

"Okay, Falcons," Lulu told us, looking relieved. "Let's look at this like real campers. We are in the woods, so basically we're invading the snake's house. She belongs here. It's her habitat. We are invading her space, not the other way around. You gotta remember she did not invite us over for tea and cookies."

Athena cracked up. Then she asked, "What's 'habitat'?"

"'Habitat' refers to where an animal lives. This is her living room and dining room, and we have parked ourselves in the middle of it!" Lulu paused, then said, "Okay—quick science lesson. Like Jocelyn confirmed, this is definitely a corn snake."

Athena said, "I bet it's got fangs!"

Jocelyn shook her head. "Nope, no fangs."

Well, that was good to know!

Lulu added, "And it's non-venomous."

"What does that mean?" Karyn asked.

I knew, but I wasn't gonna be a show-off.

"It means it's not poisonous."

"But aren't all snakes poisonous?" Athena wanted to know.

Lulu wrinkled her forehead. "Y'all watch way too many scary jungle movies."

I didn't think I'd ever seen a movie where the snake was a hero. I was feeling a little sorry for snakes in general at this point. They never get to be the good guys!

"Would the rest of you like to touch her?" Lulu put out there.

Hesitation hovered.

"How do you know it's a girl?" Athena asked.

Lulu laughed. "I honestly don't know for sure. I just figured she was looking for some cool girls to hang out with, and she chose us!"

Karyn raised her hand at last. "I'm not scared of it," she admitted. "It just . . . surprised me, showing up like that."

Exactly how I felt.

"I'll tell you what we're gonna do," Lulu announced. "Jocelyn, if you'd like, you can bring the snake—"

"Her name is Cleopatra," Jocelyn announced. The snake curled around her wrist like a bracelet.

Athena asked, "How do you know that's her name?"

Jocelyn shrugged. "Uh, 'cause she told me. I promise she's nice, nice, nice. You wanna touch her?"

"I'm no scaredy-cat!" Athena carefully adjusted her glasses, then gently touched the snake with one finger. "She's so smooth!" she cooed. "Not snaky at all!"

Snaky—great word!

Jocelyn was rocking back and forth. "Snakes are not slimy," she told us.

Lulu agreed. "She's right—they're sleek and smooth. When we go on our nature hike, we will probably see squirrels and birds, but I bet we won't see a single snake. We're actually lucky we got to see this one."

"How come?" Athena asked.

"'Cause snakes are smart and know how to hide from noisy folks like us!"

"Hide where?" I tapped.

"Under leaves. Behind bushes. In the undergrowth. That's their home. They know all the safe places to hide from birds and squirrels and foot-stomping campers."

"Snakes don't have ears," Karyn said with a thoughtful frown. "So how do they hear us, or anything that's trying to sneak up on them to eat them?"

Athena found the idea of ears on snakes hilarious. "Ears on a snake! Ears on a snake! That's *soooo* funny!"

I was trying to draw a picture in my head of a long, skinny snake with protruding ears attached to each side of its body. Maybe wearing headphones! Okay, yep, pretty funny.

"Snakes listen for vibrations through their jawbones. Odd, huh?" Lulu asked. "So when we pound through the woods this afternoon, Miss Cleo will be as far away as she can be!"

Jocelyn had come over to me with the snake. Lulu asked if I'd like to touch Cleopatra before we let her go.

I nodded and lifted my right hand. The snake was so pretty—golden brown with orange splotches on it. I couldn't believe I was actually sitting there, thinking about touching a beautiful snake!

Everybody there knew by now that my hands sometimes had their own agenda. It's actually one of the things that's most frustrating about having cerebral palsy. I just want my body to be still sometimes. This was one of those times.

Slowly I reached out. I wasn't scared. But what if *I* scared *it*? *Be still, hand!* I ordered my right hand. Miss Cleo had tiny black button eyes, and it stared right at me.

As I touched the snake, it still didn't move, and neither did my hand! It felt a little like cool, smooth leather on my fingertips. Look at me! Getting all cozy with snakes and stuff—Mom and Dad would never believe this!

Once we'd learned more about snakes than we ever imagined we wanted to, Lulu announced that she was going to let this one go home. "Everybody good with that?"

She opened the cabin door. Jocelyn went outside about ten yards from the cabin, then gently placed

Cleopatra on the grass. "Bye, bye, bye," she whispered.

Trinity snapped a quick photo.

"Thanks for visiting us," Lulu called out, "but go find a safe place to sleep, okay? These campers think you're very pretty, but they want you to go back to the forest."

It raised its head, seemed to look around for a second, then—*spfft*! It slithered off into the warming-up morning.

CHAPTER 25

So, we had a snake come to visit us. And now they wanted us to go on a trek into snake territory *on purpose*? Actually, that sounded like a fair trade—I was up for it, ready to go and check out Cleopatra's neighborhood.

We were getting a rep as the late cabin—it was Cleo's fault—but we hit breakfast just in time to gobble down yummy pancakes, slathered in caramel syrup. If they made those every day until the end of camp, I sure wouldn't complain.

The guys from the Panthers joined us on the hike. That pretty much guaranteed we wouldn't see even one squirrel or chipmunk or bird on a branch. They hooted and shouted and called to each other as we bumped along the plank-covered walkway toward the woods. If the forest was usually silent, it sure wasn't gonna be this morning!

"Hey, Firefly Girl!" Noah called out as the Panthers jostled past us. I did manage to wave back, but I'm not sure if he saw. Jocelyn noticed, however.

She grinned at me. "Lightning bug! Lightning bug! Lightning bug!"

I flicked out my hand like it didn't matter. But I had to work hard to hold in my smile.

The guys tramped just ahead of us the whole time. *That's okay,* I thought. We'd save our energy for a *real* competition! I was impressed with the power of Devin's chair—must have had shock absorbers too, because he never even bounced. Malik passed us in his solid-gold-looking chair, shouting, "Hey, Falcon Girls! You can't catch us!"

I didn't think we were trying to get anywhere fast, but he seemed to think we were in a race. I remember reading about competitions like balloon soccer or something, but so far, nobody had talked about those. It seems to me that Malik, for sure, would love something like that.

Parts of this path were rockier and bumpier and muckier than others. I was glad my dad had switched out my wheelchair tires for ones he called "industrial-strength." They weren't as thick as Santiago's—he could actually roll himself on his own for short distances!—but they were wider and sturdier than my regular wheels—kinda like what BMX bikes have. They can roll easily over rocks and through mud. The wheels on Karyn's chair were thinner, and I could see the concentration on Kim's face as she occasionally had to strain to get Karyn through the muck.

Penny had seemed to be sure that I was going to spend my whole time in the "forest," but this was our first real venture into the actual woods. I'd gotten used to the bright sunshine everywhere, but in here, it seemed like somebody had put the sun on a dimmer switch. It glimmered through the tangled branches above, but sent down more shadows than sunbeams. Pine trees dropped fat cones—plop—right in front of us. Thanks to all the studying I'd done for the Whiz Kids team, I could identify just about every species of trees we passed—birches and black oaks and bitternut hickories. It was nice to able to reach out and feel their bark, instead of just looking at them online or in a library book.

I spied the parade of tiny black ants. There must have been a hundred of them, in the skinniest line dance I'd ever seen. They marched in almost single file from the base of a hickory tree, up the trunk, to the branches. They seemed to know *exactly* where they were headed and what their job was. How much time had the guy who wrote that *Atta* book spent watching lines of ants? These ants never seemed to stop, and yeah, they seemed to help each other as they took stuff from the ground, up the trunk, and on to whatever their goal was. When I got home, I thought I'd do a search on ants and how they survive. *Okay, Mrs. V—get out of my head!*

Then *into* my head came, **"You think we'll see any bears out here?"** It was Santiago.

"Not likely," I heard Harley answer. "If a bear saw all of us, he'd probably run in the opposite direction. We're pretty fearsome-looking!"

"Betcha I spot one!" Santiago insisted.

Lulu chimed in with, "The park rangers around here haven't reported any bear sightings in years." I guess she was trying to reassure us. But now I was peeking around every tree—just in case. A bear might have decided to move back to his old territory. Or maybe come back to visit some old friends. I'd seen photos of bears online—their claws are like three inches long.

Just as I was laughing at myself searching for invisible grizzly bears, I saw . . . the skunk.

It was most definitely not invisible. It was sleek black,

with two white stripes making a V shape down its back.
And right down the middle of its face was another thin
white stripe. The same time as my brain was screaming,
A SKUNK!!, what was also flashing through it was that
the little animal was kind of pretty when you thought
about it—like a black-and-white painting that stood out
in contrast to all the shades of green and brown around
it. But skunks were not designed for cute—they were
designed for secret battles they never lose.

Bright eyes peered at us, unblinking. Even though
we were making all kinds of noise, it did not run away.
Not one inch.

I think Trinity saw it just as I did because she jerked
my chair to a stop and held up her right arm in warn-
ing. In the loudest whisper I've ever heard, "Uh, skunk,
guys! Skunk just ahead!"

We Falcons froze. *What should we doooooooo?* my brain
was yelping.

"What's up?" one of the guys called out.

Trinity, her voice betraying a hint of a quaver,
repeated, "Skunk! Skunk!"

It stood not six feet away from us, to the left of the
path—like a traffic cop whose job was to move the cars
in another direction. It was silent. So were we. I'm not
sure if any of us even breathed.

As for the skunk, it tilted its head as if to say, *Who are all these noisy intruders in my forest?* It continued to peer at us, but also began waving its tail. That couldn't be good! As I thought about it, we *were* large and clunky and noisy. But the skunk had stealth, silence—and a not-so-secret superpower.

Trinity whispered, "Let's back away slowly. Very, very slowly. Don't say a word, guys. Sh-sh-sh."

One inch we backed up. Two inches. Three. The skunk didn't move a millimeter. And why should it? We were the intruders! It was almost as if it were challenging us to cross its path. We were all so very quiet and careful. Then, just as I thought we had backed up far enough, my body decided to spazz up on me. Maybe it was the tension. Maybe it was the fear. I honestly don't know. But right as we were slowly and silently backing up, my upper body jerked. My lower body kicked. I tried not to, but I couldn't help it—I squeaked, just a little. *Oh no, oh no, oh no!*

But the little animal only stared toward me—yep, I think it made eye contact! But still it did not move. I read someplace that skunks only attack if they feel threatened, so I did my best to give it an *I mean you no harm* kind of smile while we girls slowly, slowly continued to back away. Four inches. Eight. A foot! Ten feet. Fifteen. Complete silence.

The skunk must have decided we weren't worth

the trouble to raise a stink—*ha, I made a pun*—because it started to trundle back to wherever skunks live in the woods. And that was when Santiago and Devin decided to roll themselves over to see what was going on, doubling back toward us. Harley and Charles whisper-shouted for them to stop, but the boys seemed mesmerized. So their counselors hustled back as well to yank them away. But then they all froze, big-time, Noah and Malik not far behind them. Santiago's speaker said, **"Zorillo,"** which I knew meant "skunk" in Spanish.

The skunk must have understood Spanish as well, because it suddenly paused, mid-jog, cocking its little head as if checking out who had dared to speak. Then it started tippy-tapping its front paws and slapping its tail against the ground. This most definitely couldn't be good! We Falcons kept creeping backward slowly, slowly, twenty feet away, then thirty. But the Panthers were closer and clearly kind of freaked. They finally started moving backward, five feet, then ten. . . .

And then the skunk stopped its odd dance, and, as if it had been devising this battle plan for years, it lifted its tail, aimed directly at the boys, and let loose. *Arrrrgghh!!* It smelled worse than an aerosol can full of funky farts! Worse than a bucket of armpit funk! Worse than a pile of yesterday's dog poop!

The entire group of Panthers—counselors as well as

campers—howled, screeched, gagged! *Oh man, what a STINK!* They got sprayed! Big-time!

As we all screeched, Trinity, Lulu, Sage, and Kim swiveled us around and *RAN* us back to camp. Even though none of us had been directly in the line of fire, we headed straight to the showers. Double doses of sweet-smelling body wash. And triple rinses. I wondered what the boys were using. . . .

We stayed in there a very long time. "Wonder if the guys'll have to change their names from the Purple Panthers to the Silver Skunks!" Karyn hollered from her stall.

Jocelyn laughed and yelled back, "Bet they would have rather seen a bear bear bear!"

But I did wonder if the guys who got skunked were okay. When we got dressed in fresh, never-worn-at-camp-yet clothes, I took a minute or two and looked it up on Elvira. I found out that the sulphuric acid in the skunk spray can cause breathing problems and, ohmigosh, even blindness. I'm pretty sure the guys were far enough away so they didn't get a direct hit, but they were for sure gonna need a commercial skunk odor remover! We had laughed, but this was NO joke!

So I tapped out to the girls some of what I'd discovered. Our laughter turned to concern. Karyn rolled over to me. "My dad got skunked once," she told us.

"He took a bath in tomato juice! And then he took a bath in milk!" We cracked up. "But he still smelled like a rancid bowl of cream of tomato soup when he finished. Mom finally went to the hardware store and bought some professional stuff, but I didn't hug my dad for a while after that!"

Athena kinda summed it up when she scrunched up her face and said, "Skunks rule for sure! I hope the boys are okay."

Jocelyn stood by the window, gazing in the direction of the boys' cabins. "Stinky but safe, stinky but safe, stinky but safe," she whispered.

As we sat in the cabin, discussing how stinky the boys would be, and what you could wash the stench out with, I wrote a quick email home.

> Dear Mom and Dad and Mrs. V—
> Today's science lesson was about
> skunks! You think trash bags left in the hot
> garage are stinky? That's sweet perfume
> compared to the funk of a skunk! Thanks
> for packing the peppermint soap! Bye
> for now!

Smelling sweet and really thankful, we headed to the rest of the afternoon activities. The guys weren't anywhere. I bet they did *nothing* but shower all afternoon.

We zoomed through art and music and even a swimming lesson before dinner, so I was starving by the time we rolled over there. The camp kitchen staff must have had industrial-strength equipment; they've managed to come up with some pretty good stuff. Tonight was a surprisingly yummy mystery casserole—Jocelyn guessed it was some kind of tuna—and a strawberry parfait for dessert. Cassie proudly announced that the strawberries were from the camp garden. I hoped some were being delivered to the Panthers!

CHAPTER 26

I really started to look forward to the fire gatherings. I'm usually never out at night, except in the back seat of our car, all strapped in while we made a last-minute grocery run or something ordinary like that. There *was* that amazing moment with that real live lightning bug on Mrs. V's porch. But here, outside was every day, and every night. And every night blazed with crackling sticks and drifting sparkles. Killer awesome.

Tonight the guys from the Blue Badgers seemed to be in charge of setting up the fire. When our team arrived, it was already crackling.

I sniffed the air; no residual skunk smell—yet.

"Whoa, I'm crazy about that fire, fire, fire," Jocelyn said, reaching out toward the warmth.

"Yep, it's hot, hot, hot," Athena replied. She tilted her head and looked at Jocelyn for a second. "I only said that three times because it's triple cool," she said, I guess to let Jocelyn know she wasn't making fun of her.

Jocelyn gave Athena a high five, and they plunked down together in the only two unoccupied folding chairs near the fire pit. Everybody else either sat in chairs, or on the ground with blankets or mats, or attached to whatever device made their lives function best, like I do.

As I got settled in my spot, I made Elvira shout out, **"Hey, now!"** Lots of kids, even those I hadn't met yet, waved or hollered in reply. Karyn, who evidently had tucked her bunk-bed blanket under her chair, rolled up next to me. She snatched up the blanket, flicked it open, and smoothed it over both our legs. I elbowed her in thanks. She elbowed me back, *You're welcome!*

Trinity and some of the other counselors made a dash to the kitchen. They were back a few minutes later with bags of marshmallows (the big ones—not the teeny ones Mom puts in Penny's hot chocolate), dozens of bars of Hershey's chocolate, and two boxes of graham crackers. Trinity let me know, however, that she had my back: she'd packed some caramel sauce for me! I don't need crackers—I like my caramel sauce by the spoonful. She's the best.

The Panthers were the last to arrive, all wearing brand-new-looking purple T-shirts, looking both embarrassed and victorious at the same time. Santiago, whose legs were covered by a fuzzy purple blanket, rolled in with his Medi-Talker playing really cool, really loud salsa music. All right! Apparently the guys had managed to recuperate!

When Jocelyn saw them, she murmured, "Stinky, stinky, stinky." I had to press my lips together not to laugh. The Badgers were a lot less subtle. They made a big show of holding their noses and fanning the air as the Panthers rolled in, but to my total shock, the Panthers didn't reek. I sniffed the air hard, but all I caught was that crisp smell of branches on fire, and maybe a hefty dose of aftershave lotion.

Jeremiah came and stood by Trinity. I heard him tell her that they used up all the baking soda from the kitchen to wash the stink off—and Cassie had to drive into town, where she bought out the entire supply from the grocery store there. Who knew baking soda helped with skunk smell? Cassie, apparently.

The fire tonight sparkled and blazed as if its job was to entertain us. Which I guess it was! Stacked beside

it were dozens of twigs, along with broken branches
and boughs—way more than the night before. I hoped
they didn't run out before the end of camp. Nah, we
were living in the woods—we're good. As if on cue, the
Badgers brought over armfuls of even more fire fuel
and dumped it by the blaze.

Santiago, who clearly survived the skunking with
no problems, made his machine shout, **"You ever hear
the joke about the skunk?"**

A few kids shouted back, "No!"

Santiago, his machine cranked up to its loudest
volume, shouted, **"Never mind—it stinks!"**

I caught Jocelyn's eye, and we tried not to, but we
laughed so hard we were holding our stomachs. The
freshly scrubbed, probably majorly embarrassed guys
tried to act like they didn't care. But I bet they did, a
little!

Which made it even more of a surprise when
Noah, bopping on his walker, headed over to where
I sat and plopped down—right in the folding chair
beside me.

Acting like this was the most ordinary thing in the
world, to get sprayed by a skunk and then come sit by
me, he grinned and said, "Hey, Firefly Girl."

And—I couldn't help it, I just couldn't—even while
I waved hello, I took a little sniff. I *might* have detected

a slight leftover odor, but mostly I smelled a combination of woodsy-spice soap and a ton of the type of aftershave lotion my dad uses.

"Did you get hit bad?" I tapped.

He made a face. "No, not directly. I was behind the other guys when it happened. But Santiago and Devin! Those poor dudes nearly took a direct blast! Good thing we'd all moved back when we did! Jeremiah had to throw their clothes away. And even though the counselors scrubbed our cabin with pine cleaner, and sprayed it with a whole bottle of aftershave, it still reeks like a skunk factory!"

I tapped out, **"That's terrible!"** But I couldn't keep from laughing. Luckily, Noah started laughing too.

"We spent the *entire* afternoon in the showers—almost three hours!" he exclaimed. "That lake is probably only half-full now."

Poor Panthers. No crafts. No swimming. No art. Just showers. All afternoon. I was sorry it happened, though it was a little bit funny.

The fire blazed gold and red—just being fiery and stuff like it was supposed to. Noah stared into it and joked, "I hope the smoke smell is helping with the skunk stink a little!"

I wondered if stars had any smell to them—the sky was loaded with them tonight. If they did, they should beam some down! But seriously, the smell was hardly noticeable.

I was about to tell Noah that when Cassie hollered out, "Who's ready for s'mores?"

Everybody raised their hand or shouted out something. To be honest, I'd never had a s'more in my life.

Jeremiah ambled over and held out a very long stick with a marshmallow stuck on the end to Noah. "Here you go, buddy!" he said.

But Noah replied, "Uh, no thanks. I'll pass."

Well, *that* blew me away.

He shrugged and grinned. "Don't tell anybody, but I don't like chocolate! Or marshmallow."

"Seriously? Me neither!"

"Where do you land on caramel?" he asked.

"Top of my list!" I told him.

"I just need this fire, and I'm good."

Me too! my insides were saying. *Me too! Me too!*

CHAPTER 27

Wednesday started off kind of weird and wild. When we got to art, we were told to take off our shoes. Huh? Trinity laughed, teased me about stinky feet (I'm sure they weren't), and explained that we were going to make footprints.

For somebody who had never walked before, this was intriguing. Trinity gave me a choice of colors, so I chose orange (trying to stay loyal to the Fiery Falcons) and purple (hmm—because of the Purple Panthers? Nah.). She pulled out two trays and placed the bottle of purple in my hands. "Squeeze, girlfriend," she ordered. So I did. Gushes of paint splurted into the tray. When my foot touched the paint, it felt kind of cool, kind of like how I felt the color violet ought to feel. The other foot, which got plopped into a tray of orange, actually felt different—almost fruity. My toes wiggled tangerine.

Since I don't walk, I hardly ever think about my feet, except to make sure I'm wearing the latest kicks. But this made me think about what feet were made for—for running and dancing and actually propelling the body to move ahead. We made several imprints of my feet because our first tries got smeared—I should get an Olympic medal for supreme extreme foot-kicking! But that orange-and-grape-colored "foot art" ended up looking awesome! Mom was gonna love this one.

When it was over, we cleaned up, although flecks of purple remained between my toes, and headed to swimming. I guess the rest of the purple washed off in the pool because I didn't notice any on my feet when we got my sneakers on for music.

At music, I got to bang on some drums. Who says I can't play an instrument? *Pow! Pow! Boom! Boom!* The drums were hooked up to a speaker, and *kapowie!* There was no right way or wrong way to do it. So whenever I hit the drum any kind of way I made lots of noise—*woo-hoo!*

But this was not Jocelyn's happy place. She asked Lulu to take her outside. "I don't like the boom boom

boom," she whispered, her eyes wide and distressed. Lulu rushed her out, and the two of them spent the rest of that session sitting on a bench, checking out the breeze.

Bam-bam-bam! Athena's drums beat out. *Bam-bam-bam!* Karyn found some maracas and we had ourselves an instant band. We shook and hooted and performed for the counselors. I had no idea if we were any good, but we were loud, and yep, that was fun.

"I *like* being noisy!" Athena said. "Teachers always tell me to sit down and be quiet."

I had to agree with her. A girl who can't talk needs all the noise she can get!

By then, it was just about time for lunch, and we gathered a much more relaxed Jocelyn and headed back to the cabin.

"You okay?" Karyn asked Jocelyn, concern in her voice.

"Yeah, all good now," Jocelyn replied, looking over toward a swath of yellow daisies decorating the edges of the grassy area by our cabin. Athena spied them too. She picked one and tucked it behind her ear. Then, her face radiant, she cried, "Ooh, this is a perfect place for a picnic! Can we eat out here—just the four of us?"

Karyn spun around in a little circle. "Ohmigosh, yes! A picnic!" she joined in.

As quickly as I could, I made Elvira say, **"Yes, please!"**

Our counselors looked from one to the other and nodded simultaneously. "You know, we haven't done that in years," Lulu said, all cheery. "Yes! Let's have a picnic together!"

Karyn and I looked at each other. When the counselors said *we*, they included themselves with us. But when we talked about *us*, it meant just the four of us. Athena's face fell, and Jocelyn pulled at the grass.

"You four sit right here, and we'll go get everyone's lunches," Trinity said. "Shouldn't take ten minutes."

She and Kim made sure our chairs were locked.

"You good?" Trinity asked me.

"Fine," I typed back. But not really. *WE?*

"Sure you're all good?" Lulu seconded, looking at each of us.

We assured them that we were, so finally our counselors hoofed it to the dining hall, looking back about every hundred yards to check on us. But then they turned the corner past the cabins and they were Out. Of. Sight!

Ohmigosh. It was the first time the four of us had been totally alone. We all looked at each other, almost stunned.

Athena said it first. "They're doing a picnic *with* us?"

"Yeah."

"Yeah."

"I guess so!"

"They're super nice to get our food, for sure, but . . . ," Jocelyn said, "they are always, always, always around!"

"Yep," Athena sighed with a roll of her eyes.

"Always around," I typed.

"I know!" Karyn said, groaning. "They're like my mom. She worries wayyyyy too much. When I'm at home, she checks in on me every single second!" She pulled at a lock of hair. "She's probably peeking from behind one of those bushes right now!"

"Mine too!" Jocelyn exaggeratedly looked around in every direction.

"Our counselors are the exact same way," Karyn said with a sigh.

"Yep. Like camp moms."

"Helicopter counselors!" Karyn exclaimed.

"It's like we're little kids!" Jocelyn added.

We were all scowling now.

Athena picked up some grass and tossed it around her head. "They just expect us to do what they say—"

"Like we're *babies*!" Karyn added, huffy. "Like we aren't even *capable* of breaking a rule!"

"You ever break a rule? A rule? A rule?" Jocelyn asked.

"Never had the chance!" I typed, rolling my eyes.

Karyn's eyes went suddenly bright, a sly smile on her face. "So let's break one!"

"How?"

Jocelyn pointed to a path off to the left. "What's down there?"

We had no idea.

"So let's go see!" Karyn announced gleefully. She leaned to her right, unlocked her wheelchair, whirled it around, and headed for the path. Athena broke into a skip right behind her, Jocelyn by her side.

"Uhhh!" I said as loudly as I could. I wasn't going to be left out of this little adventure!

"Melody!" Athena cried out. "We got ya, Melody!" She ran back, unlocked my wheels, swiveled my chair, and ran-pushed me to catch up.

Then . . . we just left! As quietly as we possibly could. Chipmunks skittered in front of us as we rounded the first bend. We went a little farther, and for *this* adventure, we didn't care about National Geographic facts or the height of pine trees or what little mammals darted by. Well, maybe a skunk, but I had my eyes peeled for *that*!

When a bird swooped and landed on a low branch right in front of us, we all froze. Its feathers were black, except for a patch of flaming reddish-orange and yellow above each wing. It had a sharp, pointed beak. I knew exactly what it was.

"Red-winged blackbird," I tapped.

"Cool, cool, cool," Jocelyn whispered.

The bird squawked, I guess saying hello to the four runaways in the forest, before lifting up and flying off.

As we rolled, walked, and skipped along a well-worn path, we reached an area that was a bit of a dip. The bottom looked soggy.

"It doesn't look *too* wet," Karyn decided.

Jocelyn ran ahead and pressed her foot hard into the muddy area.

"Not too bad," she confirmed.

So off we went—down the slight incline, and then . . . uh-oh . . . !

My thick tires rode easily over the mud. But Karyn's—not so much. Then, uh, not at all, despite how hard Jocelyn pushed. And pushed. And pushed. Karyn was stuck in the mud.

She turned around to give me a look that clearly said, *This isn't good!*

Athena hurried over. "We're gonna be in such big trouble!" she wailed, tugging her ponytails. She and Jocelyn got on either side of Karyn's chair and pushed. And heaved. And pushed some more. Karyn's face was red with exertion from trying to roll the wheels with them. Even I managed to give Karyn's back wheel a kick.

"Keep pushing!" Jocelyn cried.

The chair swayed forward, and just as we cheered, it rolled back.

"Again!" Athena yelled. And with one mighty, perfectly coordinated *heave*, the chair trundled forward and up onto firmer ground.

Jocelyn and Athena fell to their knees, panting. But we all looked at each other, our faces smeared with sweat. The looks of shock broke into smiles.

"We did it! We got her out!"

We knew better than to press our luck—we weren't even sure how long we'd been gone. Maybe ten minutes? It seemed like hours. So instead of risking another super-stuck situation, we headed back. Jocelyn and Athena together pushed Karyn around the dip by going off the path for a few yards, then Athena ran back for me. And we cheered again.

And I had an idea. I did a quick search on my board and found the song "Elvira." I hadn't played it in forever—it used to be my most favorite feel-good song! I turned up the volume as loud as it would go, and as we headed back, Jocelyn, Karyn, and Athena all scream-sang the words, *"Elvira! Elvira! My heart's on fire for Elvira!"*

We laughed, we sang, and it was right at the second playing of the *"oom papa, oom papa mow mow"* part of the song when our counselors found us.

They. Looked. Mad.

Really mad.

It wasn't like we were lost or anything, and the music let them know exactly where we were, but I think we were in trouble! And you know what? It was worth it! And you know what else? I realized I'd never been in trouble before!

BEST. AFTERNOON. EVER!

As our counselors walked us back, the silence was LOUD. Yep, they were mad. But I grinned at Karyn, who rode beside me, and she gave down-low high fives to Athena and Jocelyn, who stomped through the underbrush.

Sure enough, the counselors had a purple hissy fit when we got back to the "picnic" site. Trays of food sat waiting for us in the grass. At least the ants hadn't reached them yet.

"Okay, Falcons, we need to have ourselves a little talk!" Trinity started in first, scowling. "What were you thinking, Melody?"

Me (scowling back): *I bet you've had fun with friends before!* (I didn't type it out, but I'm sure she could see it on my face.)

Kim: "Karyn, I expected more from you!"

Karyn (hands on hips): "But we didn't *do* anything!"

Sage: "Athena, this could have ended so badly!"

Athena (frowning): "How? We were just having fun."

Lulu: "Do you have any idea how upsetting it was to come back and find you all gone? We were terrified."

Jocelyn: "We weren't lost."

It went eerie quiet again. My friends had to be wondering what was going to happen next.

Then Trinity spoke up again. Her voice was gentle and kind of blue-sounding, but the edges were bright orange. She was still mad. "What were you *thinking*?" she asked again, sounding honestly perplexed. "You all could have gotten *hurt*!"

But we *didn't*. Had it ever occurred to them that we had the need for, uh, *more*?

Athena responded, her voice sullen, "Nobody got hurt. We had fun."

I tapped out, **"We're almost teenagers!"**

Karyn and Jocelyn crossed their arms in agreement.

I watched the faces of our counselors closely, the frowns, the pursed lips. And I realized, *They seriously don't get it!*

"My mom treats me like I'm a baby! So do you guys," Athena said, her voice bolder than I'd ever heard it before. "But I'm NOT!"

"For real, that's not what we were trying to do, Athena," Sage said, her voice purply sad and confused.

"Our job is to keep you all *safe* and make sure you experience all the best parts of camp."

Karyn sighed. "Yeah, but can't we be safe and not have our every breath monitored? We just wanted a picnic by ourselves," she went on. "But we're sorry we took off. We didn't mean to scare you." She paused and looked over at us.

Athena added, "We're really, really sorry!"

Jocelyn added to that, "Can you just *not* be like our moms, at least not all the time?" Karyn and Athena and I nodded fiercely.

After a few more moments of utter silence, our counselors began to look at us with something close to understanding, the annoyance and concern on their faces turning into something else. They raised their eyebrows in some weird camp counselor eyebrow communication, until Trinity spoke up again. "Well, we've *never* had a group of campers who started their own revolution! But we understand your point. A little breathing room. Everyone needs that. And while it's a little tricky to know what's enough, or—ahem!—what's too much . . ."

Like our forest trek.

". . . I'm actually pretty proud of you all for letting us know how you were feeling."

Lulu, looking thoughtful, asked, "Where do the

four of you suggest we go from here? Got any ideas?"

Now it was time for *us* to blink in amazement!

Karyn spoke up first. "You know, thanks for actually asking. So many times grown-ups just 'do stuff' for us and never ask what we want. Like, uh, just because I'm in a wheelchair I can't make a decision. It stinks!"

I feel ya, Karyn. She is 100 percent right!

Then I tapped, **"How about some free time? Just the four of us?"**

Our counselors looked at each other, clearly shocked. I'm betting that no camper had *ever* asked for that before—to be left alone a little! They honestly looked like they didn't know what to do.

"Well, okay, then!" Trinity finally said. "After we finish the lunch you four escaped from"—she paused and gave us a half-scolding smile—"we'll check the schedule and see what we can carve out for some plain old quality free time in the next day or two."

"But first, if you girls don't mind," Sage said, "can we have lunch now? I'm famished."

The chicken noodle soup had gone stone cold, but somehow, it was especially delicious.

CHAPTER 28

After another swim lesson—hey, I might even get beyond jellyfish level!—and art, where I focused on maroon and pink this time, we realized we had an hour to kill before dinner. I'd glimpsed what looked like a playground off past the boys' cabins as we left the arts and crafts building. *Ooh*, I thought, *is it for us?* You know what? It occurred to me that I'd never actually played on a playground! How messed up is that?

So I tapped to Trinity, **"Can we go there, pleeeeeease?"**

"Please, please, please!" Jocelyn added.

Athena was the winning plea, however, because

she started singing, *"Girls just wanna have fun!"*

The counselors thought it was a great idea, so we headed over there. As we got closer, we literally all stared. Basically, this was like the playground of our dreams!

I'm pretty good at sitting on the sidelines watching while the kids at school play soccer or hacky sack or even something easy like cornhole, shooting hoops, or slamming volleyballs across a net. Occasionally, they take the time to wave, but not often.

I sometimes watched when Dad took Penny to the park to swing and slide, but we never stayed long because there wasn't a whole heck of a lot I could do.

But this one—whoa! This one had all the hookups for kids like us. For starters, there were swings, of course, but they were massive. A whole wheelchair could fit into each one. Karyn flipped out.

"So we just wheel right up into it?" she asked Kim.

"Yep! Here, let's try." Kim rolled Karyn onto a metal platform, snapped and clicked her chair into place, and woo-hoo!—Karyn was flying! On a swing! Her chair flew back and forth and she screamed, "I've wanted to do this my whole life!"

A minute later, I was right beside her. Snap, click, pull me back, and yesssss!

Oh my gosh! Oh my gosh! I was swinging!

Back—*whoosh*. Forward—*whoosh*. Again and again and again. I couldn't get enough of the feeling of the air as it tousled my hair, forward, then back.

I looked to one side and saw the whole park soar past me. And then to the other side, where it happened again. In my head, I was yelling *wheee* just like every little kid I'd ever seen on a swing. So I was a few years late, but I was *swinging*!

No wonder little kids go *wheee*.

When I got off the swing, I was flushed and grinning and breathing hard.

Then Athena noticed that the slide was painted a dazzling pink. That was all she needed. "Pink slide next!" she called out.

"Next ride, Super Slide!" Sage agreed. I glanced up at the slide. When I touched its support poles, they felt soft and spongy as well as superstrong. It looked like it had been thought up by the mind of a kid like me, who grew up and said, "Hey, world—this is what we need!" It had two sides—one for sliding down while in a wheelchair, and one side for sliding simply by lying flat.

Trinity asked me, "Which side?"

I told her, "Both!"

And so we did. First we loaded my chair onto something that looked like a flat forklift, rolled me off, then slid me over to a specially designed wheelchair slide. They double-buckled me in, then *whoosh*! Me and my chair and even Elvira slid down! So fun! It was over in seconds.

"Again!" I pleaded. And so we did. Several times.

By this time Karyn had noticed where we were and hurried over to try the slide. A few minutes later, I smiled as I heard her shrieks of joy.

"Wanna try the other slide, the one that you slide down your self, Melody?" Trinity asked.

Well, duh! Absolutely!

When I touched this other slide, it was so different from what Penny slid down. It reminded me of the stuff that Dad's camping tent was made of—soft yet sturdy. It must have been designed by a parent who had a kid who really wanted to slide, but for some reason couldn't. Basically, us. Thank you, parent!

Jocelyn and Athena went first, then Trinity rolled me up a ramp, hooked me to a couple of latches, and *whoosh*, I was gliding down a slide like Penny. I was slipping and not falling, faster, faster, then *ahhh*!

The bottom was so soft and squishy that even if all those fasteners broke and I wiped out, I wouldn't get hurt in the least.

Seriously, the folks who invented this place had to be geniuses.

Karyn had her turn, and then the three of us just had to try the slide a few more times while Jocelyn and Lulu went off to explore the rest of the playground. After about her fourth or fifth slide, Athena ran over to see what Jocelyn was up to, and moments later came bounding back, insisting we come to the other side of the park.

The counselors checked their watches and decided we still had time to spare before dinner. So off we went to where Jocelyn and Lulu were taking turns tossing a volleyball into a basketball hoop. The hoop was half as high as what I'd seen on playgrounds at home, so Jocelyn easily made all her baskets. Still, she was amazingly accurate, because she was standing really far away. She hit seven in a row, then went on to make another. She raised both her hands in victory each time. When her streak broke at eleven, she turned to us.

"Come play! Come play! Come play!"

I had no idea how to do this, or if I even could, but why not? So I rolled onto the court and Lulu tossed me the ball. It landed right on my lap—great shot! It felt soft and kinda squishy too, like the slide.

"Two points for a great catch!" Athena cheered.

"Huh?"

"Fiery Falcon rules," Karyn quipped.

All right then. Two points for me. I took both

my hands and put one around each side of the ball. Well, balls don't actually have sides, but I grabbed the squishy thing with two curled palms. *Okay now, hands, you behave—you hear me?*

I glanced over at my friends. As if they'd choreographed it, they all gave me a thumbs-up.

Lifting the ball, I checked out my arms. Yeah, they were skinny, but hey, they were holding that ball up. I looked from the ball to the basket only a few feet away.

Karyn yelled, "Shoot, Melody! Just do it!"

I tossed it. In my head the ball was arching in the air, spinning perfectly. The reality? The ball missed the basket by something like two hundred miles. Well, maybe two hundred feet. Didn't matter. It was still a miss.

"Do it again, again, again," Jocelyn called. Trinity placed the ball back on my lap.

I chucked it.

This time the ball missed by only a hundred miles.

Athena ran over, picked up the ball for me, and plunked it back in my lap.

So I hurled it.

"Are you even trying?" Karyn teased. But she wasn't being nasty—I could actually feel her belief in me.

So I flung that sucker! *Unhhhh!*

This time the ball missed by only a few feet.

"Do it! Do it! Do it!" the three of them shouted from the sidelines.

I wanted to give up, but I refused—my friends were watching. I chucked it again and again and again. Twelve times. Fifteen. I was getting thirsty. My arms were getting trembly.

"Heave it!"

"Punch it!"

"Fire in the hole!"

I hugged the ball to my chest for a second, catching my breath. Okay. *I am DOING this!* I gave them a ragged high-five sign with one hand while I clasped the ball with my other. I took a deep breath, stared directly at that hoop, and with all the power I'd ever used to do anything in my life, I threw that ball!

It arched into the air. It spun so fast I couldn't see the logo on it. And then, as if it had been thrown by a WNBA player who shoots hoops every single day and twice on weekends, the ball dropped into the net, *whoosh*, right through it.

Jocelyn cheered, "Hoop! Hoop! Hoop! There it is! Hoop! There it is!" Karyn gave me so many fist bumps I lost count. Athena shimmied around, pumping a fist into the air over and over. The four of us grabbed hands and they shouted, "Don't mess with the best! Don't mess with the best!"

Then more hurrahs behind me. The counselors! *They* were also cheering and applauding as if they were the ones who'd made the basket.

I looked back at that hoop, and that ball sitting a few feet away. I did that. Me. Melody. With my friends. So yeah, Hoop! There it is!

We played in the park until Lulu told us we could *not* be late again for dinner. We made up games—my favorite was something Jocelyn named Dizzy Divas, where she spun me and Athena spun Karyn around in tight circles until we all got dizzy. So dizzy that Athena actually fell over, laughing so hard she couldn't get up. I wanted to stay on that playground forever. Did the others feel the same? Had any of them done this before?

Me? For the first time in my life, I'd played outside. With friends.

CHAPTER 29

After a smooshed spaghetti dinner, a nice cool slushy drink—ah! strawberry! I drank three—and the inevitable change into orange shirts—yep, that box was truly bottomless—it was Fire Time.

I was glad Trinity had insisted on sweatshirts again—it was a little chilly out. Mine was two sizes too large—sweet—and it had a hood, so I hunkered down into it, all cozy.

"Welcome to Wednesday Night Wonders!" Cassie announced when it seemed all the cabins were there. I looked for Noah but didn't see him. Probably in the back, I thought. "Actually, I just made that up!" Cassie told us with a laugh. "Every night is a wonder, but tonight it just sounds good!"

She made sure the speakers were working, then said, "I'm ready for a fire fiesta tonight, so please join me! I hope tonight we play your song." She began with one I really liked by Miley Cyrus. When the song got to *"So I put my hands up,"* that's what I did. I put my hands up and swayed to the music.

After the song ended, I was thirsty again, and just as I was getting ready to ask Trinity for another slushy, I made a real quick mental U-turn, because crossing the road from the boys' cabins came the Panthers. Noah headed straight toward us in kind of a hippety-hop trot. Jocelyn, sitting next to me, noticed, smirked, and told Trinity that she had to go to the bathroom. I knew exactly what she was up to—leaving a space by the fire for Noah . . . next to me! *So that's what friends are for!* Sure enough, Noah spied the opening and veered toward it.

Cassie had already started another song—I think it was "Old Town Road"—so most of us started either singing or trying to dance, or acting like they were riding a horse.

"This seat taken?" Noah asked when he reached me, rubbing his hands over his head.

I waved my hand, hoping it translated into *It's all*

yours. I guess it did, 'cause he stopped there and leaned into his walker like he was leaning against a wall—all nonchalant. He stood there for a minute, then plopped into the chair as if he'd planned to all along.

Okay, okay, I'm screeching inside. I put on my best smile like this kind of stuff happened every day.

"You like this song?" he asked.

I hit **"Oh, yeah"** on my board.

"Me too," he said.

We listened in silence for a minute. He seemed a little nervous. Me, I had "Flight of the Bumblebee" playing inside my head. Thanks, Mrs. V, for giving me the perfect background music! I gave a little laugh.

"What's so funny?" he asked.

I scrunched my nose. I was not going to tell him I had bumblebees in my head! **"You like music?"** was what I tapped.

"Yep. All kinds."

"Hip-hop?"

"For sure."

"Bebop and hot rock?"

"I guess—whatever those are!"

We both laughed.

"Look them up when you get home. They're pretty cool," I typed as fast as I could.

He tapped his temple as if he was making a mental note. That made me smile.

"R and B?" I asked.

"Oh yeah."

"How about blues?" I tapped out.

"I could listen to B. B. King all night!"

"Jazz?"

"Some, like Herbie Hancock, but sometimes I don't get it—too way out."

"Same! Like they get lost in their heads!"

"Totally!"

I continued to nod. **"Heavy metal?"**

"Nope. Makes my head all jangly."

"Country?"

Now he lit up. "My mom loves country! She says those songs tell the best stories." His eyes kinda sparkled. "There's always a girl that somebody lost, and a guy to cry over, so we listen to it *all* the time."

"Oh, you're lucky!" My brain was frantically trying to remember everything Mrs. V and I had ever listened to on the huge, amped-up stereo in her living room. Then I tapped, **"What about classical?"**

"Okay, so this might sound weird, but guys like Beethoven and Mozart help me fall asleep."

I wondered if he'd get what I wanted to tell him

next. I didn't want him to think I was some kind of nutso. But what the heck.

"Not weird," I tapped. Then I went for it. **"When I hear music, I see colors."**

He leaned forward so fast he almost fell. "No way! You too? I tried explaining it to my parents, but they don't really get it."

No way. I'd *never* met anybody who really understood this! And now I get to camp with a counselor and a friend who both do this!

So I took a chance and told him. **"Jazz to me sounds brown and tan and it smells like wet dirt,"** I tapped carefully. Okay, now he was gonna think I was crazy.

Instead he almost shouted, "And Beethoven is the color blue!"

"Like fresh blue paint!" I tapped with excitement.

"What about country?" he asked.

"Orange!" I tapped triumphantly.

At this point Cassie was playing that song about a horse with no name. Noah couldn't resist singing the la-la-la parts while I did my best to tap out the rhythm on my board.

Clouds gave the moon an almost night-light glow. It was all so . . . comfortable. I spied Jocelyn back from the bathroom, sitting squished beside Athena on a towel. She had a little smile on her face, and I told her *thank you* in my head. And I just *knew* that she knew I'd done that.

I thought about how Cassie had called tonight a night of wonders. True that. But to me, the *real* wonder was that three days ago, none of us knew each other! And here we were, all comfortable. And I was talking to a boy, and acting like this happened every day. How did that even happen? That's what *I* wondered!

CHAPTER 30

Just when I thought nothing more could happen in one day—something did. I rarely have this problem, but tonight, in the middle of the night, I had to pee! It was probably all those strawberry slushies, but I couldn't wait until morning. I tried, but when you gotta go, you gotta go.

Trinity was sleeping pretty hard—I could hear her steady breaths in the bunk above me. But I couldn't wait, so I tapped on the wall. Nothing. I thumped harder. Still nothing. Could I wait till morning? Uh, probably not. So I scooched myself to the edge of my bunk, stretched over, and managed to touch my shoe—the new white Nikes. Slowly and carefully, I pulled it up. Thump. I dropped it. Dang!

I reached again. Grabbed again. Pulled again. Annnnd . . . I got it! Now I could thump the bottom of Trinity's bunk. This time one thump did it. Trinity woke up right away.

"What's wrong, Melody?" she whispered, hanging over the side of her bunk, braids dangling. "You sick?" She jumped down and unhooked our lantern.

I let her know I had to go to the bathroom.

"Okay, no problem, kid," she chuckled. Both Jocelyn and Athena had had nighttime episodes since we'd been here, so I didn't feel *too* bad.

She slid on her flip-flops, grabbed a thin blue bathrobe, pulled it on, then plopped me into my wheels. With a Falcons blanket around me, the lantern hung on the arm of my chair, and a flashlight in Trinity's hand, off we went.

Dark in the city and darkness way out in Penny's "forest" were two different things. Here, it was like the dark had sucked all the essence from the day and taken hold, and like they said in horror movies, Darkness Rules! From a distance it was hard to distinguish trees from bushes, branches from brambles. Was I scared? Well, not really. It wasn't like there were Penny's lions or tigers waiting to pounce. And probably not even any squirrels or birds—they had to sleep sometimes too! But I did hear squeaks and squawks I couldn't identify, as well as the scrurries of little creatures—maybe mice or possums? Hopefully, no skunks. They're nocturnal; it was pretty rare that we met our stripy buddy yesterday. They had their business to do, and so did I—I wasn't out looking for introductions!

I blinked hard at the purply-colored lights in the girls' bathrooms, and I did what I had to do in a hurry—maybe I could still catch the last part of that sleep train.

We were halfway back when something darted across our path—a raccoon, maybe? And something fluttered past—a soft flutter, but it sounded big.

Trinity whispered, "Ohhh! I think that was a horned owl—it flew right by us!" Wow! That was extremely cool. I'd have to look that up, too. I needed to start me a "look up" list.

But then, another noise. What the heck was *that*—that scrape-and-thump, scrape-and-thump noise coming toward us? My brain jetted to one of the songs from *The Lion King*—maybe the lion wasn't sleeping tonight! Maybe it was stomping tonight? Either way, if there was a lion in front of us, we were in trouble. Then I laughed at myself. That'd be a great story to tell Penny—how I scared myself silly in the nonexistent jungle at night at camp. Trinity heard something as well too, because she said, "Uh, let's boogie out of here, Melody!"

But the sound got louder . . . and closer! *Scrape—thump, scrape—thump!*

I was so close to screaming, but I made myself hold it in. "Who's there?" Trinity finally called out, spreading the full lights of the lantern and flashlight ahead of us.

"Just me! Gotta pee!" a male voice I immediately recognized replied. Noah! Jeremiah was right behind him.

Okay, so what was the first thing that went through my head? Yep: How messed up was my hair? Oh well—it was what it was at this point. And anyway, guys get bed head too—my dad sometimes comes down for breakfast with some serious hair issues!

So I waved at Noah quickly, glad for once that I didn't have Elvira. I wouldn't have known what to say to a boy in pajamas in the middle of the night anyway!

"G'night, Firefly Girl," he said as he passed us.

I might have heard Trinity swallow a "mm-hmm," but she thoughtfully made no comment as we hurried back to our cabin.

I wasn't going to be able to get back on that sleep train in a hurry, that's for sure!

CHAPTER 31

After our morning swim—and gee, who would have ever dreamed that I'd end up loving that?—and a quick zip line to make *sure* we were dry, I guess, Trinity called us together for a cabin chat.

"Okay, my Fiery Falcons," she said, all kinds of dramatic, "let's get ready to rumble!"

Say what? I gave a giggle.

"What's so funny?" she asked.

"I've never rumbled in my life!" I tapped.

Everyone cracked up. And yeah, I pretty much loved that I made everyone laugh.

Trinity rolled her eyes at me half in jest and went on.

"Well, Falcons, we've got an idea. And we'd like to know what you think of it."

Sage took over. "Remember how I told you that I almost made the Olympic swim team and ended up helping them train? Well, I'm pretty good at running a competition."

Competition? Where were they going with this?

"What do you guys think about having a sports challenge with our whole team—Gazelles, Badgers, Panthers, and of course, us?" she asked.

A challenge, eh? This could be interesting. Malik was *so* going to be into this.

"We talked to Cassie and some of the other counselors last night, and if you agree, we could have a sort of sports contest. Any of you ever play Balloon Ball?"

Hmm . . . What the heck is Balloon Ball?

I realized that Jocelyn had been staring out the window the entire time, so I thought she hated the idea. But, with a frown of determination on her face, she blurted out, "Do they know how fierce, fierce, fierce we are?"

Trinity gave a big *uh-huh* nod. "They better! If not, they'll find out, right?"

"I can run faster, faster, faster than anybody I know," Jocelyn asserted. "Let's do it. Do it. Do it!"

I asked, **"How do you play Balloon Ball?"**

"Well, Balloon Ball is a little like soccer, but not really," Sage explained. "The object of the game is to get balloons across the field and into the goals, and . . ." She thrust her hands with a *who knows?* kind of shrug. "See, balloons are notorious for not following any rules at all! They just float and glide and drift on the air. . . ."

"And pop! Pop! Pop!" Jocelyn chimed in.

Sage nodded. "Yep, they pop, which makes the game so unpredictable. The best kicker doesn't necessarily win. The fastest runner might not win either."

Huh? We all looked a little amused and a little confused. For sure none of us ever had a class on the physics of balloons!

But then Athena declared, "Okay by me," the rest of us agreeing.

"Great! We'll need goals and signs and such, so let's head over to the arts and crafts barn and see how creatively orange we can be! I'll check back in with the other counselors, but we'll aim for the games to start after lunch."

Sage draped us in the plastic bags (good thing, because I had on a cute yellow outfit!) and we were on it.

"Do us proud!" she told us as Kim, Lulu, and Trinity led us out the door and to the paint.

The art room was a giant orange mess by the time

we finished. I'd sloshed dabs of orange paint on a couple of sheets of poster board—I guess they were supposed to be balloons. They actually looked pretty good!

Karyn painted a giant bird—and you know what? Anyone who looked at it closely would be able to tell it was a falcon. It was perched as if it was about to take off in flight.

And Athena decided to paint an orange flag. Jocelyn sat next to her and made two more.

I gave them all a thumbs-up.

Trinity had grabbed us each two types of T-shirts from that box before we left the cabin. Now she held them up and asked, "Long-sleeved, or the short?"

Karyn eyed them for a second, then suggested, "Cut the sleeves off all of them!"

"Well, maybe not *all* of them," Lulu responded. "But for sure we're gonna look like we mean business."

As the scissors snipped, I laughed to myself, thinking of how Mom would have heart failure seeing us "ruin" perfectly good shirts! And there were still dozens of them stacked in that box. We were prepared for any T-shirt emergency—that was for sure.

Done with redesigning T-shirts, Trinity created a playlist of songs with the word *orange* in the title with a few clicks on her phone and cranked the volume up real loud. Most of them I'd never heard of, but they got us even more hyped up.

Trinity side-whispered, "You up for this?"

I tapped back, **"How fast can you run?"**

She laughed out loud. "Just you wait and see!"

Next we painted four cardboard boxes, one each of blue, green, purple, and of course orange—those would be the goals.

Turns out Athena had a hidden talent that came in pretty handy—she was crazy good at blowing up balloons with a hand pump. Apparently we needed about a bazillion balloons for Balloon Ball. She grabbed the pump from Kim, and soon she'd filled two extra-large garbage bags with orange balloons.

Kim then gave her a bag of pink balloons. "These are just for you!" Athena hugged her and happily blew up two dozen of those as well.

Jocelyn took crepe-paper streamers—orange, of course—and wove them through the spokes of the wheels on Karyn's and my chairs. She taped shorter streamers to the handles on the back as well, so if we went fast enough, they would fly out behind us. I felt like a parade float. Karyn did whirlies in her chair, checking out the streamy-ness of the streamers. They streamed perfectly.

"Thank you!" she called out as they floated behind

her. We were so busy prepping that we didn't want to stop for lunch. But the counselors made us go eat, and good thing, because it was what my mom called "hamburger beanie-weenie." It was *almost* as yummy as hers—squished-up hamburger meat, mixed with baked beans, and swirled with maple syrup. It was probably *not* served to any diabetics at the camp, but I had doubles. Plus, for the first time since I'd been here, they served fries! They were better than McDonald's. I'm not kidding.

The Panthers and the Badgers began our competition early by starting a fry-eating contest. A Badger boy named Xavier won, and then he won again for the loudest burp! Once they started talking about a fart contest, the counselors said it was time to clear our tables and get going.

We hurried back to the cabin and changed into our sleeveless T-shirts, and we were ready.

Let the games begin!

CHAPTER 32

The event took place on that fenced-in grassy field behind the boys' cabins. Some of the counselors had already divided it into four lanes, each labeled with a team's initials, using lawn paint. Cassie passed out cans of the paint, getting us psyched up.

"Paint?" Jocelyn asked.

"You can paint grass?" Karyn added.

I took a quick minute to look it up on Elvira. I'd never heard of that either! I had the answer in seconds. **"Grass paint comes in lots of colors! It does not hurt the grass or animals. It washes away with rain."**

Huh, maybe that was how they marked up football or soccer fields. I never thought about it before.

"Thanks, Melody," Athena said. "You and Elvira are so smart!"

"Yeah," Karyn said. "I wish I had an Elvira or a Melody around all the time."

I gotta admit—that made me feel pretty good.

The Green Gazelles were already at the field. Since their color was green, the *GG* in their section had been painted neon yellow. They'd had the same streamer idea we'd had, but they stepped it up—mixing silver metallic wrapping ribbon with their streamers, so they glittered in the afternoon sun. AND, they'd painted their faces GREEN! Why didn't *we* think of that? Totally cool. A minute later the Blue Badger guys showed up. They'd gone the streamer route too—blue metallic— plus banners.

Only the Purple Panthers hadn't arrived, and yeah, I felt a twinge of worry. I'd really hoped Noah would be there. While we waited, the counselors ran up and down the field, setting up the goal boxes and the flags. Then, wait, what was that? We heard music, BLARING music—the theme from . . . *Chariots of Fire*? Whaaaaaaaaa?

I looked at my cabinmates—I think we all rolled our eyes at the same time! Devin, in his awesome purple

chair, rolled into sight first, Charles wearing a huge
pair of purple shades, right behind him. Devin carried
their still-wet banner, decorated with what I guess was
a panther. Not that I would say anything, but it pretty
much looked like a kitten.

Santiago rolled in next. He and Harley wore hats
they'd made out of purple pool noodles, and they carried bags of what looked like purple confetti.

When Malik rolled in with Brock, I couldn't believe
it—not only did he have purple streamers flying from
the back of his chair, but his *hair* was purple!

Athena was thunderstruck. "How'd he *do* that?"

"Red and blue food coloring from the kitchen, probably," Sage said, sounding impressed.

Totally awesome!

With a purple-striped bath towel wrapped around
his neck like a superhero cape, Noah strutted forward on his walker. I wondered if he had actually
packed that. Probably. Since he'd been here last
year, he'd have known about the cabin colors. Unfair
advantage!

Jeremiah brought up the rear, toting a massive plastic bag of purple balloons.

"The Purple Panthers are in the house!" he
announced through a megaphone. So extra!

Cassie then pulled out her own megaphone and

said, "Welcome, Panthers! What's your color again?"
Everybody laughed. "Now we can begin our event,
even though we have no idea what we're doing!"

Jeremiah hollered back, "We *never* know what we're
doing!" to which Noah said, "True that!"

We cheered. They cheered. I don't think anybody
knew why we were cheering, but that was okay. Nobody
seemed to know exactly what to do next, but Sage, our
only connection to the real Olympics, took charge.

"Okay, people!" she announced once Cassie had
passed her the megaphone. "Here's the primary rule
of the game: Get your balloon down the field and in
the goal the best way you can. Kick it, hit it, any way
works. And if nothing works, no big deal!"

Huh? Okay, good; I relaxed a little. It wasn't like this
was going to be recorded in official Olympic records
someplace! Balloons in a box—why not?

Sage cleared her throat. "The rest of the rules are
loose and flexible. Here's how we score."

Okay, I was listening.

  —Balloons that pop: one point—but you have
    to get a new one and start over.

  —Balloons on the field: two points—just for
    showing up.

—Balloons that go over the fence: two points.

—Balloons that fly into the sky and never
   come back: three points.

—Balloons you capture from another team:
   five points.

—Balloons that land in your team's basket:
   five points.

—Balloons that land on your lap and stay
   there: fifty points because that never
   happens!

—Balloons that fly away with Peter Pan and
   never come back: ten thousand points!

Everybody loved that one. There would be four
rounds, two kids from two teams at a time. And each
round was six minutes.

When Sage was satisfied that we pretty much knew
what was going on, she announced that the first teams
up would be the Fiery Falcons and the Purple Panthers.
"Green Gazelles and Blue Badgers, you'll be up next.

Devin and Santiago from the Panthers, Jocelyn and Athena from the Falcons, you're in the first round," she declared.

Phew! At least I didn't have to go first!! Now I could see how this game was played before I went out there and made a total fool of myself.

Athena and Jocelyn trotted over to the top of the *FF* lane, flexing big-time in their sleeveless T-shirts. I hit **"GO FALCONS"** on Elvira, loud. Devin, with his electric wheelchair, could maneuver on his own, and Santiago, with Noah behind him to help, lined up at their start, looking all kinds of smug. Their counselors handed them each a purple balloon, while Kim gave orange ones to Athena and Jocelyn.

How hard was it going to be to navigate these chairs on the grass? This would be interesting.

Cassie double-checked that they all had a balloon, then bellowed, "Are you ready?" Fist pumps said YES! So she rang a bell—an old-fashioned, ding-a-ling school bell like you see in movies—and Athena, Jocelyn, Devin, and Santiago were off! They went into an immediate kicking frenzy, and the balloons couldn't care less! Jocelyn's perfectly executed soccer kick sent her balloon sideways. A gentle tap from Devin caused another one to pop; he had to speed back to the start for a new balloon! Santiago's flat-foot kick sent his balloon floating high into the air, landing exactly where it had started. It was almost too hysterical to watch.

I'd thought Devin would have the advantage, since he had a motorized chair, but his chair had only one speed—slow! It moved easily over the bumpy terrain, but not quickly. He was soon overtaken by Santiago and Noah. Then Santiago gave a monster kick and his balloon floated high, higher, higher still . . . backward! We roared with laughter as Noah swung him around to go get it, and Devin was able to take the lead once more. Then a gust of wind took his next kick, and his balloon floated over the fence.

"Two points for the Panthers!" Cassie shouted.

But neither of the Panthers could keep up with Athena. She ran full speed down the field. She kicked, and ran, then kicked again and ran, so focused, connecting with her balloon over and over, but the balloon seemed to have other ideas. Her face was flushed, and her forehead sweaty. I hollered so loud for her my throat got raspy.

But—gotta be honest—at the same time, I was hollering for the boys' team as well. Santiago and Noah were great together. They'd clearly played this game before. Most of the time, their balloon zipped across that grass like it knew where it was going. Noah's towel-cape flared behind him like in superhero cartoons. I really wanted them to win this round, but oh, there goes my girl Athena! I had to switch my cheers back to her. I wanted my Falcons to win too! Athena landed a balloon in a basket. Hooray!

"Five points, Falcons!" Cassie called out. All of us on the sidelines roared for her.

As for Jocelyn, she was so fast that even though lots of her kicks floated sideways, she kept barreling forward. But then, oh no! She made a massive kick just feet away from our goal, and her balloon popped! Gahhh! She looked furious as she raced back to the starting line. C'mon, Jocelyn! But I couldn't stop cheering for the guys too!

Then I came up with a genius idea—I set Elvira to her loudest setting and let her holler **"Yay"** and **"Hooray"** and **"Great shot"** over and over.

Just a few feet from the Panther goal, Noah rolled Santiago right over the balloon! *Ka-plooey!* That one wasn't gonna feel air again!

"I'm trading you in for a new chauffeur!" Santiago's machine shouted as Noah spun him around to go get another balloon. I bet he'd typed that in ahead of time—he had a great sense of humor.

Then Athena, who had steadily worked her way back to the goal, went to tap her balloon in. It got caught on a wisp of air, and, oh no! It floated right into the *guys'* box! Arghhhhh! Everyone froze—how was that counted? Cassie ran over and declared that Athena got *double* points for getting it into a goal that was even farther away than her own! Woo-hoo! Athena ran to get another balloon.

Maybe we Falcons woo-hooed too soon though, because Cassie then added that the boys also got five points for "technically" capturing Athena's balloon. But then we realized, we still got five more points than the boys, and woo-hooed all over again!

And the bell rang. It was the end of that round.

We thought that the score was about tied, but nobody was entirely sure, and no one seemed to care.

And as Noah left the field, he gave a chin nod. In my direction. I was sure of it.

The next round was a blur. The counselors handed out slushies while we watched a pair of Gazelles versus a pair of Badgers. The Green Gazelle girl—Alicia was her name—who'd had the streamers in her wheels on the very first day of camp kept having the worst luck. Her balloon was captured twice. But then, somehow, she and her partner, a teeny-tiny girl who seemed hardly taller than the wheelchair she was pushing, were total Energizer Bunnies and ended up scoring three goals—in a row! The Gazelles' face paint was dripping down their shirts in the heat—good thing those were green too.

And the Badgers were really good at . . . popping their balloons. They jokingly blamed the freshly cut grass. Balloon death by grass, ha! In the end, the Gazelles creamed them. I was having so much fun that I forgot I was up next!

CHAPTER 33

Okay, so now it was my turn to get out there. Karyn was supposed to be with me, but at the last minute, she needed the bathroom and told me to get goals for her. I told her we'd wait but she insisted. Okay, yikes! I needed to double-psych myself up. I could get all sweaty and mess up, or I could glow and be magnificent. That might be hard. I already had some skills at the sweaty, messy stuff. But I did have a secret weapon—I could kick! I channeled my dad, who was always yelling at soccer players on TV, telling them what they should do, or should have done. If he were here, he'd be saying, *Melody, you are a kicking machine! Just get out there and do you!*

Jocelyn stepped in to be my driver—and she was *so* ready. I raised my arm to let her know I was ready too. Yep, psyched!

My wheelchair actually has straps on the footrests that keep my legs from kicking out involuntarily. Trinity unfastened them, and if my legs cooperated, I felt like I could knock a ball, or, in our case, a balloon, a hundred feet in the air. Or at least a few inches.

"We got this, got this, got this," Jocelyn said, her voice steely serious. "The Panthers don't know the power of you and me together out there!"

I reached for her hand, and we did a quick squeeze.

The midday sun above was a ball of fire. Perfect, because that was what I felt like. I was already feeling sorry for that balloon—because I was ready! And I better be, because Kim thrust an orange one into my hands.

Ding-a-ling! And we were off! I could hear my girls screaming behind us, "Go, Jocelyn! Go, Melody!"

Definitely not a phrase I hear every day.

I ran my job through my head: kick this thing across the field and hope it landed in one of the goal boxes at the other end. If the balloon popped, I had to start over. If I captured the other team's balloon, five points! Easy, right?

Dozens of runaway balloons were bobbing on the grassy field.

But here we go! I gotta tell you—Jocelyn was fast. She gave my chair a twenty-degree turn in the direction of our balloon, which I'd thrown ahead of us. A wind kicked up again, and we were suddenly in the center of blue balloons. They seemed to be floating away from their "team" and landing near me. Did I try to capture some, or just kick? I thought fast—*I'm better at kicking than catching*—so I kicked out, and I connected! Yes!!!

I tried again—and I connected again. This one floated just a few inches, then landed. Still, *I did that!* Then I managed to boot *another* one, but while it soared for a few seconds, it floated away, landing on the dirt road on the other side of the fence.

We got a new balloon, then Jocelyn was racing back down our lane, yelling at the top of her lungs, "Kick, Melody! Just do it!"

From the sidelines I could hear the rest of the Falcons. "Kick it, girl! Kick it!" and "Go, Jocelyn! Look at you go!"

I'm not even sure what a dropkick is, but that was the energy I gave my next punt. That helpless balloon was under *my* power this time! And that Felt. So. Good. It was in *my* control! It spun and whirled in a perfect arc and in the exact right direction. Jocelyn raced after it so fast we rode right into it, and—oh my gosh, it connected with my head and still went forward! I heard kids, even from other teams, screaming, *"Go Melody!"*

And you know what? I was sweaty and I thought my underarms were funky, and I didn't care!

In the middle of all that noise and excitement, I glanced around and couldn't help but grin. All around me were kids screaming with passion, screeching with excitement, and sweating in the summer heat—playing a game with crazy rules and cheering for each other to win. And I was right there in the middle of it—I might even be a key player! For just a second I let my mind drift back to the playground at school, where my classmates would play stuff like four square or Heads Up or whatever they felt like. I was, of course, never included. I sat under a nearby tree and watched them scream and run and giggle. It never occurred to me that I could play too. Not once.

So I was in this to win this! I kicked again—the balloon floated sideways toward the Panthers' lane, but Jocelyn got us over to it just as Malik charged toward it.

"That balloon is mine, Melody!" Malik growled, Brock swinging him to the left for the kick.

But not if Jocelyn had anything to do with it! She was unstoppable! I never realized how strong she was.

She never stopped running, never stopped maneuvering my chair exactly where we needed to be. Zoom! Glide! Swivel!

She set me up, and . . . I gave it one more kick right toward the box, up . . . up . . . up. . . . It tumbled over itself, and it landed—no, not in the goal, not in the Panthers' lane . . . it hovered in the air as if hesitating, then it spun and landed in my lap. I grabbed it like it was a treasure. I hugged it close. Fifty points!!

I saw Noah on the sidelines—he was waving wildly, and I waved my balloon.

Then out of the corner of my eye I could see the two guys from the Panthers rolling across their lane, running toward us. What? Could they do that? Noah and Santiago were laughing from the sidelines, and Noah was yelling, "New rules! New rules!"

Was this an attempt to steal—literally steal—the ball? Or in this case, the balloon? Nope, not today! Jocelyn took off so fast, I nearly got whiplash.

I hugged that balloon with both hands and hunched over it to make sure it didn't decide to bounce away. Jocelyn managed to do a fancy twist, and we jetted off in the opposite direction.

Malik and Brock tried to do the same maneuver and ha! Malik's chair got stuck in the thick sod! By the time they'd backed up and turned around, we could not be caught! I raised my right arm and waved good-bye, 'cause they were in our dust.

Cassie was laughing so hard she could hardly ding the bell for us to stop.

The rest of the competition was a blur. One guy from the Badgers scored four goals but had three other balloons captured by an amazingly quick Gazelle. The final whistle sounded. We all gathered at one end of the field—just a bunch of hot and sweaty kids in orange and purple and blue and green. It seemed that no one really had a clue who'd actually won! And it didn't matter, at all. Balloons bobbed everywhere, and we started throwing them at one another—there must have been dozens left over that hadn't been used.

"We oughta let them go free, free, free!" Athena suggested.

"Nope. Nope. Nope. Can't do that!"

"How come?" Karyn asked.

"People have already put too much junk, junk, junk in the sky and the land and the water." I beamed with pride at Jocelyn. I never even thought of the environmental aspect of this. Karyn, her face scrunched up with thought, finally said, "After my birthday party last year, we donated them—so these might be my balloons all over again!" She laughed.

"So let's splat, squash, and store these for next year," Athena suggested.

"Except for this one." I touched the balloon on my lap. **"She's going home with me."**

And even if it wouldn't work, a bunch of kids dumped out the rest of the balloons from the plastic bags and deflated them all, including Athena's bag of perfect pink ones.

My balloon was sitting at the foot of my bunk now, slightly deflated, but proudly unpopped. Trinity sprayed it with hair spray when we went back to the cabin to shower. She said that might make it last longer. I was taking it home—I hoped it would last forever!

CHAPTER 34

"You ready for our flames tonight?" Trinity asked as we
**got ready after a quick dinner of red beans and rice that
was almost as good my mom's.**

I smiled. I think I blushed. She knew the answer.

"By the way, you and Jocelyn did an awesome job on
the field today."

"Thanks! It's a great game."

"Hey, I've got some neon-orange nail polish in my
bag—plus a bunch of other colors. You want me to do
your nails before heading out?"

Even though I knew that orange fingernails would
not make one teeny bit of difference to anybody else, I

tapped, **"Yes, please."** Mom hardly ever has time to do my nails—she has a ton of other stuff to do.

"You got it!" She dug down in her backpack and whipped out a plastic bag, which held at least twenty different-colored bottles of nail polish. Wow.

She asked me to choose. First I pointed to a bottle called Jungle Drama. Then I thought, *Why not?* And I typed out, **"Let's do one of each!"**

Trinity loved that idea. In just a few minutes, the nails on my left hand were transformed from ordinary pale to carrot-colored orange, hot pink, soft peach, sunshine yellow, and fire-engine red. For my right hand I chose coral, lime, aqua, maroon, and navy blue.

"You like?" she asked when she finished the last layer of clear polish "to protect the colors from chipping."

Yeah, I liked! **"Thanks for doing this, Trinity."**

"Shake them to help them dry."

Now that was funny! I was being asked to shake on purpose!

I looked away from my rainbow fingers, and there sat Karyn, Jocelyn, and Athena, pitiful looks on their faces.

"Can you do theirs, too?" I tapped.

"Just leave the tips on my table!" she teased. Jocelyn chose a deep blue. Karyn chose metallic gold and silver.

When it was Athena's turn, Trinity asked, "Which pink do you want?"

Athena looked at every single jar in Trinity's bag. Then I heard her mumble, "Everybody thinks they know me," and she picked out a deep golden apricot color. "Falcon Orange, please," she said, as if she was at a fancy salon.

I smiled to myself—so sweet that our pink-loving Athena was choosing orange tonight. Soon we were the fanciest-fingernailed Fiery Falcons ever!

When our nails had finished drying, and we'd changed into . . . yep, another T-shirt, we were ready to head out into the night.

The guys were already there. I could hear them trash-talking and howling with laughter.

"Hello, Melody!" Jeremiah called out.

I lifted one arm. *Hello back!*

He said hi to all of us. Such a nice guy.

We found our usual spot and set up like we did every night, but somehow, it felt different.

Pine cones tossed into the fire? Check.

Flickering flames against the starlight? Check.

So what was different?

I think the difference was *me*. I was sitting around chilling with my friends—yep, my friends. How cool was that?

So it was perfect that one of the Gazelles' counselors began the music tonight with show tunes from famous musicals. Mom and I sometimes have movie nights, just the two of us—and we binge our favorite productions and sing along with the music. She's got a really good singing voice, and of course, in my head, I am Beyoncé!

I was seated next to Karyn; Athena and Jocelyn sat on the ends. The four of us sang along—loudly and out of tune, with me making the best noise I could. Karyn squeezed my hand. The stars sparkled brightly, and I felt sparkly myself—just because.

Then Sage announced, "Okay, campers, we're going to try something new—a circle dance my grandpa taught me. I was on the phone with him last night. It was his birthday, and he reminded me of it. Don't judge! He used to be a dancer on Broadway!" She gave us a *don't mess with me* look, but followed it with a big smile. "It's super easy—all we do is form two circles, one inside the other. It doesn't matter who is in which circle as long as we've got an equal number of folks in each one. When the music starts, one circle walks or rolls clockwise—the other counterclockwise—around the campfire. When it stops, you introduce yourself to the person next to you and say one cool thing—about anything you like. Got it? Told you, easy! Let's try it."

I heard lots of groans and complaints, but everybody

pretty much followed the directions. Sage put on "Getting to Know You" from *The King and I*. Mom would totally be singing along. Some rolled, some walked, some were pushed. Then the music stopped. I was next to Devin.

"Hey," I hit on Elvira.

"Hey there, Melody," Devin answered. "They got a Balloon Ball team at your school? Cuz you should definitely be on it!"

"Well, thanks," I replied in surprise.

"For real, you have some seriously stealthy skills—first the headbutt, then the fifty-point catch. Only one in the match!" But before I could respond, the music started up once more. And we were off! It was way more fun than I thought. I talked to some kids from other teams, and also got to tell Alicia from the Gazelles how cool I thought her wheel streamers were when I'd seen them on the first day of camp.

The last round stopped me right in front of Noah. "Hey, Firefly Girl," he said, all casual.

Heat rushed to my face, and it wasn't from the fire. *Say something!* I screamed to myself in my head. Then I tapped out, **"The games were awesome today!"**

Okay, that was pretty pitiful.

But it was enough, because he said, all hyped, "You did great! Wish you'd been on our team!"

My heart literally started thudding. *Okay, chill out, Melody*. But it was just, no one had *ever* wanted me on their team—for anything! Well, I was on the Whiz Kids quiz team in fifth grade, and we won the regionals, but the kids on it were NOT happy about it.

Noah went on. "You were the only fifty-point scorer!"

So I swallowed hard. **"And I *rule* Balloon Ball!"** I tapped out. I even managed to push the speak button.

He cracked up. "True that, for sure! And just wait till horseback riding tomorrow—you'll love it!"

Tomorrow? Eek! I'd actually kind of forgotten about horseback riding.

Sage interrupted by thanking us all for doing such a great job. She said she hoped we'd enjoyed it. Kids started breaking away from the circle, but Noah and I stayed right where we were.

"I'm a little scared about the horses," I admitted.

"Easy like breezy!" he boasted. "It's like a roller coaster—scary the first time, then you can't wait to try it again."

I racked my brain trying to come up with a clever response—anything, really—to keep this conversation going. So I tapped, as quickly as I could—come on fingers, cooperate!

"You like roller coasters?" Okay, not brilliant.

Still, Noah wobble-nodded. "The faster the better!"

I thought about the coaster near where I lived. **"Ever heard of the Super Serpent at Meadow Valley Amusement Park?"** Now *that* took a minute to type out!

"Wait! You know that park?"

"We go every year." I didn't mention all the rides the place wouldn't let me on—which were most of them, including that roller coaster—but he probably had a pretty good idea.

"My family goes there all the time too!" Noah's head double-wobbled. "That coaster is sick! I tell you what—have your people call my people and we'll do the challenge together!"

Well, that would be awesome! And did that—maybe—mean he wanted to hang out . . . outside of camp?

We sat in the moonlight, talking about the speed of coasters and the best flavors of cotton candy. He liked lime—bleh! I liked cherry . . . a bleh from him! "But that means more lime for me!" he said. And I laughed.

He waited patiently for me to type in questions for him as well as answers to the stuff he was asking me.

"You like cats?"

"I've got a three-legged one named Peggy. We call her Peg for short! You have a cat?"

"Nope. A dog. Her name is Butterscotch. *Best* golden retriever in the world!"

"Is she fierce?"

"Nah. She once showed my dad a baby bird that had fallen out of its nest. Dad picked it up and put it back."

"Did it survive?"

"I guess so. There are a million robins in our yard every year!" That made him laugh.

"Is Butterscotch a service dog?"

I thought about that for a minute. Then I typed, **"Not officially. But she looks out for me and she's with me all the time except for school. I kinda miss her."**

"My cat probably hasn't noticed I'm gone, and won't even care when I get back!" he said with a shrug. "But hey, I heard you had a snake in your cabin!"

"Yeah. *Not* in the camp brochure!"

"Did everyone freak out?" Noah asked.

"Not really—a little at first. But actually, it was pretty cool. Don't want one for a pet, though!" Wow, that took forever to write, but Noah didn't care at all. He was seriously patient.

"My science teacher used to keep several snakes in glass aquariums in our classroom. He'd feed them little mice and we'd watch!" he said.

"Ooh—that's kinda yuck!"

"Yeah, and during the summer he'd take them home. He told us that a couple of times a snake or two had gotten loose in his house!"

"Seriously?"

"Yeah—no big deal. He said he knew where they liked to hide."

How was this happening, just . . . talking like this? It was like we'd been doing this for years, not just figuring it out as we sat here.

"You ever been in a tornado?" I asked next.

"Yep. Once. You know how Ohio gets lots of tornadoes every summer?"

I tapped yes.

"Well, once, when I was like six, a tornado ripped the front porch off our house!"

My eyes went wide, asking for more.

"My parents flipped out because they'd left my new walker on the porch, and bye-bye, walker! It got whirled off to OZ!"

"You ever get it back?"

"Nope. I hope it landed on the porch of some kid who could use it."

We laughed about silly stuff—online games and downloads, the latest apps, even armpits and toenails, and boogers that get stuck in your nose.

Noah got quiet then. "Yeah, that sucks," he said. "I hate when I've got like personal issues and somebody has to help me."

I typed, **"Me too."**

"But hey, I get to board an airplane before anybody else. Gotta take the perks when I can get 'em!"

I nodded in agreement.

"So, what's your story?" I tapped out. I wasn't being nosy—just curious. I watched him carefully, ready to type *Never mind* if he seemed bothered by the question. But instead he leaned forward, ran a hand along his walker.

"They named me Noah because I was born in the middle of a hurricane," he explained. "My folks lived in Florida at the time. They barely made it to the hospital, so I was born right outside the emergency room doors!"

"Whoa! That's a trip!"

"I was like seriously impatient to see a storm, I guess, so I popped out early to check it out!"

I gasped.

"My dad delivered me like he was some kind of professional, or so he tells me. By the time the medical folks had rolled out a gurney, I was already here."

He paused. "But there were complications. The doctors tried to convince my dad it wasn't his fault, but I know he still kinda blames himself that I wasn't breathing when I came out."

I didn't interrupt, but wow.

Noah continued, "I ended up with what I call a

'brain fart.'" He breathed out in a sort of wistful way. "How about you?"

"I'm not sure if I was born too early or too late," I told him. I've never actually discussed the details of my birth with anybody other than my family and Mrs. V, but for some reason, Noah was so easy to talk to.

Noah bit his lip, then blurted out, "Can I ask you something?"

I nodded.

He looked me straight in the eye. "Do you ever feel annoyed being in that chair twenty-four/seven? I don't mean to be rude or nosy or whatever, just . . . using my walker isn't always a walk in the park, you know?" Then he laughed at himself. "Hey, I surprise myself sometimes! That was pretty deep—I gotta post that one day!"

I didn't even have to think about the answer to his question! I typed, **"It sucks scissors sometimes!"**

He nodded. "Yeah, I get it, I really do."

I returned to Elvira, tapping as fast as my body would let me. Still, at least a minute went by. Finally I hit speak. **"I'd give anything for people to see me first, not my chair, and to do more stuff on my own, like hanging out with my best friend . . . if I had one."**

He looked up at the star-speckled sky. Then he said, "Well, you've got one now!" And then he reached out and touched my hand. His fingers felt cool, yet my hand went instantly warm. And I was aware of only one thing. No flickering fire. No lightning bugs. No stars above. Just the touch of three of his fingers on the back of my hand.

I didn't dare look at him. But I couldn't not look at him. And so I did. And I smiled.

And that's when Santiago showed up.

I doubt he noticed, but he just about bumped his chair into Noah's knees. **"Are you Falcons going horseback riding tomorrow?"** he asked. Evidently he'd set his volume to the highest level. It was like he was shouting. So that's what I sound like when I'm on loud. No wonder Mom's always saying, "Volume control, Melody!"

Noah slowly removed his hand.

"I'm pretty sure it's on the schedule," I tapped.

"Dude, I'm ready for tomorrow!" Noah said.

"Me too. I love riding!" Santiago replied. **"See ya at the stables, Melody."** And he turned to talk to Jocelyn.

"He's super nice," I said to Noah.

"Yeah, I would have been mega bummed if he hadn't come back to camp this year."

"So you _did_ have a Balloon Ball advantage!" I teased.

"Guilty!" he laughed.

We talked about school (he loved it), rainy days (he

hated them), and NFL football. We both liked the Cowboys. Crazy!

The fire blazed like it had every night since I got here, orange and gold, with an occasional pine-cone flare-up. Despite its heat, I felt a little shivery. Of course, some of that shivering might have been because I was sitting there with a boy who maybe, maybe seemed to like me for no other reason than that I was Melody.

The song that played over and over was "Count on Me." But then, Cassie also played the funky chicken song several times, so I wasn't taking messages from music tonight! I told Noah what I was thinking and he burst out laughing.

The fire was nearly out. The moon was playing peekaboo with the clouds, with less and less peeking. I hadn't even noticed how dark it had gotten. Trinity walked over to where we sat. It was time to go.

"Sorry to interrupt, but horseback riding is tomorrow—gonna need a good night's sleep."

Like, uh, seriously? I felt a flare of annoyance, but, actually, she was right.

She stepped away to gather up our stuff.

Noah pulled himself up on his walker and playfully poked my shoulder. "See you tomorrow," he said.

I sure hope so.

CHAPTER 35

So here I was, a girl sitting there in a wheelchair at a stable. And hulking over me was a six-hundred-foot-tall horse. Okay, maybe six feet. But IT WAS A HORSE! I don't usually think much about being able to walk or run, but at this very moment, I really needed to spurt, sprint, hustle out of there. Immediately. Like, right this minute.

This thing was big enough to eat me and not even burp! I couldn't even see the top of the horse from my chair. I could see the side of a saddle, and some dangling foot-holding things.

Cats swish their tails when they're annoyed. Do horses? Because this big boy's tail was swishing away. It tossed its head as we approached; it made a snorty kind of sound. But to my astonishment, it did not move.

Trinity had her hands on her hips. "All right, Ms. Melody, this is gonna be a day you'll never forget. Brace yourself for some serious adventure!"

Actually, I was! But at the same time, well, I wished a little bit that I was at the library *reading* about horses instead. But I also really wanted to ride a horse. My chaotic brain was working overtime, but the *Let's do this!* side was winning.

I looked at the horse. The horse did not look at me. Evidently, it did not find me unusual. I guess I wasn't even worth a second look. Fine with me!

Trinity put on a French accent and made introductions. "Melody, this is Jolie. Her name means 'pretty' in French."

It was a girl horse? I was good with that. Jolie was the color of cinnamon-flavored chocolate. Her mane, black and flowing, made my hands want to touch it. Was it as silky as it looked?

Jolie wore a band around her mouth. It was connected to leather straps that led to the saddle—which these people thought I was going to sit in. That was a joke! I'd slide right off!

"What's great is that Jolie has been specially trained to work with children," Trinity told me as she stroked the horse's nose. "And then she went to college for advanced training in working with kids with unique needs."

I was imagining a horse sitting in a college classroom, taking notes on how to deal with kids like me, who just might freak out when they got close to her. I'd like to see those notes!

Trinity continued to explain. "A female horse is called a mare. And a male is called a stallion or a gelding. When Jolie was born—right here on this property, I might add; she's a hundred percent Green Glades!—she was called a filly, the horse word for *girl*. But she's considered to be completely grown now, even though she's only twelve."

That was all very nice, but she wasn't telling me what I most needed to know: How the heck was I going to get on that thing? And then stay on? Because I watched horse races like the Kentucky Derby on TV every year. And Dad's cowboy movies. Those animals got major speed!

So I asked.

"Yeah, thought you'd be wondering," Trinity said. "I get on first—I put my foot in that stirrup and swing my other leg up over the saddle, so I'm sitting there."

Good for you! I thought grumpily. *What about me? That animal is like a million feet off the ground!*

Trinity held up a hand as if to say, *Calm yourself*. She was right, I did need to calm myself! "As for you, you get airlifted into place. See that machine by the stable hands over there? It'll lift you up, place you in a specially designed saddle right in front of me. I'll buckle you into place, and off we'll go!"

She fit a black riding helmet on my head—just like the ones that real equestrians wear. I hoped those picture-taking people were catching all this!

"You look like a professional, my friend!" she said, tightening the helmet strap under my chin. Then she did exactly what she'd said—foot in stirrup, other leg swung, and boom! She'd hefted herself up onto the back of the horse as if it were nothing. But in a minute, I was going to be up there too. And I thought the zip line had been scary!

Two assistants, wearing T-shirts that said TRUST ME— I'M A STABLE PERSON!, joined us. Everybody had jokes. Before I even had time to object, I was unbelted from my chair, scooped up, and slid into the lift device. As I was hovering right over the saddle—which felt like I was dangling from a crane!—a third stable hand guided me gently into a saddle and buckled me into place right in front of Trinity. The whole thing took barely a minute! And Jolie stayed still as still could be. I couldn't believe it. Maybe one ear flicked. That was it.

Annnnd—hello, people!—I was sitting on the back of a real live horse! Gotta say, as tall as a horse looked from the ground, it was even taller from on top!

Using stepladders on each side of the horse, the stable hands made sure Trinity and I were buckled and strapped and secured. If we had an earthquake, I don't think I could have fallen off—there were safety straps around my waist, my hips, my shoulders, and even my legs. I felt a little like a knight in armor about to go into battle. Okay, maybe that was a little over the top, but still—this was me, Melody Brooks. On. A. Horse.

"How you feeling, cowgirl?" Trinity asked. Without Elvira, I had fewer answering options. But a hum always means happy. So I hummed.

An assistant handed Trinity the reins, and Trinity said, "In a second Jolie is going to start walking. Just ten steps, then she'll stop. So you can get the feel of it, okay?"

I nodded. I think. The helmet made my head feel funny—heavier and more unbalanced than usual. So I couldn't quite tell.

Jolie moved forward, and I gasped and lurched forward, but then I was okay. She literally took ten steps—I counted—and stopped. This was gonna be awesome!

"You good?"

I was more than good. I hummed louder.

Though Trinity held the reins, she tucked a part of them into my hand so I could hold on as well. I was mostly managing to keep them there too. Jolie began to walk again, her muscles rippling as she moved. Her ears flicked this way and that, her mane shining in the sun. I found myself wondering what they washed horses with—some kind of special apple-scented horse shampoo?

Plop. Kerplop. Plop. Kerplop. I bounced in the saddle with each step she took. *Thump! Ka-bump! Thump! Ka-bump!* When she rose up, I plunked down. I laughed out loud. My skinny little butt was having trouble finding the rhythm. But I gradually smoothed out as I focused on every step that Jolie took.

Plop. Kerplop. Plop. Kerplop.

Thump! Ka-bump! Thump! Ka-bump!

Look at me! I was riding a horse!!

The only animal I'd ever been around on a regular basis was Butterscotch, who was soft and huggable. But Jolie—the power and energy that I felt pulsing through her neck and body made me feel safe, and not afraid at all. This horse knew what she was doing. It was like she was telling me, *Chill, Melody. I got this.*

So I chilled. And let the horse do her thing. She kept on going down that path.

Plop. Kerplop. Plop. Kerplop.

Gentle stepping of her hooves.
Bronze dirt.
Gold sun.
Pink breeze.
Purple shadows on a dirt road.
And I was riding a horse.
How 'bout that?

CHAPTER 36

The sun glimmered above. The pine-needle-covered path muffled the rhythmical thumps of Jolie's hooves. That made me think of our music session the other day. I wondered whether Athena, if she patted her drums real softly, could capture that sound. After a while, I let the greens and golds envelop me.

Plop. Kerplop. Plop. We headed deeper into the woods.

Jolie's walk was a little like a sway—almost like a sideways rocking chair! I wondered if she was bored. Or tired of folks riding on her back day after day. I'd seen documentaries of wild mustangs galloping in herds across fields. It made me sad to think that Jolie probably never had the chance to do that.

But I was glad she was my horse.

The more I relaxed, the more I became aware of more than just me. Duh! This wasn't just riding day for *me*. I'd forgotten that the rest of our team were having their own adventures! I saw Athena and Sage up ahead on a black horse in front of me. Athena kept rubbing her helmet—she must have known that she looked really regal in it. Even though nobody was looking, she waved like her job was to greet her cheering fans.

I decided to try waving as well. *Look at me! I'm holding on with one hand!* Then I quickly grabbed the reins again, just in case.

Karyn and Kim clomped up next to us. Karyn's horse was pure white. Wow—pretty! In movies, the good guy always seems to ride a white horse. And for sure, that's Karyn. She was on the perfect horse.

One other thing I noticed? Lots of poop!

CHAPTER 37

As we rode, I started daydreaming—imagining this was the movie of my life, except this *was* my life. I was gradually understanding Trinity's instructions to pull the left side of the reins to turn Jolie to the left, and pull to the right side to turn her right. My right hand sometimes obeyed, but the left just wouldn't. But it was okay. Because today I was riding a stinkin' horse!

Just as I was thinking how this movie was going to develop, how I was gonna remember this moment forever, a commercial came on! Well, not exactly, but the silence of the forest was suddenly rudely interrupted by boisterous laughter.

Oh yeah—the Panthers were riding today too. I guess it had just temporarily tiptoed to the back of my mind—ha-ha!

Jeremiah, leading the charge, shouted out, "Yee-haw!" and "Passing on your right, passing on your right!" and Trinity, slowing down, pulled Jolie to the left, letting him by. He and Noah were going lots faster than we had been! But then I remembered Noah had ridden before. Jeremiah gave Trinity a salute as they bolted by. "Sorry about that—Devin got a head start, and we want to stay together!" Birds fluttered away in alarm as more Panthers rode up hollering, "Wait up!" And the director of my movie shouted *Cut!*

"Noah's horse is called an Appaloosa," Trinity told me, as Brock and Malik, who was looking a little sun-burned, scooted by with a wave on what I was pretty sure was called a palomino.

Bringing up the rear were Santiago and Harley. Santiago looked totally chill—and was even holding the reins all on his own; I wondered how often he'd ridden before. Harley bellowed, "Excuse us, excuuuuse us!" as they slipped by.

The Falcons ahead of us had moved to the side as well, and our horses took advantage of the stop, grab-bing mouthfuls of leaves from nearby bushes. They also peed and pooped without caring who saw! Oops! No manners here!

"You wanna catch up with the guys, Melody?" Trinity asked, her voice playful. "Or let them go on alone? Left hand up, we stay on this path. Right hand up, we follow their route to the right."

I thought for a moment. Okay, half a moment.

Right it was!

With Trinity's gentle tug on the reins, Jolie tossed her head and turned slightly to the right and back onto the path. Trinity made a *click-click* sound with her mouth, and I felt her heels thump twice into Jolie's side, and Jolie started walking again. Then Trinity repeated the clicks and thumps, and Jolie started trotting! Well, it wasn't exactly a gallop, but it was faster than before.

The Panthers were hooting and shouting and yee-hawing ahead of us. It took just a few minutes to catch up. And Trinity—she was so sassy! She pulled up right beside Noah and Jeremiah.

I was trying to picture in my head what Noah saw—a wobbly girl wearing a black helmet, bouncing along on the back of a lovely brown horse.

Hey, that wasn't such a bad image!

Just then Jolie whinnied, stretched out her neck, and snorted—hard! I jumped in my seat in surprise.

Noah yelled, "Bless you!"

I must have looked confused, because he told me that was how horses sneezed! Trinity added that horses also snorted to talk to one another.

Noah laughed and said, "Yeah, sneezing usually involves a lot of snot!"

Okaaaaay, that was reasonable. Horses didn't have tissues to blow their noses on . . . or wait—ewwwww! I'm sorta like a horse—my sneezes can get ugly! Okay, that was a little bit weird. But interesting, too. I'd have to tell Noah later.

As if he sensed me thinking about him, Noah said, "Hey, there, girl with a name that sounds like a song. I hope Jolie's giving you a good ride!"

I nodded in what I hoped was a dignified manner and reminded myself that he couldn't know how fluttery I felt inside. Oh, how much I longed to speak.

The path was wide enough for several horses, so we could ride side by side. I did not hear the chirp of a bird. I did not hear the chatter of a squirrel. If there had been a Category Five hurricane at that moment, it would have blown right past me. I was on a horse. Noah was on a horse. And we were riding horses together. Well, sort of. But still!

A minute later we caught up with Devin as well.

"Hey, Melody," he hollered. "You are prettier than your horse, and your horse looks good!"

Wait—was that a compliment?

"Man, you are seriously lacking any chill," Noah joke-dissed him.

But I waved at Devin anyway.

Jeremiah looked me over with a nod of approval. "Hey, Melody, you *do* look like a pro!"

Then he asked Trinity, "What time does the dance start tomorrow?"

On the outside, I was trying to look chill, no big deal. Inside my head I was silent screaming. A dance? *A dance?*

"Last year they put up the dance floor during dinner," Trinity said, "so probably a half hour afterward—give the kids time to change."

I was sitting there listening to this, so astonished by the idea of a dance that I was speechless. Now that was a good one! But seriously, no one mentioned a dance in that brochure I'd read seventy-four times!

"Okay, thanks," Jeremiah was saying. "I just needed a ballpark." Then he added, "Want to ride with us, Melody?"

I managed to make a noise that let him know that absolutely I did want to ride with them.

"We'd love to," Trinity added, just in case he didn't get it.

We picked the pace back up to a trot, heading deeper into the woods, Devin on one side of me and Noah on the other, Trinity and I tucked in the middle.

My brain has always been stuffed full of words and thoughts and clever expressions. But at that moment, I was almost grateful for the silence. There was no need to say anything to what was already pretty perfect. Riding! As we rode along, I lifted my face to the dappled sunshine . . . until I noticed there wasn't any.

Clouds were gathering. The branches had begun to sway with a wind that abruptly gusted around us.

Trinity must have noticed the same, because she said to Jeremiah, "Looks like we better cut our ride short—we might get some weather."

Jeremiah looked at the darkening clouds. "Huh. I heard there was a front coming in, but the forecast said this evening. You're right, though—we're in for a downpour! I'm gonna get our guys back before that happens." He gave a turn-around motion to his team.

"We're right behind you," Trinity agreed.

CHAPTER 38

Long, low thunder rumbled off in the distance. I felt Trinity's arm tighten ever so slightly around me as she pressed her heels into Jolie's sides, and the horse picked up speed.

"Melody, I'm having Jolie hurry up a bit—we're cantering. We might just beat the rain!"

I looked again at the dark, dark sky and got goose bumps. The colors of the ferns and vines shifted. Yeah, it was a little spooky. Even Jolie seemed uneasy—more thunder rumbled and her ears flattened back.

"Well, looks like we won't be having our bonfire tonight. Every camp week has to have one rainy day,"

Trinity said in an overly cheery, keep-Melody-from-freaking-out voice. I could tell. I was also wishing I could tell her that I loved . . . cantering. Was that what she called it? I had that "in a movie" feeling again. . . . Jolie was going so fast, yet so smoothly. Kids who love sneakers are sneakerheads, ballet girls are called bunheads. What was the word for loving horses? A horsehead? Nah, too weird, but whatever it was, I could see myself turning into one.

I also wondered if getting off the horse would be as easy as getting on. Probably easier because of gravity, I decided. My calves and thighs were tingling—just not used to the stretch of being on horseback. My physical therapist was always wanting me to stretch more. Maybe I could get her to prescribe daily riding lessons. Aha—a plan!

And that got me wondering if they had stables with specially trained horses like these at home. Well, I for sure was gonna find out.

I patted Jolie's mane, giving her a silent thank-you for allowing me to have such a smooth and easy ride. And I made a mental note to tell Mom and Dad that they should definitely send Penny to camp when she was old enough—she would love it!

A few fat plops of rain landed on my arms just as we reached the stables. The other Falcons had arrived moments earlier. Oh no—Athena was crying! "I'm scared of thunder! I'm scared of thunder!" she insisted. Sage assured her it was miles away still, and that we'd be back in our cabins soon.

As if to prove her wrong, the sky gave another long, low rumble. If I could talk, I would have told Sage that it was clear the storm was going to win this race.

Trinity looked from me, to the sky, to me again. That's when the clouds opened. And the rain. Came. Down. I was getting soaked, but I didn't mind—it was totally worth it for being able to have my first-ever, never-could-have-imagined-in-a-zillion-years, ride on a horse.

Karyn was waiting for her turn at the harness. Noah was in front of her, and as he was being lifted off his horse, he hollered, "My name might be Noah, but I'm not taking the blame for this flood!" Yeah, he was pretty funny.

But Trinity wasn't laughing. She was looking around, frowning. "We're gonna be just fine, Melody," she suddenly declared. "I'm going to get off and slide you down myself, okay? Your chair is right over there!"

I gave her a hesitant head nod, but Trinity was strong—she could totally do this. She could probably carry me *and* the wheelchair if she had to. Thunder continued to rumble.

I grabbed for the reins as Trinity let them go, worried they would fall away. My fingers don't always cooperate, but somehow they hooked the leather straps and I clutched them tight.

As Trinity slid smoothly to the ground, Jolie snorted and tossed her head, but she had done this for years. She didn't even take so much as a step. Horse school clearly works!

But then a bolt of lightning blazed like fire, seemingly right at us, and the sky lit up. I'd never actually watched lightning this close. It crackled bright white against the almost-black sky. It was actually really pretty.

But what followed—two more jags of lightning— wasn't. The thunder, no longer a low rumble, but a huge *ka-boom*, sent Jolie's ears twitching. Karyn's horse pawed the ground.

Trinity unfastened my legs, then ran to grab one of the stepladders leaning against a stable door so she could climb up and unhook me. Just as I was thinking how Trinity pretty much knew how to do anything, my tingly calves got even more tingly. And my legs did what they always seemed to do—they kicked!

Yep. My legs kicked, then kicked again, right into Jolie's sides. Exactly the way Trinity had gotten Jolie into a trot. So Jolie listened to my legs, and she did what she'd been taught—she trotted!

And my legs—they did it again! Because that's kind of what my legs do!

SO. SHE. RAN!!

I heard Jeremiah yell, "Hey! Runaway horse! It's Melody!"

Too late.

Jolie was pounding toward the path we'd just come back from, at full canter. With me firmly strapped into my saddle. And Trinity running after us, screaming my name with shock and alarm and I guess helplessness.

But I was gone.

CHAPTER 39

I had to stay calm. I had to stay calm. *Nothing will happen to me if Jolie stays on the path,* I told myself. And Jolie would get tired, right? The rain beat down. I was soaked—those cute jeans and new green shirt were a sopping mess. Jolie didn't care. I guess horses like being in the rain—it probably cools them off. But I've got some awful memories of rainy days and almost tragedies.

No! No! No! I wasn't going to go there. . . .

I bounced with Jolie's every stride, knowing I couldn't fall off, but wondering where this horse might decide to go. *If she stays on the path, we'll be okay,* I told myself again. I said it—*we'll be okay*—like a mantra.

Still, terror crept up my throat. I stuffed it back down. Jolie's ears went flat against her head at the next rumble of thunder, closer still. Trees above me swayed—just like I was swaying in my seat. I knew I was securely fastened into this special saddle—they had me buckled into place like I was a passenger in a spaceship. But we had to stop!

Then I tried to think what Trinity would do.

The reins, I told myself. The reins. Why my hands and thumbs decided to cooperate at that moment I do not know, but they did. Well, one hand did, but one was all I needed. So I did what I'd seen Trinity do. I pulled the reins. Just a little. Was it enough? I couldn't get a strong enough grip to pull harder. I tried again. I pulled.

Then I felt it—Jolie, almost imperceptibly, slowing down.

I pulled again. Incredibly, Jolie slowed to a trot. Rain was streaming off her neck, her mane slick.

The rain pelted, the sky growled. I pulled once more. And slowly, slowly, Jolie slowed her pace to a walk. Oh, how I wanted to tell her she was a good horse. I settled for humming. I hummed so stinkin' loud, Jolie's ears flickered this way and that. So I thought, *Now, how do I make this horse turn around?*

I tugged gently to the right, willing my hands to hang on to those reins.

And.

She.

Turned.

Oh, thank you! Thank you! Thank you!

Okay. Ohhhkay! What next? What next? I wanted to wipe the wet from my face, but no way was I letting go of the reins—what if I couldn't grab them again?

I had no idea where we were, or where to go, or how to get back. But then it dawned on me that Jolie must have done this ride a thousand times. She was born here! She'd know the way back to camp! Of course she would. So I let her do just that.

And Jolie clip-splash-clopped down the well-worn path, which I hoped, I prayed, led back to camp. She moseyed along as if we were on a Sunday drive.

As we rode, between yelling at myself not to cry, I argued with myself over whether I should ever tell my parents about this. They'd never let me ride again.

That was when I heard Trinity and Lulu screaming my name. I tried to answer, but my voice doesn't have a lot of volume. Jolie sure heard them, though. Her ears flicked and she picked up her pace.

CHAPTER 40

When Trinity finally saw me, she sobbed, "Oh, Melody!" from the horse she was on. And that was what nearly made me cry!

"Are you okay?" Lulu asked breathlessly. "Are you hurt?" It seemed like they were moving toward me in slow motion. I couldn't figure out why until it occurred to me that they probably didn't want to spook Jolie and send her racing off again.

Trinity, her voice hoarse with anguish, cried out, "Are you cut anywhere? Bleeding? Anything broken?" I wish I could have told them I was perfectly fine—just wet. I shook my head no, smiled, even tried to wave. *I'm fine! I'm fine!* I said in my head.

Jolie neighed to the other horses, ridiculously calm, as if she'd just decided to go on a rainy-day stroll—no big deal.

But as soon as they reached us, Trinity and Lulu couldn't dismount quickly enough. As they did, it occurred to me that neither of them had a way to get onto the back of Jolie. They'd been so anxious to rescue me that they hadn't thought of what to do when they found me!

Trinity untangled Jolie's reins from my hands, which, by the way, deserved a medal themselves. She brushed tears—or was it rain?—from her face. Truth!

"You sure you're okay, girlfriend?" She checked my legs, the saddle, the reins. I just kept smiling my *I am okay* smile and hoped it translated.

I could tell she was calming down because she finally said, "Girl, you are a hot mess! But no worries! You just got a free daytime shower! No extra charge!"

Gah! It was so frustrating not to be able to tell her that I was totally fine! And that this was the most excitement I'd had in my *entire* life! All I could do was smile harder and hope I didn't look like I'd lost my mind.

We trudged back to the stables sopping wet, but yeah, also a little victorious. Trinity walked on one side of me, holding Jolie's reins, Lulu on the other, watchful and careful while she held the reins of both her horse and Trinity's. And I came to a decision. No way was I telling Mom and Dad about this. They'd never let me near a horse again! And I was *not* gonna let that happen.

CHAPTER 41

Of course, because of rules and regulations and stuff, just before dinner Trinity told me that she was required by both the rules of the camp and the laws of the state to call my parents to report the "incident." Cassie was already getting the necessary paperwork ready.

Nooo! Mom would pull out her hair with worry, and Dad would get into the car and come bring me home immediately. *Nooo!* So I tapped, **"What if you help me write a message to them first?"**

She agreed that was an excellent idea.

This was what Trinity and I composed together:

Hi, Mom! Hi, Dad! I'm having a great time at camp! Today I got to ride a horse! Yep, me on a big brown horse. The day started out sunny, but then it rained and I accidentally kicked her and she ran down the road. Oh, forgot to mention—I was on her back when she did that! I was only a little scared. Well, maybe a lot. But I pulled the reins and stopped the horse—all by myself. I was so proud of me! I am fine. Cassie will call you. Don't freak out. Camp is awesome. Love, Melody

We all got totally drenched again going to dinner— the storm laughed at our pathetic raincoats and baseball caps. But it was worth the trek, if only for dessert. Lemon meringue pie!

CHAPTER 42

When we got back, Trinity took the time to wipe down my wheelchair to make sure no water had collected in the moving parts. Fortunately, I'd left Elvira in the cabin, so she was safe and dry.

The wind continued to whistle and the thunder crashed overhead. Our battery-powered lanterns flickered just enough. Athena, snuggled with Blankie, seemed more relaxed now.

"So, how about we do our own private story time tonight?" Lulu suggested.

The four of us looked at each other in dismay.

"Maybe we can tell ghost stories," Trinity suggested, all perky.

"Or tell jokes." Sage, perkier.

None of us replied—louder this time.

"Maybe have hot chocolate or caramel?" Trinity offered. Perkiest!

That got the loudest no reply!

Jocelyn interpreted our silence for them, her arms tight across her chest. "Boring. Boring. Boring."

I looked from Karyn to Athena to Jocelyn, and the four of us nodded at the same time, like a visual fist bump.

I put Elvira's speaker on her *loudest* level. **"Can we have some chill time alone? Please?"**

The rain pelted the roof of the cabin. Lightning lit the sky—a storm bonfire! And the four of us waited for a reply.

"Well!" Trinity said at last while pulling her braids into one thick ponytail. "In my four years of being a counselor, I've never had a group of young women who've bonded so well and deserved some time off more than the four of you. So how about this? We get you all into your PJ's, then we 'helicopter counselors!!'"—and here she gave us a sly look—"will disappear for an hour or so, and the four of you can do your thing?"

We all double fist-pumped into the air, whooooo!

It took just a few minutes to get us changed and meds taken. And true to their word, the counselors actually left us alone in the cabin! Okay, they were three minutes away in the kitchen, and they made us swear on Athena's blanket that we would not, under any circumstances, leave the cabin. We pinky promised.

I couldn't believe how *good* it felt to have the cabin to ourselves. The room was warm, and we all felt like friends at a sleepover staying up past our bedtime.

"Sooo, what do we do now?" Karyn asked with a giggle.

"What do you think of camp?" I asked, starting off the conversation.

"I like swimming and art," Karyn said.

"And the zip line is the bomb," Jocelyn said next. "Feels like flying, flying, flying."

"Yeah, before this, not much flying in my life— actually not ever," I admitted.

"Me either!" Athena added.

"This is fun—I've never been able to hang out with my friends before." Then I added, **"Okay, truth. I've never *had* friends before!"**

Karyn said, "I have a couple of friends at home, but they don't always get it. We hang out sometimes, but lots of times they're 'busy' when I call them."

Jocelyn said, "Yep, yep, yep," as she slid off her bunk to the floor and leaned against the bedframe. "Friends to giggle with—never had that before." She didn't repeat herself, but hugged her shoulders three times. We all exchanged smiles.

Then Athena, cozy-looking in fuzzy pink pajamas, suggested, "Hey, I know what! Let's tell stories!"

I'm in! I thought.

"Can I go first?" she asked.

"Go, girl," Karyn urged her.

Athena stood up, Blankie wrapped around her shoulders like a cape. She took a second to wipe her glasses with a tissue and put them back on.

"Once upon a time," she began. Then she stopped and asked, "Do I have to say 'once upon a time'?"

"Nope!" Jocelyn confirmed.

Athena thought about that, then said, "Twice upon a time there was this girl named Athena." She paused, and made a tiny curtsy.

"Athena loved dancing, so she asked her mom if she could take dance lessons. Her mom thought it was a good idea, so she called a dance studio. They said no.

"So her mom called another studio. They also said no. Athena cried. She just wanted to dance like they do on TV. Finally her mom called a place that said, 'Sure, bring Athena to our studio.'

"So Athena went to her first ballet class. Her mom brought her special pink shoes and a black leotard. At her first class, Athena was shy, but the teacher and the other dancers were so nice. And the music was very pretty. So Athena learned to turn, and lift her arms, and point her toes. She learned how to take a bow at the end. Dancing made Athena smile every day."

And then she took a bow.

"That's why you dance so well!" I tapped. **"Didn't they say something about a dance on the last night?"**

"I think so," Karyn replied. "Let's ask in the morning. That'll be fun!" Then she added, "Uh, I have a story too."

"Ooh, let's hear it!" Athena said, nodding over and over.

"It's a little embarrassing," Karyn admitted.

"We won't tell!" we all promised.

Karyn took a breath. "Well, okay. So, when I was in third grade," she began, "I was the only kid in my class in a wheelchair."

I sure could identify with *that*.

"The other kids were nice enough to me at school, but I never got invited to the birthday parties I heard them talk about after a weekend break. I guess it was too much trouble to deal with a wheelchair kid when your party included a bouncy house."

Oh, boy, did we get *that* one.

"Anyway," Karyn continued, "one day we had a substitute teacher. There was a fire drill that afternoon."

I caught my breath. I bet I knew what was coming. But no, it was worse than I could have guessed.

"Did I mention the classroom was on the third floor?" Karyn asked. "It was music and was the only class I had that wasn't on the main level. The regular teacher was a big guy who could easily carry me down the stairs if necessary. Even though that was *way* embarrassing!"

Our eyes went wide.

"Anyway, that stupid fire alarm went off, and everyone in class stood up and marched out like we'd practiced at a million fire drills before. The substitute looked at me and announced to the class, 'Let's head to the elevators, children!'

"A few kids looked at her like she was crazy, but nobody said anything. So we got to the elevator, which, duh, DOES NOT WORK DURING A FIRE EMERGENCY, and so the substitute said, 'Let's take the stairs. Hurry!'

"'What about Karyn?' one girl asked.

"'She'll be fine. It's just a drill. And we'll be right back.'"

Jocelyn stared in disbelief as I gasped.

Karyn bit at her lower lip, her eyes full of hurt. "So the rest of the class hurried down the three flights of stairs. The substitute hesitated for a minute, but for real, she did not know what to do!

"'We'll be right back,' she told me.

"'You're gonna leave me in here?' I asked.

"'These things are over in five minutes. Just relax,' she told me. Then she ran down the steps after the others!"

"Oh no, she didn't!" Athena was quaking with rage.

"And she left me in the hall by the elevator door," Karyn continued.

Our mouths fell open.

"What happened?" I asked though Elvira.

Karyn brushed away a lone tear. "Well, when my mom found out, she went ballistic."

"I know that's right!" Athena shouted furiously.

"What about the teacher?" Jocelyn asked, making frantic circles on the floor with her finger.

"Well, the substitute got fired," Karyn told us. "And barred from ever teaching anywhere again."

"Yes!" we all shrieked.

Karyn looked at each of us, blinking hard. "I'm not crying!" she said, then choke-laughed. "Well, I *am*. But not why you think." She paused. We waited.

"It's just . . . I never thought anyone else would understand."

Athena jumped up and held out her Blankie. "Need this?" And now Karyn was full-on crying. But smiling, too.

"Thank you. I do need Blankie!" She hugged it close and wiped her eyes with her pajama sleeves. "Soooooo! Who's next?"

Jocelyn stood up. "I got a story. Story, story," she said softly, staring down at the floor. "It's . . . well . . . sad."

"Tell us, Jocelyn," Karyn said just as softly.

Athena sat on Jocelyn's bunk and patted it for Jocelyn to join her. "Nobody here but us!" she said. When Jocelyn sat, Athena gave a happy bounce.

Jocelyn took a breath, then began, "I'm in a special class at a regular school."

"Yeah, us too," Athena reminded her.

"But sometimes the kids in 'regular' are kinda mean, mean, mean."

We all knew *exactly* what she was talking about.

"Well, you know how I like things in threes. It just makes sense to me, and my doctor explained that it makes me feel safe."

We nodded. Whatever works!

"So I sit at lunch by myself every day. It's just . . . less complicated."

She wasn't looking down anymore.

"My mom always gives me extra lunch money, and my teachers try to keep a lookout, but sometimes kids are, well . . . One day, on my tray I had three juice boxes, three bags of apple slices, and three chocolate pudding cups. But kids kept swiping them. I can't start eating unless I have three in front of me, so I had to go back to the lunch lady and explain."

"That's awful!" Karyn exclaimed angrily.

"After a while, the lunch lady wouldn't give me any more, and I ran out of money anyway, and I never did get to eat because the bell rang. . . ." She sniffed, hard.

Karyn rolled close and grabbed Jocelyn's hand.

"I told my mom, and she told the teacher, and the teacher gave the whole class a lecture on being kind to 'special' kids, but nothing really changed. So I ended up eating in the back of the teachers' lounge every day, all by myself. But I still like the number three," she added. "It's just right for me!"

We were all dead silent when she finished. Our cozy room was filled with . . . deep blue.

I knew the counselors would be back any minute, and I hadn't told a story yet. I wanted to tell them about what happened with Whiz Kids in fifth grade, how the entire team ditched me because they were too embarrassed to be seen with someone like me and didn't like the attention I got. But even more, I wanted to do something, say something, to make everyone feel better.

That was when I remembered Mrs. V's present.

"Look in the outside pocket of my backpack. Look for the small orange bag!" I tapped fast. Jocelyn, her face a question mark, hopped right up, unzipped that pocket, and pulled out the small cloth bag.

"What's in there?" Athena asked, peering forward.

"Friendship bracelets!" I paused. **"Something for my *friends*!"** I grinned huge.

"Awesome! Awesome! Awesome!" Jocelyn said, squatting down in front of me.

Karyn murmured a happy, "Wow!"

"Open the baggie!" I insisted.

Jocelyn pulled the drawstring, then emptied the bag onto my tray. The four braided bracelets tumbled out. How did Mrs. V know?

One was red. One was intense pink. One was orange. And one was yellow and gold.

"Pick the one you like," I told them.

Athena, of course, chose the pink one. Jocelyn said she liked the red. Karyn chose the one that was woven with both yellow and gold. I was glad the orange one would be mine—orange for Fiery Falcons. Orange for my friends. Athena helped me put it on.

"When Trinity comes back, I'm asking her to take a picture of us all with these on!" Karyn said, holding her hand out to admire her bracelet.

Jocelyn, twirling hers around and around on her wrist, said, "That's a perfect idea."

I couldn't agree more.

The rain had finally stopped. I could hear nighttime creatures peeping and whispering outside. The counselors eased back in, armed with jugs of warm milk and cocoa for us all. "Thank you, thank you, thank you," we said, again and again, as we were tucked into bed, beds that had felt so strange when we first got there. We thanked them for the cocoa, but also for everything else they'd done for us that evening.

"We take it you Falcons had a good time?" Lulu asked. We broke into giggles and held up our arms. That pretty much said it all.

CHAPTER 43

This morning I woke up excited, but with a pebble of sadness in my stomach. It was our last day. How had zip lines and boats and skunks and swimming and runaway horses and six thousand different ways to serve pasta slip by in a blink? Mom will be amazed when I tell her.

Today we had our last swimming class. Mrs. V would be so proud to see me kick and roll and move myself with my arms. Okay, fine, Trinity was always holding me, but I finally let myself float on the surface of the water, knowing that she would not let me sink. I'd never do the butterfly like an Olympic swimmer, but I was officially no longer a "sinker"!

As I did my last set of kicks and rolls, Karyn, Athena, and Jocelyn sat on the sidelines, full of jokes and useless advice.

Karyn: "You couldn't drown if you wanted to. There's a foam shortage in the state because you're wearing it all!"

Jocelyn: "Lookin' good, good, good, girlfriend! Orange foam is your color!"

And Athena, who had just received her Level One Swimming Certificate and didn't hesitate to tell every person she passed by about it, assured me that if I needed her, she could jump in and save me.

I was thinking that maybe when I got home, I'd ask Mom about swimming—and horseback riding lessons too! Lessons for *both* me and Penny. Classes for kids like me had to be around somewhere—it just never occurred to us to ask! And I got excited about thinking about horseback for Penny, giggling just at the thought of her riding a small brown pony. I'm gonnna ask Mrs. V and Mom to help me with those searches. I'm determined!

After we dried off and ate a quick lunch (funny—lunches kept getting shorter and shorter because we kept wanting to get to our next activity, instead of sitting around munching), we had our last art class as well.

Classical music played over a speaker as we donned our designer garbage bags. Beethoven's Fifth Symphony came on and we all improv chanted to it: "Who's at the door? DUM-dum-dum-DUM!" I imagined a scraggly robber covered in maroon rags, yet wearing velvet gloves as he pounded on the door of a medieval castle. So that was what I painted—dark gray swirls with red splotches to match the rhythm of the music.

Next was "Morning Mood" by a composer named Grieg, Kim informed us. It was filled with flutes and violins and yep, when I heard it, I could see yellow daisies blooming in Mom's garden, and the sun coming up over the trees like it had every morning here at camp. Trinity rinsed the grays and reds off my hands and I plunged them deep into the yellow, and then the orange. I could actually hear birds singing as the music played. My painting became swirls of sunshine.

Ooh! I already knew the next song she played—Moonlight Sonata, also by that Beethoven guy. It sounded sad and mysterious, and suddenly, maybe because I'd just been thinking about it yesterday, the music brought back that time I got ditched at the airport by the Whiz Kids team, kids who I thought were my friends. And maybe because of what the girls had told me yesterday, too . . . I chose dark purple and royal blue for that song. Trinity looked at it pensively.

"Hmm, I can really see what you're feeling. Sorrow?"

I nodded.

"Anger?"

Yep!

And as I swirled those purples and blues together, I thought about what those kids had done to me, taking off without me, not letting me know the flight had been changed, despite how much I'd practiced for that competition, and how much I helped the team.

The colors under my hands began to blend into one giant bruise. I shoved at the paint harder and harder. Who cared if I ripped the paper? And as the paints blurred, becoming indistinguishable from one another, I hesitated. The colors had become a whole new color. A night sky color, like the color of the sky here—at the campfire!

And an odd calm kind of feeling came over me. Those Whiz Kids, they weren't part of our Green Glades night sky. They weren't part of *here*!

I made a grunt to get Trinity's attention, pointed to the bottle full of orange. She went to squirt it onto the dish, but I shook my head no and reached out. She pressed the bottle into my hand, and shakily, shakily, I squeezed. Just me. All by myself. One drop. One more drop, and then another and another fell on the paper. Then one last one.

I dropped the bottle, but that was okay. I was done. My hand was trembling, but I had done it all by myself!

Trinity came back, looked over my shoulder. "Melody!" she exclaimed, her voice full of wonder. "You painted fireflies!"

I nodded yes, but in my heart, it was no. What I had painted . . . was friends.

CHAPTER 44

"There, I think you're all set," Trinity declared as she put the finishing touches on my hair.

My curls looked bouncy, my red rhinestone earrings were perfect, and a couple of well-placed flamingo-shaped clips made me look like, well, almost like a teenager!

"So, are you ready to kick it? The sky is full of stars, the night is warm, and the stage is set," she said in a low, fake-movie-star voice.

I ignored her, trying to suppress a grin as I rolled over to the only mirror in the cabin, hung crookedly near the door. I gotta admit, the red dress that Mom insisted on packing was absolutely perfect. It had cap sleeves, a rounded neck, and a skirt that spread out over my whole lap and down past my knees. I twirled myself around and watched the fabric ripple. I felt . . . I felt . . . almost magical.

And then I realized that tonight was the last time we would all assemble around the fire! I was *really* gonna miss the songs and the stars and the flames.

Last night's storm had blown away all the bad weather, and tonight was crystal clear. This week we've covered just about every activity that a bunch of kids can do around a blazing fire at night. Except for one. A *real* dance!

Instead of trying to imagine how that would work for me, I just rolled with it. Because nothing I'd done over the past few days had been a disaster. In fact, it's all been pretty awesome.

The fire-pit area looked different as we rolled closer. Counselors had laid down several sheets of wood, like what Dad used to nail against the windows during tornado season, and it looked like . . . uh, I guess it was . . . a dance floor! A dance floor with a campfire for lighting. What could be better? Better than a movie set! Even the fire somehow seemed to spark and shimmer more brilliantly tonight, as if it were dancing itself. Ramps on either end easily smoothed out the problem of wheelchair and walker access.

I heard oohs and aahs as groups of campers who we'd only seen at meals or waiting for their turn on the zip line or the pool filed in. An artist could not have painted a better backdrop for the dance than what the sky already provided. Swaths of the last of the burgundy sunset ran through it, and stars, high, high up, gemlike, dotted their own sparks here and there. I heard an owl hooting in the distance. And yep, teeny little lightning bugs weren't going to miss this party— they flickered on and off above our heads.

I settled in, wondering exactly what would happen next. Cassie and Charles fiddled around with their phones, making sure they were connected to the speakers, I guess. With a thumbs-up, Cassie walked into the middle of the dance floor.

"Are you all ready for my personal favorite night of the camp?" she called out, doing a little shimmy.

As we all roared YES, one kid, one of the Badgers, I thought, shouted, "How we gonna dance if we can't walk?"

"Great question!" Cassie shouted out. "We dance with our hearts. We dance with our minds. We dance with our souls. We dance for fun. So tonight, that's just what we're gonna do."

Lulu, joining Cassie on the floor, then suggested, "Maybe some of you would like to come up first and show the others how it's done. One at a time, or in a group—"

Ummm . . . nah . . . I'm good.

But before Lulu could even finish her sentence, Athena stood up and cast off her blanket, revealing a ruffly peach-colored dress, then ran to the center of the stage. "I love to dance!" she announced.

All right, Athena!

Cassie flicked through her phone, probably looking through her playlist. A moment later and—ohhhhh, Penny loved this one—on came "Let It Go" from *Frozen*.

Athena moved to the music as if it had been composed just for her. I could tell those dance classes she'd taken had taught her a lot. While her movements were solid and deliberate, at the same time they were intricately delicate and lovely. Her pink hair clips sparkled as they caught the firelight.

She closed her eyes as she moved to the sound, to the moon and the stars and the breeze, and she danced. And she looked so happy. And I felt a swell of happiness, just watching her.

When Athena finished, she bowed, of course, like nineteen times. We all clapped and cheered—all nineteen times!

Once she was off the floor, Harley announced that Santiago wanted to go next. "He's practiced and rehearsed for, uh"—Harley checked his watch—"a full four minutes. So he is *ready*!"

Santiago rolled to the center of the stage and nodded at Harley, who was whispering to Cassie, and "Electric Slide" boomed from the speakers. Dad always sang this in the car: *"It's electric! Boogie woogie woogie!"* He told me that he killed it on the dance floor with that song in high school. I'd always laugh, because there was no way I could imagine him dancing to anything!

Hands gripping the rims of his wheels, Santiago managed to hit every spin, every turn, every circular zoom. He had serious wheelchair dancing skills! A bunch of kids started dancing on the sides as well. When the song finished, he clasped his hands together and shook them over his head in victory. We burst into applause.

The next dancer was Malik, with Brock right behind him. His hair back to white, Malik had decorated his golden wheelchair with what looked like a zillion (well, maybe a couple dozen) gold-painted paper plates. He must've used up all the gold paint in the arts and crafts barn, but he, uh, literally glowed. The song he chose was so slick—"Goldfinger." I loved it! He kept his face serious, his eyes squinting a little, James Bond–like, as he wheelchair-sashayed across the floor. It was awesome. When he was done, lots of whistles joined the cheers.

Jocelyn, her head down, smoothing the front of the cute cropped pants she had on, made her way across the floor next. "I'm gonna dance to 'Twinkle, Twinkle, Little Star.' I know this is a baby, baby, baby song," she said, fierceness in her voice. "But I don't care. Every night during Fire Time, we look up at the stars. And I love, love, love the stars!"

We broke into applause immediately—why *couldn't* she dance to any song she wanted to? Cassie gave her a thumbs-up, and "Twinkle, Twinkle, Little Star" tinkled through the speakers. Oh, I knew this version, by Jewel—Mom used to play it for me. The song was perfect—for the star-filled night, and for Jocelyn.

> *Up above the world so high,*
> *Like a diamond in the sky . . .*

Jocelyn quietly, quietly began reaching for the stars, slowly, gracefully, until she was almost on tiptoe. Then she swept left, swept right, almost as if she were gathering them up. It was simply enchanting. She looked around, like she was surprised, and head down, trotted off the stage as everyone clapped and cheered for her. But her smile was huge.

The next few kids, I didn't know real well. But it was fun to sit huddled in a blanket and watch them do their thing. I hoped I remembered some of these songs; I wanted to add them to my playlist.

As the next song blasted onto the speakers, Noah and Devin, along with two of the Badger boys, literally *slid* onto the dance floor. Okay, I sat up a little straighter—Noah was in a chair! Probably because it was easier than a walker for dancing. It looked like the one he'd used for that pontoon trip.

And the two boys from the Badgers wore wheelie shoes! I always thought it would be a blast to have sneakers that you could just lean back on and suddenly you're rolling. As they maneuvered Noah and Devin in their chairs, they spun and jerked and jammed around to "Old Time Rock and Roll" as if they'd practiced for months. Sleek and liquid-smooth one second, hip and funky the next.

A bunch of the guys started playing air guitar along with the beat. At the end, the guys bowed and applauded themselves so many times that Jeremiah had to shout at them to quit it to get them off the stage. Loved it!

A group of girls, all in short-short skirts and white T-shirts tied at the waist, all of them on walkers, asked for "Macarena," giggling hysterically. They must have

been here last year, as they were READY. I had no idea
what the steps of that dance were supposed to look
like, but they sure looked like they were having a blast.
Soon everyone was shimmying their shoulders to the
rhythm, including me.

I wish I could have had the chance to get to know
them, too. But hey, maybe next year! Oh, was I already
thinking about next year? Mom would be cracking up
if she knew. . . .

When the cheers and laughter had quieted, Cassie
asked if anyone else wanted to solo before she opened
up the dance floor to the whole group. I hesitated. But
then I raised my hand. Then I snatched it down fast.
What was I thinking? *You can't dance—you can't even
walk!*

I'd seen those weekly dance competitions on televi-
sion, where stars and ordinary people performed for
fame and money. I'd watched Fred Astaire and Ginger
Rogers on the old black-and-white movies Mom liked.
I'd seen videos of ballroom dancing and boogie blow-
outs and hip-hop rhythms I could barely follow with
my eyes—let alone my feet. That kind of movement
was for someone else, for someone who would walk
and run and glide on cushions of air.

So never in my life had I considered . . . this. I asked
the insides of me, *Should I even try?*

"Melody?" Cassie said encouragingly. Rats! She must have seen my hand up, gahh! But then, *everyone* else began to clap in perfect time, as if this was the most ordinary event in the world—a girl who could not walk getting up on a stage to dance. I know, I know, a bunch of kids just did that. But not . . . ME. I had to be nutso. But everybody continued to clap—wow, synchronized clapping was loud! And all for me to get out there and embarrass myself—and yep, dance. It was an ordinary starry night and I was hanging out with my friends. No, I was a total liar. This was not ordinary at all. This was me. *And I am gonna dance!*

A wisp of wind blew across us, making the edge of my dress flutter. Even my dress wanted me to dance! I poked Jocelyn's arm. She seemed to read my thoughts immediately. "Let's do it. Do it. Do it. Me and you. Me and you. Me and you!" she said in a whisper. She grabbed my hand grips, and we rolled to the front and up the ramp, Karyn and Athena hollering like crazy.

Cassie beamed at me and searched for just the right song. I heard her say, "Yes!" when she found the one she was looking for. The first few bars of the music floated up, and oh yeah—I knew this one! It was "Wings" by Little Mix.

"You ready, ready, ready?" Jocelyn asked.

Yep. Yep. Yep. I nodded.

Jocelyn pushed and twirled and swirled me. My red dress rippled and ruffled around my legs. I hummed along with the singer, and lifted my thin arms up to the night sky like wings. And. I. Danced.

CHAPTER 45

When my heart stopped pounding long enough for me to actually begin to hear again, what I heard was Cassie shouting over the cheers—cheers for me?!—for people to quiet down, quiet down. Then she announced that the floor was now open to everyone. So many kids got on that floor! Walkers and wheelchairs and canes and braces. I watched as friends danced with friends, guys got silly, and girls got sillier. Campers twirled each other's chairs around in circles, nearly causing a few collisions but swerving at the last second. They played all the latest songs. I was going to have the BEST playlist when I got home! Then "Y.M.C.A." came on and everyone went

ballistic! Even I knew what to do for that one, and it didn't matter if my arms went wild.

Malik and I nearly bumped into each other. "Hey there, Melody," he yelled above the music. "Planning on any more joyrides with the horses?"

I didn't have time to tap out much, so I smiled and said, **"Absolutely! At midnight tonight!"**

He laughed and said, "Seriously, though, I would have totally freaked out. You should have seen Trinity. She nearly had a heart attack! But you were so chill when you got back. Even Santiago was impressed, and he rides all the time."

That was so nice to hear! But before I could answer, Athena bounded up. "Malik, wanna dance?" I watched them spin away.

It was getting late. We'd been out here much longer than on previous nights, but the fire still burned bright and nobody seemed to want to leave. I sure didn't.

And then it happened.

"Hey there, Melody," Noah said, ambling over, back to using his walker again. He glanced up at the sky as if he was concerned about the weather or something.

Then he said, "You and Jocelyn looked good up there."

I gulped but managed to hit **"Thanks"** on my board.

I hoped my smile wasn't as wobbly as my insides were feeling.

"Uh, I'm not much of a dancer," he mumbled.

I took a chance.

"Neither was I," I tapped.

"What do you mean?"

"Until tonight. I never danced until tonight."

"You are kidding me," Noah said. "Really?" And then his face went red. "I've actually never danced before in front of . . . anyone. Not all by myself. Or . . . with someone, for real. I mean, not being crazy with my friends . . ."

He glanced at me, and I took one more chance. Because, why not?

"Um, if you dance with someone for real, then you won't be dancing by yourself. . . ." That took so long to tap. But Noah watched patiently while I typed every letter; I could literally feel him watching.

And before I could tap out the next word, he said, "Okay, Firefly Girl, before they close the place down, do you, uh, do you wanna dance?"

He is nervous too? I wondered in amazement.

Then, *of course*, I accidentally hit the volume button on my board as I went to respond, and it screeched out, embarrassingly loud, **"YES!"**

I wanted to sink down in my chair. No, under it!

Noah, however, didn't seem to be even remotely bothered by the world's loudest response. He touched one edge of Elvira, waggled his finger like he was scolding her. That made me giggle. But then he gently touched the back of *my* hand. Now *that* made me shiver.

Devin and Malik were chanting, "Go, Noah! Go, Melody! Dance! Dance! Dance!"

Trinity stepped close and offered to help, but I shook my head because Noah was already swinging behind my wheelchair, pushing his walker out of the way, and grasping the wheelchair handles. He pushed me up the ramp and onto the dance floor Just. Like. That.

The song was the one I loved, the one about dreams. And suddenly I was dancing—with Noah. A boy who wanted to dance with me. Me! A boy *I* wanted to dance with. Could this be real?

He leaned on the back of my chair for support, and the wheels did the rest of the work. Yep, my chair knew how to take care of me! And Noah must be strong; he swirled my chair around like it was weightless. *Swinging on a walker must be good for the biceps,* I couldn't help thinking when my brain could process anything other than the fact that *I'm dancing with Noah.* I spread my arms as wide as I could—yes I did, like wings—and swayed with the rhythm of the music.

I gulped down the words as the song went on about how it's gonna take a million dreams. . . . Then—brain freeze. Noah touched my shoulder. On purpose. He made it seem like it was part of the dance, but when I stole a glance back, I saw him smile shyly. And, yes, I smiled back. My brain unfroze and began whirling as fast as the wheels of my chair.

Even though I was pretty sure that Cassie played the song all the way through at least two more times, and other kids were dancing around us, our time on the dance floor was over way too soon. The last strains of the music faded away. The firelight was barely a glow. We did one last twirl, then Noah spun me to face him and gave a deep bow. I pretend-curtsied back, and we both cracked up.

"Thanks for the dance, Firefly Girl," he said, reaching for his walker, which Jeremiah had at the ready.

And as he swung back to his group, he turned around once to wave good night. I waved back. I noticed lots of fist bumps and such from the rest of the Panthers when Noah joined them. And my circle of girls surrounded me as well, with whispers and smiles and hugs.

It was time to head back. I looked for Noah in the shuffle of packing up, but the Panthers had disappeared. It was late. It was time for bed. Tomorrow, I realized, we would all leave, go back to our own homes, and all this would be a memory. Home! I couldn't believe it, but I felt like it was too soon, like I hadn't done enough here. That made me laugh a little. I had worried so much. I'd fretted and stressed. And now I wasn't sure if I was ready to leave.

Had I made it all up? Had I really danced? Did that really happen? Trinity came over to tuck a fleece around me, but I shrugged it away.

I felt on fire.

Tomorrow, I'd go home.

But tonight, I had danced!

CHAPTER 46

We were all up early. Trinity rummaged through the clothes I had brought and pulled out a really sharp outfit—skinny jeans, a hot-pink cutoff shirt, and fresh white sneakers.

I pointed to the box, still not empty of orange T-shirts and sweatshirts.

She laughed and said, "Not today, you orange-wearing horse whisperer! We're wearing cute instead of camp. Fair enough?"

At first Athena picked out a pink T-shirt, but then she exclaimed, "I need to wear orange today—we're the Fiery Falcons, right?"

Sage hugged her and pulled out a shirt for her. And no, the box was still not empty!

The chatter seemed noisier, the giggles gigglier. And Karyn, Athena, and Jocelyn each had on their bracelets. Me too!

Thanks to Karyn, breakfast today was caramel oatmeal. She'd swirled gobs of caramel syrup into her bowl, tasted it, and announced, "This is the bomb! I am an inventor!!" So Jocelyn added three beige dots to the side of her bowl. "Decoration, decoration, decoration," she explained.

I told Trinity, **"Caramel me up!"**

She shook her head in semi-disgust but cheerfully transformed oatmeal into a delicious caramelly delicacy. I couldn't wait to show this to Penny—she'd love it.

I tapped out, **"When do our parents get here?"**

Trinity checked her watch. "In about an hour. Gee, the week went by so fast! It always does." She looked at the four of us and gave my hand a little rub. "I'm gonna miss you guys." I could tell she meant it.

Athena went from giddy to frowning. "I miss my mom. But I think I'm gonna miss camp—maybe a lot." She squeezed another huge glob of caramel into her oatmeal and stirred and stirred and stirred.

Sage looked her in the eye. "I know, Athena. It's always hard to say goodbye to friends."

I glanced at Karyn. Was she sniffling? I bumped her elbow with mine. Sometimes you don't *need* words.

Lulu, I guess trying to lighten our mood, said, "Oh, and we meant to tell you! Everybody will receive a souvenir T-shirt and sweatshirt to take home. . . ."

Well, *that* broke up our moping! Jocelyn laughed so hard she had to go to the bathroom.

Back at the cabin to do some last packing up, Sage explained a bit about the closing ceremony. Parents would sit with us on lawn chairs with little boxes of tissues placed under each chair because, apparently, they always, always cry.

"For real?" Karyn asked.

"For real!"

I knew Mom could sniffle with the best of them. She cries when we watch *movies* of graduations!

"I'm gonna text you all when I get home," Karyn declared, looking teary. "Okay? That way we can all stay in touch!"

Jocelyn chanted her phone number out; she knew it by heart. I gave her my best thumbs-up, reminding myself to make sure our parents met. Athena said she was gonna ask her mom to make sure Karyn's mom had all the info. "I'm gonna have online friends!" she squealed, bouncing on her toes. I was thinking the exact same thing. The idea that I'd have friends to talk to online almost blew me away! Then Athena ran around the room, giving us each a hug. Even Jocelyn, who wasn't crazy about being touched, hugged her back.

Sage's phone pinged. She glanced down. "Hey, Athena! I just got a text. Your parents have arrived at the check-in gate. Do you want to go out and greet them?"

"Super-duper!" Athena cried out. "Yes! Yes! Yes!" Then she paused, her face distraught. "Bye, guys—I hope I see you next summer!" She gave us each one more hug, and she was out the door, Sage racing after her.

And once again I thought about the possibility of coming back next summer! *Oh yeah!*

I looked at Karyn and Jocelyn. Karyn still looked teary, her eyes on the door Athena had just bounded out of.

"Next year?" I tapped.

They couldn't answer quickly enough. "Yes! We have to! For sure! We gotta make a pact or something!" Karyn and Jocelyn did a fist bump. "Falcons! Falcons!" Then Jocelyn grabbed my right hand and Karyn held my left. They squeezed at the same time. Karyn was full-on crying. Jocelyn grabbed a tissue to wipe her tears. Then she grabbed another one and wiped my eyes. Yeah, we were a mess.

Karyn's parents arrived about the same time as

Jocelyn's. One more quick round of hugs—Karyn's strong, Jocelyn's as light as firefly legs on my hand— and they both hurried out to the greeting area.

And then I was alone with Trinity. I looked at her, and she glanced back at me with a smile. "You're not worried, are you?" she asked, checking her own phone for a text.

I shook my head no. But yeah, I was a little worried. Were they gonna just leave me here? Funny not funny. I thought back to the beginning of the week. Hadn't I said the same thing when I got here? I'd been so clueless!

I took one last look around our cabin, now almost as empty as when I'd arrived. Then, the hard bunks, the dim lanterns, the well-worn wooden floor had seemed cold and uncomfortable. But this morning, with the sunshine streaming through the cabin window and the luggage packed and ready for parents to load up, it felt like I was leaving home.

And that was exactly when Trinity's phone dinged. "They're here!" she told me.

I let out a joyous screech, and we booked it out the cabin door. And then I saw the car, the blue SUV that Dad keeps saying he's going to trade in soon. It's a good thing I was strapped in—I kicked, I screeched, my arms wiggled in every direction.

They're here!

The car had barely come to a stop when Mom jumped out. She ran over and engulfed me in a bubble-gum-flavored hug. Dad, who'd just unbuckled Penny from her seat, could barely keep ahold of her as they hurried over right behind Mom.

"Dee-Dee!" Penny wiggled out of Dad's arms and ran to me at full speed, launching herself right onto my lap. She babbled about ice cream and Barbie and Butterscotch and Doodle. "Did you like living in the forest, Dee-Dee?"

I hugged her tight.

I wanted to tell her there were no lions or tigers, but the forest, as she called it, was both beautiful and exciting.

"Your fingernails look awesome, Dee-Dee," Penny said as she touched each color.

I noticed Trinity grin, then take a few steps back, not interfering. Did she look a little sad? I guessed she was used to this. But I was going to *miss* her, for sure.

Mom kissed my forehead and Dad enveloped both me *and* Penny in a giant bear hug. Gee, he smelled good.

Mom, who's pretty good at getting the most information out of me, asked the most, and the most typically mom-type questions.

"Did you have enough to eat? Was the food good?"

Yes and yes.

"How was the boat ride?"

Awesome!

"Are you traumatized by the runaway horse incident?" Her face went instantly from deliriously happy to severe and concerned.

Nope! It was exciting!

Mom gave me a "look," which meant *she* didn't think it was exciting. There had been, in fact, several phone calls between my parents and the camp about me and the horse named Jolie, but she was going to let it go—for now. She continued her questions.

"Did you make new friends?"

Yes.

"Are you glad you came? Would you like to go back next summer?"

I put Elvira on speaker. **"Yes. Yes. Yes. Yes. Yes."**

I wished I had more words to explain it all. But we'd have time in the car. I was definitely keeping Elvira in the seat with me.

I waved Trinity over. She held out her hand to shake, but instead Mom gave Trinity the biggest hug ever! "I—we—can't thank you enough for taking such good care of our girl," Mom blubbered. Yep, tears already.

Did I see Trinity wiping a tear as well? Gah! So she

was gonna miss me! And yeah, I'd never ever forget her.

"I have seriously enjoyed getting to know Melody this week, Mrs. Brooks," Trinity said. "She is truly a gem and a delight!"

Just then Cassie's voice reverberated out of the same megaphone she'd used during game day. "To all campers and their families, we will begin our closing program in just a few minutes. Please join us around the fire pit!"

CHAPTER 47

Even though it was morning, a fire in the center pit burned brightly. I felt like it was probably a little insulted, saying like, *You expect me to perform in the sunshine like this? I had to laugh at myself.*

It felt weird sitting around a blazing fire in the morning rather than at night, but it felt so good to have my family sitting here with me! I looked at all the kids and their parents gathered around, and I felt grateful all of a sudden—folks doing these camps all summer so that kids like me, Karyn, Jocelyn, Athena . . . Noah . . . could go to camp just like any other kid.

I glanced at the group sitting across from us. Noah

sat with two adults who had to be his parents, and a man who looked like Santiago's twin—just much larger—had to be his dad. Santiago caught my eye and waved. And so did Noah.

Mom whispered, "Friends of yours?"

I touched **yes** on my board. Twice.

Mom gave my shoulder a happy little squeeze.

On the speakers—I couldn't believe it—was that song, "Wings." Noah's eyes met mine just as Penny, who sat on Dad's lap looking every which way, asked VERY loudly, "Wow, Dee-Dee. Are these people all your friends?"

And I typed the truth. **"Yes, they are!"**

Cassie, baseball cap on, walked up to a podium that I hadn't seen before. It was time. "Welcome, parents, friends, and caregivers! We are so glad you are here to share with us our final activity at Camp Green Glades. Oh, and we're also glad you decided to show up to retrieve your campers!"

Little murmurs of laughter followed.

"Camp Green Glades," Cassie continued, "is so very proud to introduce you to this week's graduates!"

Whoops and hoorays!

"During our week here, we made friends, created art, learned music, rode horses, cruised on a boat, zipped on a line, and hiked in the woods. We learned more about snakes—and skunks—than we wanted to." She paused as we all cracked up. "But Cleopatra safely found her way home, and Stinky left us a message we'll never forget!"

Now everyone was flat-out laughing.

Cassie continued. "We sang songs, played Balloon Ball, and yes, we danced!"

She got a lot of whoops for that.

Mom whispered, "You danced, Melody?"

Yep!

Mom's mouth fell open.

"And we want you to know," Cassie continued, "that we have treasured sharing this week with your loved ones. The trophies and certificates they are about to receive show their growth and success."

Now Dad whispered, "You're getting a trophy, my Melody?"

I tapped, **Of course!** Well, I hoped I was.

To be honest, as I looked at the lineup of little gold trophies on the table behind Cassie, it was clear that everybody would receive one. Yeah—because we rock!

"We will call the names in alphabetical order by cabin," Cassie explained, "and counselors will give their campers their awards."

She opened the folder she held in her hand and

paused, I guess for dramatic effect, then shouted, "Let the ceremony begin!" She nodded to Sage, who began playing the song called "Pomp and Circumstance."

Last year, when we went to my cousin's high school graduation, Mom cried when that song played. She basically boo-hooed through the whole thing. So as soon as the first few notes of the graduation song played, Mom was already fishing under the seat for a tissue, sniffling.

Dum, da de da dum dum, dum, da de da dum.

I didn't laugh. I know what any graduation for me meant to her, but that music playing for me today had to really touch her heart. She was going to *really* lose it when I graduated from high school!

Jeremiah came up first. "What can I say? If every group of guys was as cool as my group, I'd be a counselor year-round."

His campers belted out, "Panthers! Panthers!"

Jeremiah shook his head in a way that said *quit it* and *I love you guys* at the same time, and continued. "Our first graduate is a young man who showed strength and fortitude and mighty slick dance skills! Congratulations, Noah Abercrombie!"

Noah, wearing a crisp new Panthers T-shirt, waved to the crowd as he bopped up to the front on his walker.

I slapped my hands together as best I could. I made Elvira shout, **"Yay."** Several times. At maximum volume.

I looked over at Mom, who was looking at me. Her face was a question mark. Mine was a blushing grin.

CHAPTER 48

Noah got more applause as he returned to his seat, catching my eye as he did.

Jeremiah then gave certificates and trophies to the rest of his crew. Malik threw candy to the crowd, even as his mother laughed and scolded, "Now, stop that, son!"

Trinity was up next. "Well," she said, "that's going to be tough to follow! We don't have any candy!"

She cleared her throat as folks chuckled. "The first graduate from the Fiery Falcons is a young lady of great grace and dignity. And she's got the loudest scream on the face of the earth! When she took her first swim, ladies and gentlemen, I think they must have heard her on the planet Mars!"

Everyone started chanting, *"Melody! Melody! Melody!"* Mom and Dad looked thunderstruck! I can laugh about it now, but I really was sure I was gonna die that morning.

Trinity continued, "So I am pleased to award this trophy to Melody Brooks, who conquered fear and learned to swim, to paint, to explore, to ride a horse— alone, I might add—to dance, and to fly!"

I thought, *Gee, I did that! Me—Melody—I did that. Yes, I did!*

Cue the applause—Mom and Dad jumping out of their folding chairs and clapping loudest of all. Penny didn't know exactly why, but she cheered along also. My mother turned to push me to the stage, but I gently signaled *No.* Mom nodded.

Trinity shook my hand once I rolled myself over to her, her face aglow. "You are a victory, Miss Melody," she low-voiced. "Never forget that. And I shall never forget you."

And you know what? Every time I smell the fragrance of jasmine and hibiscus, and maybe burning wood—ha—I will think of Trinity.

Then, with great seriousness, she placed several certificates and a trophy on my tray. She shook my hand once more. I swiveled my chair around and waved to everyone. Then I placed both hands on my heart. And you know what?

I.

Was.

So.

Proud.

Of.

Me.

I rolled myself back to Mom and Dad. Yeah, Mom was now on Dad's pack of tissues!

As their counselors took turns presenting certificates and trophies to Karyn, Athena, Jocelyn, and the rest of the cabins, I couldn't stop thinking how a week ago, all of them were strangers. But now they were my friends!

I. Was. Also. So. Very. Proud. Of. Them.

In our schools, most of us are considered misfits. We are often ignored, mistreated, teased, or overlooked. Each of us struggles with something—physical, emotional, mental—that makes us just a little different from others. Sometimes a lot different.

But here, we were awesome, we were noble, we were able, and we were cool!

I was heading home. I'd be taking my orange balloon (which, amazingly, has not popped yet), my trophy, my gloppy artwork—including my footprints—and my certificates of success and completion in hiking and dancing and painting and yep, horseback riding!

It'd be really awesome to look through the photos the camp compiled and was sending home with me. But I didn't really need pictures from a camera. I couldn't wait to tell Mrs. V about everything as we sat on her porch and sipped sodas and listened to music. And when I get back to the library, I'll thank Mr. Francisco for helping me find the info on Camp Green Glades so he can show some other kid that brochure next year. I'll return my book on Atta the ant (and admit to him that I actually cried at the end!). And then I'll dive into books about snakes and skunks and storms, and forests and lakes and campfires. I'll check out books on horses, for sure. And ask Mr. Francisco to help me find out who to talk to about making better playgrounds in our town so other kids like me can do what all the other kids do!

I hoped I'd get to come back to camp next summer— who knows?

But I wouldn't have to come back in order to remember Trinity, Karyn, Athena, and Jocelyn.

And I would never forget Malik, Devin, Santiago and . . . Noah.

And the magic and mystery of starlight, fireflies, and flickering flames.

ACKNOWLEDGMENTS

I would like to give a special thanks to the following people and organizations:

Crystal Draper, who is a natural creator of movement and words, a discriminating editor, a loving mother and daughter, an incredible dancer, and my very best friend. Thank you for your wisdom, your love, and your incredible insight into the mind of a tweenager.

Ailey Rose, who loves to snuggle with a good book, loves to shop and play dress-up, and understands that beauty is found both inside a person and outside as well.

AJ, aka Anthony James, the titanic builder, the intense creator, and the magnificent dreamer, who sees the world with a golden heart and a spirit of possibility.

Horizon Emmanuelle Adams; her mom, Emily; and her dad, Kenyon. Much love to you!

Victoria and Jeffrey. Thank you for love and laughter and memories of catching lightning bugs on East Eighty-Third Street.

Damon and Cory. My sons of strength. My Peter Pans.

Wendy. My Tinker Bell.

Larry and Buddy, silent strengths.

Catherine the Great and Victor the Valiant. Without you, I would be nothing.

Caitlyn Dlouhy, my editor and my friend, whose wisdom and guidance (and yes, she found a green-tipped online marker!) helped me and Melody find our way through the forest of Camp Green Glades. I thank you for your brilliant attention to detail and gifted insight into the essence of good writing. I will forever be grateful. And yes, we get ice cream!

Nita Page, who lifted me up in prayer and lifted my spirits with laughter. Thank you!

Torie Queally—thank you for your wisdom and guidance. And yes, you got the VERY FIRST copy!

Camp Stepping Stones and Camp Allyn and Camp Cheerful. Thank you for summer days full of adventure, exploration, discovery, and respite. And thanks to the hundreds of volunteers at camps like Stepping Stones who make the magic happen each year for dozens of young people like Melody.

Larry Gross, the computer tech magician who saved my lost data, including the manuscript of this book! He retrieved, revived, and reloaded my missing information on a holiday weekend, and did it all with a smiling graciousness. Bless you, my friend!

Cat Denton and the amazing Richlynn team. They spread the word so gloriously.

Janell Agyeman, who remains my forever friend and giver of wisdom.

Karen Brantley, who became a lifelong friend when we met as new mothers of new babies with incredible needs.

Denise Bykes, whose calm assurances got me through several very difficult times in my life. I kinda miss that pew!

Kimya Moyo, whose wisdom runs deep and whose friendship is precious.

Tanya McKinnon, my feisty friend and agent, who pushed me to reach for ever higher levels of accomplishment and belief in myself.

Elaine Harris and Darlene Hampton, who keep me connected to the straight and narrow through phone calls and laughter.

Greg Jasper . . . keep on keepin' on. You are a beacon of light in the darkness.

Jeannie Ng and Valerie Shea—incredible copyeditors. How DO you find all those teeny errors? THANK YOU for being the Marine Corps of Minutia! I bow to your excellence and attention to detail.

Debra Sfetsios-Conover, the designer of this *amazing* cover. It captures the essence completely. Irene Metaxatos, for making sure the interior looked just as good.

Alex Borbolla, thank you for everything—past and present! Carl-Eric Péan, many thanks for keeping Caitlyn sane and organized!

Justin Chanda, thanks for all you do—and you owe me a dinner!

And Michelle Leo (we go waaaay back), thank you for all of it!

And Anne Zafian, Chrissy Noh, Lisa Moraleda, Lauren Hoffman—as well as all the others I do not yet know—without all of you, none of the magic happens. We are a family, and I appreciate you all.

A special shout-out to Bethany Bookin, a magnificent dancer and teacher on wheels!

A very special thanks to the moms and dads and nurses and care-givers and specialists and teachers who took the time to read drafts and dribbles of this book, who told me, vociferously, where I didn't quite get it right, and kindly helped me to represent children of varying abilities and strengths with respect and dignity and humanity. I do not claim to be an expert on anyone's situation. I write fiction so that we can all see truth.

All my family and friends who have continued to believe in me and support me.

All the teachers who have struggled and managed and invented and created ways for students to read and learn, even during a worldwide, life-changing, school-disrupting pandemic, while taking care of their own families' needs. They juggled multiple computers and multiple screens for *months*—and emerged at the end exhausted and victorious, because learning had happened! From the bottom of my heart, I thank you.

All the students who love to read, and all the students who hate to read but found one of my books and kept on reading! I thank you for your letters and emails of love and encouragement.

All the librarians who have always managed to create ways for students and teachers to access books and knowledge, including mask-covered, hand-delivered books to student homes at the height of the lockdown. From the little girl who used to check out ten books a week from the library on Kinsman Road in Cleveland, Ohio, I thank you!

To sites like Zoom and Skype and dozens of other platforms that suddenly existed and grew appendages and became what we all needed before we even knew we did, because communication between humans is essential.

I give thanks to God every moment for the gifts and blessings.

And a very special thanks to everyone who kept asking, "So what happened to Melody?" This book is for you!

With Love from Sharon M. Draper